Rupert Gilchrist was born thirty-nine years ago on the Leeward Island of Nevis. The seventh generation of an English colonial family, Mr. Gilchrist is the first to break away from plantation life. After attending preparatory school in Rhode Island, he studied on the Continent.

He has travelled extensively in Africa and the Far East and now lives in Montserrat, in a 17th century captain's house, which he has faithfully restored himself. His hobbies include horses, skin-diving, collecting African artifacts and tuning the engine of his Lamborghini.

A Girl Called Friday Night

Slaves Without Masters volume 2

Rupert Gilchrist

CORGI BOOKS

A GIRL CALLED FRIDAY NIGHT

A CORGI BOOK 0 552 12425 7

Originally published in Great Britain by Souvenir Press Ltd.

PRINTING HISTORY

Souvenir Press edition published 1983
Corgi edition published 1984

This book is set in 10/11 Souvenir

Corgi Books are published by
Transworld Publishers Ltd.,
Century House, 61–63 Uxbridge Road,
Ealing, London W5 5SA

Made and printed in Great Britain by
Cox & Wyman Ltd., Reading, Berks.

Contents

Historical Note

Racial prejudice in America spread rapidly in the immediate decades following the Civil War, regional vigilante riders consolidating into the powerful Ku Klux Klan, White women forming auxiliary teams which offered assistance to the 'good' causes of the male groups, such as harassing Black women, especially the free Negresses who often had to eke out a livelihood by prostitution.

America's Negroes were little better than slaves without masters after their recent emancipation from slavery, and it's an interesting – and ironic – historical coda that apart from the KKK and its secret sororities, a large onslaught of hatred hurled against Black prostitutes during these turbulent years came from White females working in the South's gaudy bordellos, strumpet segregationists fighting to keep Black women and girls condemned to walking the streets, or confined to squalid sin ghettoes such as the notorious Smoky Row in New Orleans.

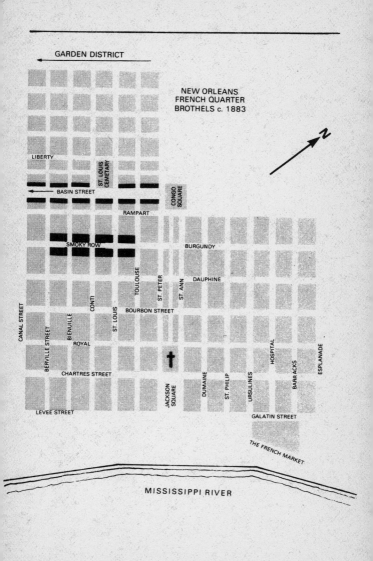

NEW ORLEANS
FRENCH QUARTER
BROTHELS c. 1883

Part One

Smoky Row

1 'Lewd and Abandoned Women'

Emmaline Rickers held one naked leg crossed over the knee of her other leg as she lounged on a narrow bed in a brothel on Smoky Row – the district for Black prostitutes in New Orleans.

Outside the room's louvered shutters, the sing-song voices of prostitutes filled the humid evening, a chorus of lewd remarks called to men walking on the boardwalk or driving buggies down the infamous stretch of Burgundy Street in the French Quarter . . .

Brazen, challenging, the solicitations continued:

'Ever have Black pussy, mister? Best Black pussy in town!'

'Want a good time? Good time waiting right here with your name on it, sweet potato.'

'Want to go to Heaven or rather go to Hell? You got fifty cents and I give you a little bit of Heaven. You got a dollar and I give you a whole lot of Hell.'

Emmaline, the youngest, the prettiest of the six prostitutes working for Big Jocasta Liddle in the two floor brothel at the corner of Burgundy and Bienville Streets, never stood in a doorway or hung out of a window like the other women of Smoky Row, never lifted her long skirts, whistled or called wisecracks to attract the attention of men passing in the street. She stayed inside her room and received a steady stream of visitors.

But not all of Emmaline's callers were as undemanding as Henry Peele, the man down on his hands and knees scrubbing the plank floor in her room, a White man who paid

11

three dollars to work as a maid for the eighteen-year-old whore.

Emmaline Rickers, skin the color of tobacco and black hair softly curling into ringlets, had first come to Smoky Row ten months ago and had been surprised to see how many of its customers were White men. She remembered that, back home in Longchamp Parish, Louisiana, White men only bedded Black women and girls in the darkness of a horse barn, or in the secrecy of pine forests. But in New Orleans, White men came to Smoky Row openly, raucously, looking for Black women, making love with them in rickety bordellos, in windowless little hutches called 'cribs' dotting both sides of the muddy street, sometimes in the back of a work wagon, on the floor of a buggy, even in the street itself, or down an alleyway.

The majority of men who visited Smoky Row, though, had dark complexions like the women who worked there - men from road gangs, the harbour and railroad yards, married Negroes with money in their pockets and not getting the sexual satisfaction they wanted at home, or young bloods out for a good time.

Emmaline had also learned that men often wanted more - or was it less? - from a prostitute than what she considered to be . . . sex.

Men wanted dirty words to excite them. Lewd poses on the bed to tease them. A whiff of her undergarments. An opportunity to kneel on the floor and adore her, perhaps even kiss the toes of her high button boots. Or feel the slap of her hand against their bare buttocks as if they had been bad boys and had to be punished. Men paid a prostitute to do things which often had little or nothing to do with the act of copulation.

Henry Peele's secret desire was to clean. Scrub the floor. Wash the window. Dust the louvered shutters. Take home a pair of old cotton sheets, launder and mend them. Emmaline had at first suspected that the little White man masturbated when she was not looking at him. But never once had she seen his fist working to relieve himself in a far corner, or at the foot of her bed.

12

So what did he do? Emmaline wondered. Masturbate on her sheets when he got them home?

'Does madam require anything else?'

Emmaline, glancing at Henry Peele crouched on his hands and knees alongside her bed like a timid dog, saw that his forehead was beaded with perspiration and his round wire spectacles were riding the tip of his small pink nose.

Lazily, she asked, 'You finish your work?'

'Does madam wish to inspect?'

Emmaline was good at play-acting but she had never excelled in showing interest in something – or someone – she did not like or understand. And not understanding why Mr Peele paid good money to clean her room, Emmaline quickly, disinterestedly ran her eyes over the bureau with its oval mirror, a straight-backed chair, a three-legged table covered with a fringed shawl.

Nodding, she said like a child playing school teacher, 'It looks pretty good. I guess you can go.'

'Is madam certain?'

'You can go.'

'Thank you, madam.' Peele turned on the floor, gathering his wooden bucket, rags, brown bristle brush.

Emmaline called, 'Oh, one thing.'

Peele, rising to his feet, turned with the cleaning equipment in his hands, the knees of his trousers soggy from the wet floor.

'I'm leaving tomorrow,' Emmaline told him. 'I won't be here next week.'

He looked at her, pushing the wire spectacles back up his nose.

'I thought you should know.' She lay on the bed, toying with the hem of her loose white cotton shift, adding, 'But I'll be back in ten days.'

He bowed. 'Have a pleasant journey, madam.'

'Thanks.' She waved him to leave.

Henry Peele, burdened with the wooden bucket, the wet

13

rags, the brown bristle brush, opened the door and gently closed it behind him.

A few minutes after Peele left Emmaline's room, the door opened and the brothel-keeper stood in the doorway. Jocasta Liddle was a large-busted woman, with skin the color of a wet raisin, wearing a low-necked purple dress, and her black hair neatly marcelled to the shape of her enormous head.

Emmaline moved to stand, pulling the hem of the smock from her waist down over her naked thighs.

Waving a pawlike hand for Emmaline to remain as she was on the bed, Jocasta Liddle shut the door and sank down on the thin mattress, saying, 'Honey, I just got my first complaint about you.'

'Complaint?' Emmaline's doe-eyes sharpened and she began to come to life. 'What'd I do wrong, Miss Jocasta?'

Jocasta, pulling on a thin black leather thong tied around her neck, slowly hoisted a piece of lead pipe from her cleavage as she sighed, 'Least I *think* it was a complaint,' baby doll.'

'What about?' Emmaline sat at the head of the narrow iron bed, anxiously watching Jocasta remove a roll of paper money from the lower end of the lead pipe.

Jocasta took three one-dollar banknotes from the pocket of her purple dress and wrapped them carefully around the money roll. She next began to poke the money roll back into the pipe, pushing her stubby forefinger into the end of the pipe, tapping the money roll as she said, 'That White goof, Peele, he just done told me you let your "house slaves" get away with too much, Em honey.'

'My *house* slaves?'

'That's what he says. "House slaves".' Jocasta took a deep breath and, holding the leather cord in front to her chin, she lowered the pipe back down her bodice, shifting herself, repositioning her breasts for the pipe to drop comfortably down her generous cleavage.

'What's that supposed to mean, Miss Jocasta? My "house slaves"?'

14

'I guess you ain't being tough enough on him.' Jocasta sat on the edge of the bed, looking around the small dingy room. 'I know this place ain't no castle, honey, but, hells bells, can't you make-believe? Inspect things after he's cleaned here? Run your fingers over edges for dust?'

'I *do* look around, Miss Jocasta,' Emmaline answered petulantly.

'Well, you ain't looking good enough. You've got to pretend you're mistress of a big fine house. Like a mansion over in that Garden District. Or some plantation place upriver. White columns out front and crystal chandeliers in the hallway. You got to get mad as a hornet when you think your slave ain't doing his job. You might even have to get yourself a whip to use on the little peanut –'

Stopping, turning to look at Emmaline lying on the bed, Jocasta said, 'You're no more than a snip of a thing, Em honey, but Peele is most likely itching to get his ass whipped good and proper. The trouble is, he can't come right out and ask you for it like a man. So leave it to me this time. I'll talk to Willy. I'll see if Willy can find us a nice little whip, something just the right size for your hand. Nothing too heavy.'

Emmaline knew about Willy the Whip, a Basin Street pimp who also made money by whipping prostitutes, a quiet, neatly-dressed White man with an alligator bag filled with whips, rods, and lashes, going from brothel to brothel in New Orleans, punishing prostitutes, both Black and White, who paid him for his expertise in flagellation.

Jocasta said, 'You got to start doing something different to that Peele man because when a customer ain't pleased, he'll go to another gal.'

Her brown eyes alive with concern, Emmaline asked, 'Did he mention somebody else, Miss Jocasta?'

'Not yet. But he had that way to him. That unhappy, wandering way. I could see he was not a pleased man when he stepped out this door.'

'But there's nobody else who could satisfy him here besides me . . . is there?'

Jocasta shrugged. 'Could be a couple of gals. Cassy's

15

good with a leather belt. Peaches don't step back from rough-ing up a man. Maybe even that new gal, Lizzie, who's going to start working here this coming weekend.'

The casual announcement surprised Emmaline. She asked, 'That White girl? You can't let no White girl work here, Miss Jocasta!'

Jocasta shot Emmaline a sharp look. 'Why the hell not? I did what I wanted to here before you came along. And I will a long time after you leave. So don't sass me, gal.'

Lowering her head, Emmaline apologized, 'I'm sorry, Miss Jocasta. I don't intend you no sass. I was just saying only Black gals work Smoky Row. White gals like Lizzie got their own places in town.'

'Lizzie's not exactly a White gal. Not in a normal way she ain't. But that's neither here nor there. Not to you. Not to nobody. Except for the fact –'

Jocasta patted her stubby fingers over the neat furrows of her tightly marcelled hair, saying, 'I might as well tell you now, Em honey, I'm allowing Lizzie the privilege of using this room while you're away home visiting your folks.'

'I pay for this room! This is my room, Miss Jocasta!'

'Sure this is your room . . . when you're here. But, baby doll, a smart woman don't let a good piece of property like this sit empty. Space is short on Smoky Row. You know that.'

Emmaline took a deep breath, then said, 'Miss Jocasta, mam, I don't mean no disrespect to you, but that Lizzie gal better not get too settled in my room. I'm only going to be away a week, ten days at the most, Miss Jocasta.'

Jocasta eyed Emmaline, saying, 'Sometimes a gal goes home to see her folks and never comes back to Smoky Row. Sometimes a gal goes home and gets herself a bad case of the guilts.'

Emmaline arched one thin eyebrow. 'What I got to be guilty for?'

'Baby doll, there's lots of reasons gals take to this way of life. Some gals get knocked-up and have no place to go but the whorehouse. Some gals get tricked into this life by their mean old man. But mostly the reason's money. Take the other gals working here for me.

16

'Peaches and Luba. They turned to whoring because they couldn't find decent paying jobs. Neither Peaches nor Luba had a husband to take care of them and saw no prospects of getting none. And Julia's here with me because she's got to support a sick old mother and two teeny weeny little babies down in bayou country.

'But you, baby doll, you're a mystery to me. I don't know why you're here on Smoky Row. You weren't no virgin when you came here. But you weren't no wild woman. You had no policeman chasing your ass. You had no sucker planted in your belly. Oh, sure, you were a country gal and had the jitters at first about being in a big city and learning the ways. But Smoky Row spooks the toughest gals.

'Fact is, baby doll, you came to me with money already stashed in your purse. You laid down twenty dollars in advance for this room. And like Queen Cleopatra herself, you refused to set your little royal ass out there in that street and hawk your sweet-smelling pussy. You were no street whore. You waited right here in this room till the men started lining up with their peckers in their hands. And they did, baby doll. The men folk sniffed out your muffin mighty fast and started making tracks straight to your bed because you're a young, tender morsel.

'Baby doll, I ain't expecting no answers from you why you're here on Smoky Row. Maybe you don't know yourself. But answer me one thing, Emmy gal. Just answer Big Jocasta one little question.

'When you stand in front of that looking-glass over there, Em honey, what do you see when you look in that looking-glass? What's the first thing you think of when you see that pretty little angel face peeking back at you? You see angel? You see whore? You see somebody's future wife? You see mother? You see a pretty gal with long silky lashes and sweet kissable lips? Or maybe you look in the looking-glass and you see nothing but a poor nigger slave staring back at you?'

Emmaline held her eyes lowered, her thin shoulders slumped forward as she mumbled, 'I don't see a slave, Miss

17

Jocasta. Slave days are over for us. You know that same as I do.'

'Over? Hog shit!' boomed Jocasta. 'Black people got no more freedom now than days when we was slaves. You listen to me. I was both. I was a slave back home on the farm. I'm a so-called free woman here on Smoky Row. But is this freedom I got? Shit! This is no freedom. This is still some slavehouse. The whole world's a slavehouse for the Black person, honey. And maybe that's why you're here on Smoky Row. Maybe you're here looking for your own kind of freedom. Maybe you came here trying, hoping to break away from whatever keeps you a slave when you're back home with your people. Maybe you turned to whoring to prove nothing more than you're a free person.'

Emmaline sat motionless on the bed, her bare feet tucked under her haunches, looking younger than her eighteen years, as if she was no more than a child.

Finally, she asked, 'Miss Jocasta, why are you talking like this to me now? The night before I go home? Why are you talking deep like this, asking me deep questions?'

'I want to know if you're coming back to me, baby doll. Coming back to Smoky Row.'

Emmaline's answer was almost whispered. 'I'm coming back.'

Big Jocasta, sitting on the edge of the narrow bed, nodded approvingly as she looked at Emmaline's small body, saying, 'You're some cute piece of shortcake, baby doll, and I'd sure hate not to see you around this house no more. I make no bones about it, neither, that I'd let you hop tits first into my bed any minute you want. Oh, yes, yes, Em honey, when a gal gets tired pleasuring a man, the touch and the feel, the hug and the cuddle of another woman's warm body is a mighty fine treat. And I make no bones about it, Em honey. I'm waiting for you. Whenever you're ready, you come tapping at my door and I'll show you how I do "the egg roll". Ummm-huh!'

Emmaline knew about Jocasta Liddle. She knew that the bordello-keeper had other women for lovers. She knew that Jocasta was as strong as a man. Stronger than most

18

men. She knew that Jocasta kept the piece of lead pipe dangling by a leather thong around her neck not only as a container for money but also as a weapon to use in fights. Big Jocasta Liddle was a powerful, strong-minded creature who fought men in the streets and made love to women in her bed.

'What's the matter, gal?' Jocasta asked, looking at Emmaline huddled limp and helpless on the bed. 'I scare you?'

Emmaline shook her head. 'I just don't want no other gal getting my room when I'm away, Miss Jocasta.'

Laughing, Jocasta slapped her fat thigh as she rose from the bed, saying, 'If that ain't a rich one! If that ain't a real rich one! Newspapers, they call us whores here on Smoky Row sinful, nothing but sinful "lewd and abandoned women". But look at you. You're no "lewd and abandoned woman". You're just a little girl, a sweet little gal worrying about another little girl taking away your bedroom, taking away this shithole of a bedroom!'

Laughing, Jocasta opened the door, calling, 'Don't forget, baby doll, you've got your Oysterman paying you a social call around eight o'clock tonight.'

Her mind miles away, Emmaline nodded. 'I remember.'

Still chuckling, Jocasta added, 'Honey, I'll keep your share of the cash Mr Peele gave me as well as the Oysterman's money. I'll put the money towards buying you that nice little whip from Willy. It can be waiting here for you when you get back from your trip home.'

A whip? Emmaline was in no mood to think about a whip, about life waiting here when she returned to New Orleans. She was still too worried about going home and facing her parents for the first time since she had come to New Orleans and become a prostitute.

Charley the Oysterman was not a tall man, but his ebony black physique was sinewy with muscle, his shoulders wide for his height, and his shoulders stretched even wider as he positioned both hands on the mattress, his naked buttocks rising and dipping like twin dark moons over Emmaline lying motionless beneath him on the bed.

Dark and shiny, Charley's fat penis moved quickly into the thatch of hair curling between Emmaline's brown legs.

He panted, 'I love you, Emmy. I love you.'

Charley the Oysterman had been one of Emmaline's first customers on Smoky Row; he was a smiling, happy-go-lucky young man who worked in the oyster beds southwest of New Orleans, and after their second meeting, he had invited her to stroll with him to Ruby Dee's Supper House on Conti Street for a bowl of shrimp gumbo, collard greens, and a pitcher of beer. Emmaline and Charley had met frequently in the following weeks, walking arm-in-arm along the riverfront, listening to the calliope and eating banana-flavored taffy from white paper bags. Charley had shown Emmaline Jackson Square flanked by the ornate Pontalba Buildings; the banks of flickering red candles inside St Louis Cathedral; the stalls of brightly colored fruit and freshly washed vegetables in the French Market; iron-work galleries as intricate as spider webs on the old Creole houses deep in the French Quarter. Emmaline and Charley had been becoming good friends when Jocasta Liddle had called Emmaline into the kitchen one afternoon, warning her about friendship with clients. And Emmaline, more eager to please the bordello-keeper than Charley the Oys-terman, began making excuses about seeing him outside the bordello.

Charley, perspiration dripping from his forehead, slicked his penis back and forth into Emmaline's vagina, saying, 'I'm going to miss you when you're away, Emmy. I'm going to miss you like crazy.'

Emmaline humored Charley's confessions of love for her. She had not been upset when Jocasta had advised her to stop seeing him but she did not want to hurt his feelings, always wanting to give him some sign that she appreciated his attention.

She whispered, 'I'll only be away a week, Charley.'

'You're special to me, Emmy. Real special to me . . .'

Charley fell onto his side, rolling Emmaline to face him, continuing his drives into her, enjoying the deeper strokes as he cupped her breasts with his hands; he whispered, 'I want to take you away from here, Emmy . . . Have you all for myself, baby . . .'

Emmaline had heard other men tell her the same thing, confessing they wanted to take her away from Smoky Row, and she knew they all had sexual reasons for saying it. She often thought, that if a man was going to take her any place, she wanted it to be Basin Street, the best, the most prestigious street for prostitutes in town.

Charley, working her cocoa-colored nipples, asked, 'You ever think you could be happy with just me, Emmy? Just me making love to you?'

'Hmm. You're good, Charley.' Emmaline knew the reason for Charley's questions.

'No lie, baby? You could be satisfied with just my pecker, Em? My pecker fine enough for you?'

'Fine, Charley.'

'Lots of men have bigger peckers than me, Em. I know that.'

'You're real fine, Charley.'

'You see lots of peckers bigger than mine, Em?' he asked plunging in, out, in, out.

She assured him, 'Charley, you're big.'

'My pecker is kind of fat but it's not long, Em. Not long like other men.' Charley began kissing her cheeks, nibbling her ear, whispering, 'How big are other peckers you see, Em? Tell me. Tell me about other peckers.'

Hearing Charley's breathing become quicker, Emmaline took it as her cue to start telling Charley the words he liked to hear in bed, the stories about other men's size.

She whispered, 'I had a man built real big last night, Charley. Fat as yours but, oh, was it long. So long I thought I was going to cry, Charley. Cry so loud . . .'

Charley began to kiss Emmaline's cheek more excitedly, driving his hips faster against her, begging, 'How long, Em? Tell me how long was it?'

Emmaline knew she was good at whispering stories, teasing men, and the room's darkness made it easier for her to speak words she would not usually say, to tell stories that would normally embarrass her to tell.

21

'Long, long and hard,' she described in a low whisper. 'Long with a big head on it the size of a baby's brown fist. And this man made love to me all night, Charley, touching places in me, making me feel things, doing things to me with that pecker I never known before, Charley.'

'You liked it, honey? You liked that big pecker?'

'Hmmm, Charley. It was . . . oh, heaven, Charley.'

'You thinking about it now, Emmy? That big pecker with the big head on it? You thinking about it now?'

Emmaline was indeed thinking of a penis, remembering the first man who had ever made love to her, the man who had taken her virginity with the penis she was describing to Charley, and always described to any customer who wanted to hear such stories in bed.

'I loved that pecker, Charley. I loved it so much. I begged for it all night. And he gave it to me that long. He came into me, holding me in his arms, doing all kinds of things to me with that – oh, Charley, I even begged to take that pecker in my mouth. My mouth, Charley. And I kissed it. I spread my spit all over it like grease. Rubbed it so slick and hard with my spit, Charley, feeling it throb . . . feeling it like iron . . . holding his balls, Charley . . . holding his balls while I tried to stretch my mouth around that head . . .'

Excitedly, Charley pulled out his penis from the clutch of Emmaline's vagina and grabbing her by the neck, he pressed her down to his crotch, ordering. 'Take me deep. Swallow it, Emmy. Swallow.'

Charley, his muscular body shaking with his sexual explosion, drove his penis into Emmaline's throat, gasping as he tossed his head back and forth on the bed.

Emmaline, feeling the penis explode in her mouth, tried not to swallow the semen, still thinking about the man who had taken her virginity, wondering if she would see him, too, when she went home to Longchamp Parish.

2 Longchamp Parish

The early morning sun was lighting the Louisiana sky from dark gray to a soft purple as the stagecoach rumbled along the weathered dirt road and Emmaline sat on the cracked leather seat with her best friend, a freckle-faced White girl, Punkin Bluedaw, who worked in New Orleans as a housemaid. The two other passengers who had boarded the stagecoach with them at the Canal Street post house had disembarked at the first stop, Twin Oaks Station, and now the four mud brown horses galloped between the dark shapes of the water oaks lining the road, racing toward the next scheduled stop – Centipede, Louisiana.

Punkin Bluedaw, unwrapping pieces of cornbread and thick slices of ham from a yellow checkered napkin spread on the lap of her thin green woollen coat, said, 'Let's start testing you with questions, Emmy. See what you remember.'

Emmaline had originally come to New Orleans with Punkin Bluedaw to work at the Shipton house on Carondelet Street. She had decided not to work there, however, but had subsequently devised a plot to keep her parents still believing she was a domestic servant like Punkin.

She asked, 'Do you really think I can get away with telling Mama and Papa I'm working as a maid with you at the Shipton house?'

'You've been writing them letters all these months you're at the Shiptons'. Isn't it a little bit late now to start changing your story?' Punkin worked as a kitchen girl in the house on Carondelet Street, and Emmaline had originally been hired

23

by correspondence to work as a laundress and upstairs maid.

'Writing letters back home that I'm a maid is one thing.' Emmaline argued. 'But to tell them lies face-to-face is just downright – I don't think I can do it.

Punkin reminded her, 'The idea seemed good enough to you when we first came to New Orleans, Emmaline.'

'Why didn't you speak-up like this back then?'

'You didn't ask me.'

'Punkin Bluedaw, you've changed.'

Punkin, lifting a thick slice of ham onto a second yellow napkin for Emmaline, asked, 'Why do you say that, Em?'

'You've learned to speak your mind.'

'Isn't that one of the reasons we decided to leave home? To grow up? To get out of our parents' clutches? To become women?'

Emmaline tossed back and forth on the seat of the stage-coach; the narrow brim of a yellow straw bonnet surrounded her face like an angel's shining nimbus, making her look even younger than usual; and the country air was already making her feel wholesome, seeing willow trees turning bright green for summer, farmers in the field with their mules, not looking, not listening to the whores squabbling on Smoky Row. Emmaline even noticed how she was talking differently, how she had already dropped the slow, drowsy drawl of Peaches, Luba, Effie, Eva, and Claire, the women who worked in the bordello.

Feeling more like her old self, she said, 'Oh, Punkin, it seems so long since we first decided to leave home. How did we ever convince our parents to let us do it?'

'It wasn't easy.' Punkin handed Emmaline her napkin of food, adding, 'You've changed, too, Em.'

'I know Punkin. I know. I feel different, too. I feel older. I don't feel like a child. But I also don't feel like going home!'

'Well, it's now or never, Em. The Shiptons have gone to Baton Rouge for ten days. You know they wouldn't let two hired girls leave work at the same time if they were in town.'

Emmaline knew. The Shiptons' brief trip to Baton Rouge had been the perfect time to go home, as well as providing the ideal excuse for not having come home sooner – and for not staying too long.

Punkin nibbled at the corner of a thick piece of corn-bread, saying more brightly, 'Hmmm. Isn't this good? It's Miss Lucy's new recipe. She puts a dozen eggs in it.'

'Miss Lucy?' Emmaline looked blankly at her girlfriend. 'I thought the Shiptons' cook was called Lorna Belle.'

'Lorna Belle? Oh, Em! Lorna Belle's gone!'

'Gone?'

'Lorna Belle ran away to Baton Rouge and got married to a shill from a medicine show.'

'When did that happen?'

'Three, four months ago at least.' Punkin sank back into the coach, saying, 'See. That's why we have to check and compare stories if you are going to tell your folks you're working with me for the Shiptons.'

Emmaline took a deep sigh, again wishing she was not going home. 'Maybe I should just keep my mouth shut and hope our folks don't compare stories.'

Punkin, picking yellow crumbs from the front of her threadbare coat, mused, 'Em, how do you think things would have been if you'd gone ahead and become a maid as you'd originally planned?'

Emmaline laughed. 'I can tell you exactly what would've happened if I was a maid. I wouldn't be here now. I would have gone home – or gone someplace – a long, long time ago.'

Punkin tried another idea. 'Or what would have happened, Em, if I had gone with that woman who stopped us on Canal Street when we first got to town?'

'Mrs Franklin.' Emmaline thought back to the sharply-featured woman who had approached them on the rainy day they had first arrived in New Orleans, two country girls carrying their possessions in carpet bags, their eyes wide with excitement – and fear – as they stared at the smart carriages, the loud horse-drawn street cars, the bells and horns and bustle of activity on Canal Street. Mrs Franklin had been wearing a long, stylishly cut black coat, topped with a red foxtail cape, and after politely introducing

25

herself, she had asked Emmaline and Punkin if they were interested in seeking immediate employment, to work in lavish surroundings where they could meet exciting people and earn a great deal more money than they would as housemaids.

Turning to Punkin in the tossing stagecoach, Emmaline asked, 'Did you hate me for going with her and leaving you stranded?'

'Don't be silly. I could never hate you, Em. But, sure, I was scared. I had to go to the Shiptons alone and tell them you found another job.'

'Was that the only thing that scared you?'

'No, I was worried, too, about what might happen to you. Em, you know you're silly and very reckless sometimes. I know you think I'm an old stick-in-the-mud. I might not say much. But I do worry about you. Like you using your own name in that . . . place where you work.'

'Fiddlesticks! Names aren't important, Punkin! My folks don't even use my real name. They've got a hundred little nicknames for me.'

Punkin asked with new concern, 'Em, are you taking care of yourself?'

'How do you mean?' Emmaline nibbled at the cornbread. She had slept little last night and was frightened by the prospect of seeing her parents. She hoped Punkin was not going to give her a lecture about her health, about prostitutes catching dreadful diseases, about dying some kind of early, horrid death. In the last ten months, Punkin had neither openly approved nor disapproved of what Emmaline had decided to do in New Orleans. And she hoped Punkin would continue being a good friend by keeping her mouth shut.

Punkin said, 'It's a little late now for me to start talking about what's done. But don't be surprised – and, please, Em, don't be angry – if I bring up the subject of your health on our way back to New Orleans. I'm your friend, and friends do worry. But for the time being . . . well, we're going home. So just don't fret about a thing. You're only going to be home a week. You'll survive. In fact, I bet you have the time of your life.'

'I hope so.'

'Why shouldn't you? Your mother is one of the nicest, one of the sweetest, prettiest ladies in the whole wide world. And your papa – why, Em, your papa is so-o-o handsome!'

Emmaline tilted her head and light-heartedly said, 'Punkin Bluedaw, are you sweet on my father?'

Punkin quickly protested. 'Certainly not!'

'Oh, oh, oh.' Emmaline playfully pointed at Punkin, accusing, 'You *have* changed. Listen to you snap! You can't even take a joke!'

Punkin lowered her head. 'I'm sorry, Em. I'm a little bit nervous, too, I guess because –'

Folding the corner of the napkin across her knees, Punkin confessed. 'Em, I'm doing something in secret, too. I'm being just as sneaky as you.'

'Sneaky? You? Little Miss Goody Two Shoes?'

Punkin nodded.

Being with Punkin always revived Emmaline's spirits. And although only a few hours had elapsed since they had left New Orleans, Emmaline already felt like a different person, like a playful, silly eighteen-year-old girl instead of the person who lived in the shuttered room on Smoky Row and spent her day wearing nothing but a white cotton shift.

Grabbing Punkin's forearm, Emmaline teased, 'You know everything about me, Punkin Bluedaw, so you tell me *your* secret. Tell me your secret or I'll do what I used to do when we were kids –'

Laughing, Punkin pushed away Emmaline's hand. But then she sank back onto the cracked leather seat, saying, 'That's the problem, Em, isn't it? We're not kids anymore. We're not two little girls. We're grown up. We left home. And . . . and . . . and . . . I'm in love, Em.'

'In love? Oh, Punkin, that's wonderful!'

Punkin looked at Emmaline. 'Is it?'

'Of course, it is, Punkin. Being in love must be the most wonderful thing ever to happen to a woman.'

Punkin's round face, splashed with red freckles, remained sober. 'Even if the person you love is not the same . . . color?'

A few seconds passed before Emmaline realized what

Punkin was telling her; she gasped, 'Oh, Punkin, no!'

Punkin nodded. 'Ben's black as midnight, Em. And I love him. I really do. I love him so much but – oh, Emmy, I'm so very scared.'

The Louisiana countryside became rougher, fewer towns and settlements dotting the wilderness as Punkin Bluedaw told Emmaline about Ben Hopper, the young Black man she had met in New Orleans who drove a vegetable wagon with his father along St Charles Avenue and the adjoining residential district dubbed the Garden District. Punkin explained how she had first bought berries and vegetables from Ben, and, then, after a few smiles and hints, she had begun sneaking out of the Shipton house at night to meet him. Punkin spoke more timorously when she reported how Ben had already told his family of his fondness for her, how the Hopper family had been very displeased with the fact that their son was secretly courting a White girl.

Punkin said, 'Em, it's very hard for White people to understand that Black people don't want their children marrying us, just like we don't want our children marrying . . . you.'

Emmaline nodded, remembering the lectures her parents had given her all her life about White people, especially about handsome young White boys with silver tongues and suave manners.

She asked, 'What are you going to do, Punkin? Run away to the North and get married?'

'The North? Oh, Em, you're so romantic. Things like that don't happen.'

'Yes they do. If you make them happen.'

'But I'm not strong like you, Em. Strong or whatever it is that makes you think and act how you do.'

The stagecoach rattled and bounced through the countryside as Punkin continued telling Emmaline about Ben Hopper, how he had wanted to come home with her to Longchamp Parish to meet her family, how he had already invited her to meet his parents but that she had so far declined the invitation.

28

Shortly after midday, the stagecoach stopped in the small town of Eustace, Louisiana; a White couple boarded the stage and, showing no annoyance that a Black girl would be travelling with them, Emmaline did not have to climb outside and ride on the roof with the driver.

As the sun turned into a blazing orange disc and began sinking down behind low, pine-covered mountains, the driver halted the four weary horses at the post house in Junctionville; Emmaline and Punkin hurried in the fading daylight, finding their way back to the same private house where they had slept overnight ten months ago on their way south to New Orleans.

The small frame house belonged to Miss Lillibelle Spooner, a parson's spinster sister; Punkin rapped on the front door and Miss Spooner warmly welcomed the girls into her home, sending them upstairs to the guest room while she went to the kitchen to prepare a light supper tray. The girls enjoyed the hot milk, wedges of moist yellow cheese, and slices of warm raisin bread while Miss Spooner sat in a fan-backed chair visiting with them. She rose as soon as the girls had finished eating, promising to awaken them early the next morning so they could resume their journey home to Longchamp Parish.

Shortly after the rooster's first crow, Emmaline and Punkin were seated back inside the stagecoach; across from them sat an old Black woman and a fat Black boy who wore a grimy felt hat pulled down over his head; the old woman stared at Emmaline and Punkin with small beady eyes but she did not speak until the stagecoach rumbled out of Junctionville.

The old woman said, 'You're too young to remember the old days, ain't you, girlies?'

Both Emmaline and Punkin, still drowsy with sleep, looked poker-faced at the old woman.

'Before Freedom Day,' the woman explained. 'You're both too young to remember them times, ain't you?'

Nodding, Emmaline said, 'My parents didn't come south from Pennsylvania until after Freedom, mam.'

The woman, tucking at a kerchief knotted around her

head, said, 'I bet your folks found no sweet bed of roses waiting for them. Not like her kin had.'

Punkin said, 'My parents only moved here from Arkansas eight years ago.'

'Arky dirt farmers, are you?'

Punkin had forgotten that country people also had their own forms of prejudice, and the slang expression, 'Arky dirt farmers', momentarily startled her.

She faltered, saying, 'My father's a farmer, yes, mam. And we're from . . . Arkansas.'

The old woman continued, 'You being Arky, you most likely heard of that Camellia bunch.'

Punkin glanced at Emmaline. What was she talking about?

'Knights of the Camellia,' explained the old Negress. 'Them troublemakers wearing sheets over their heads and carrying crosses of fire in the night. Folks say the Knights of the Camellia died out around here. But I say they ain't. I saw a band of hooded riders only a few nights ago. This side of Palmetto Landing. Course, they don't call themselves Knights of the Camellia no more. They all consider themselves to be members of that Kluxer's Klan.'

'The Ku Klux Klan?' gasped Punkin. 'You saw *them* near here?'

The old woman nodded. 'Them's the one. Ku Kluxers. White men who don't like outsiders changing this land. White folks who hate the sight of niggers – and Arky sodbusters like your kin!'

The old woman held her small beady eyes on the two girls as she dipped her crooked forefinger into a small pasteboard box, digging out a wad of tobacco, tucking it into her mouth, making a bump under her lower lip.

Punkin nudged Emmaline.

Emmaline nodded. Old women dipping tobacco. Talk about the Ku Klux Klan. Complaints about dirt farmers and sodbusters. Suspicion toward strangers. Land divided into parishes instead of counties. Yes, they were getting closer to home.

*　　*　　*

The old Black woman and the little fat boy left the stage-coach at the edge of a share-croppers' settlement called Crow Forks and, fifteen miles beyond Crow Forks, the four horses galloped into Bossburg, a small town of unpainted board buildings lining both sides of a dirt street, most of the buildings being abandoned, many collapsed from age or disuse.

A thick cloud of dust enveloped the stagecoach but Punkin excitedly pushed at the door, moving to step outside onto the street.

'Hello there, Miss Bluedaw!' called a tall, broad-shouldered man moving forward through the dust. 'And by crikey, is that my pretty little girl called Friday Night?'

Warren Rickers, with skin the color of a coffee bean and a wide-brimmed straw hat pushed forward on his closely-cropped black hair, warmly embraced his daughter, saying, 'You're even prettier than I remember, baby girl.'

Emmaline momentarily forgot all her misgivings about coming home and buried her face against her father's broad shoulder, suddenly seeing - feeling and hearing - how big, how boyishly handsome he was, the gentle way he acted and spoke.

The stage driver tossed the girls' bags from the top and, after Warren Rickers caught them and put them in his buggy, he explained to Punkin that he had made arrangements with her family to drive her home.

The chestnut mare trotted smartly along the parish road, finally turning from the road, passing between two posts, across a small plank bridge, and up to a log cabin snuggled in a copse of tall cottonwood trees.

Molly Bluedaw, a short, statuesque woman with her blonde hair knotted on top of her head, jubilantly greeted Punkin, then kissed Emmaline on both cheeks and thanked Warren profusely for being so neighborly, insisting that he and Emmaline step onto the porch for some refreshments.

Warren protested. 'Thank you, mam, but my Gemma's waiting at home. She can do nothing but talk about this little lady getting back.'

'Sure Gemma's anxious to see her baby,' agreed Molly

31

Bluedaw, and turning to Emmaline, she said, 'But your mama wouldn't want me to set you and your Daddy back on the road without giving you a cup of coffee or a nice cool glass of lemonade. Now tell me, honey, what's it going to be, coffee or lemonade?'

Punkin, with three little freckle-faced brothers and two sisters tugging at her long skirts, helped her mother produce a frosty pitcher of lemonade and a plate of apple-sauce cake for Emmaline and Warren. As everyone was gathering around the porch table, a stocky, broad-featured man appeared in the yard with a teenage boy. Neither the man nor the boy wore proper trousers, shirts, socks or shoes; their only clothing was twill trousers cut off at the thighs, and both were dripping water.

Punkin screamed with excitement at seeing her father and oldest brother. But when Molly Bluedaw saw her husband and oldest son scantily clothed, she scolded, 'Deke Bluedaw! Where's your decency? What's Warren here going to think about the way we live?'

Deke Bluedaw, unembarrassed over the near nakedness of his work-hardened body, shook Warren's hand and explained, 'Jeb and I were damming the creek. Warren, you understand about working in water.'

Warren grinned. 'Not only understand, Deke. I wear less when I jump in the creek for a cool-down.'

'See there!' teased Deke, patting his wife on her buttocks, round and firm under her long homespun skirt.

Grabbing a piece of cake, Deke turned back to Warren, explaining in a more serious voice, 'Fact is, I've got to work fast on that creek before Gus Hankley makes more trouble for me.'

Warren knew about the recent rift between Deke Bluedaw and Gus Hankley over the damming of the creek. He had even heard that Gus Hankley was calling in – or was threatening to call in – outsiders to prevent Deke Bluedaw making a dam for irrigation.

Preferring not to speak about affairs which did not concern him, Warren said, 'Deke, you better pull up a chair before we eat you out of house and home.'

32

Punkin, bringing towels for her father and brother, suddenly pleaded, 'Oh, Papa! Why don't you play hambone?'

Molly shrieked, 'Hambone? Oh, Punkin, no! Please don't encourage none of that foolishness! Not now.'

'But, Mama, I've been away so long and –'

Punkin turned back to her father, begging, 'Please play hambone, Daddy. Just a little bit.'

Deke Bluedaw motioned toward his lack of clothing, saying, 'Punkin, you're catching me at a moment when I can't rightly refuse you, now can I?'

Molly insisted, 'No, Deke. Please –'

'Mama, just one song,' wailed Punkin. 'Daddy's the only one who knows how to do it!'

When the other children joined in the request, Molly relented, saying, 'Okay. But just one song.'

Deke Bluedaw, sitting on a wooden stool, leant forward to hold both hands together in front of him as if he were going to pray. But as he started to nod his head slowly in time to an imaginary rhythm, he began slapping the flat of both hands against his bare thighs and the opposite fore and upper arms, making quick, staccato sounds on his naked flesh and whistling to keep in tune.

Punkin squealed with laughter and, throwing back her head, began pumping one foot up and down on the porch, clapping her hands; soon, the rest of the Bluedaw children, even Molly, joined in the entertainment.

Deke kept the song short and, when he finished, he rose from the bench and nodded playfully to the raucous applause.

Warren, also rising from his chair, said, 'Deke, we'd sure like to ask you for an encore. But if we don't get home pretty soon, Gemma's going to be out on the road looking for us with her rolling-pin.'

Molly kissed Emmaline farewell on the cheek, saying, 'Your mama sure must be anxious to see you, honey. You and Punkin might have flown the coop, but you're still our little chickadees.'

Punkin and Emmaline hugged goodbye as Deke Bluedaw reminded Warren, 'Don't forget. I'm taking the girls into Bossburg to meet the coach going back.'

Molly stamped her foot, scolding, 'Deke Bluedaw, you're the limit! The girls barely get home and here you go talking about them leaving!'

The Bluedaw family – happy, laughing – stood lined up in front of their log house, waving goodbye to Emmaline and Warren as the buggy bounced over the plank bridge.

Molly Bluedaw waited until the buggy reached the parish road before she sobered, shaking her head, saying, 'Poor Gemma. I've never seen Emmaline look so peaked.'

'Let's just worry about our own brood,' said Deke Bluedaw. Then turning to Punkin, he said, 'I half expected you to bring home a young gent, girl.'

Punkin smiled faintly as the image of Ben Hopper shot through her brain – big as a giant, smiling like a happy child, black as midnight, and waiting for her to hurry back to New Orleans.

'Junior Dehasset? I heard that name before.'

Ivy Bravo, a White woman with mousy blonde hair living on the outskirts of the small river town of Palmetto Landing, looked at the ruddy faced man standing in the darkness outside her doorway and said, 'Dehasset's a famous name in Longchamp Parish. From that big plantation, Belrose, west of here.'

The late-night caller, gripping a brown leather saddle bag under one arm, said in a husky voice, 'I didn't come here to talk about my family. I was told that you're a lady who can keep her mouth shut and –' Junior Dehasset smiled, '– her legs open.'

Ivy tilted her head, looking at Junior Dehasset, a barrel-chested man with a thick moustache. She said, 'I don't give away my hospitality, Mr Dehasset.'

'I got money for loving. I also got something you might be interested in seeing . . . that is, if it ain't too big for you.' Junior Dehasset grinned, thinking of what he carried inside his saddle bag.

'Too big?' Ivy smiled. 'I've yet to see a man built too big

for me.' She stepped forward to feel the crotch of his twill trousers.

Pushing away her hand from his genitals, Junior Dehasset lifted the saddle bag and said, 'What I've got is in here. I call it my "whorebreaker".'

The smile quickly faded from Ivy's slim face and, shaking her head, she said, 'Mister, you've come to the wrong woman. I'm a whore yes. A country town whore. Not a circus clown act. I take no trick gadgets up my pussy, you get my meaning?'

Opening the saddle bag, Junior Dehasset said, 'Don't you think you should see what I got before you start sending me away?'

Ivy stared transfixed at the object Junior Dehasset slowly removed from the saddle bag, an image of a phallus made from smoothly carved wood and tightly stretched horse leather, bigger than any man's penis Ivy had ever seen.

She murmured, 'It looks almost . . . real.'

Junior Dehasset asked, 'You ever seen nigger dick, woman?'

Ivy jerked her head. 'Course I ain't.'

'This is how they say niggers are built. Big like this. But they ain't. I castrated enough Black bucks to know. Niggers are built small. Tiny like acorns. Not big and strong like my – yep, I call this my "whorebreaker".'

Holding it toward Ivy's face, he said, 'Here, sniff it. Give it a little smooch maybe.'

Ivy pushed the leather phallus away with her hand. 'Get that danged thing away from me! Don't you know people might be passing behind you in the road? What they going the think, seeing me kissing that . . . thing?'

'I ain't been invited inside, mam.'

She studied him, seeing that his face was burnt by the wind, and that the moustache made him ruggedly handsome. She detected a mean, cruel glint in his eye, though, and she was old enough to remember hearing stories how Junior Dehasset had fled from Longchamp Parish years ago after he had dynamited a camptown of freed slaves with masked riders, how he had been part of a vigilante group called the Knights of the Camellia.

Slowly turning the leather phallus for Ivy to study, Junior Dehasset said, 'I tell you what. I'll give you two dollars for every inch of this you can take up your pussy. See. Look here. It's even notched. Like a ruler. You take it all, you get forty dollars cash.'

The front door of her house locked, Ivy Bravo lay on her bed as Junior Dehasset sat alongside her, easing the leather phallus – now slick with goose grease – between her spread legs as he manipulated his penis with his other hand.

Propping herself up on her elbows, Ivy said, 'I ain't never done nothing like this before.'

Junior's voice was low, assured of his actions. 'First we just got to open a path.'

'What if I can't take all of it tonight?'

'There's always tomorrow night.'

Pushing, stretching, watching the phallus slowly ease into her vagina, Ivy asked, 'You sticking around here a spell?'

'I've got work to do here in the parish. But you keep your mouth shut about that, you hear, and I'll be good to you.'

'You pay me two dollars an inch every time you stop by?'

Junior, gripping the phallus firmly with one hand, said, 'Pretty soon, woman, you're going to be paying me. That's one reason they call this a "whorebreaker". It breaks the bank of every whore who gets it. You gals just can't get enough. And, oh, yes, Ivy. I already see you're one cock-hungry woman.'

'What's the other reason they call it . . . that name?'

Ingoring the question, Junior Dehasset urged, 'Relax now, woman. Push out that pink pussy. Show me more pink. That's a girl. Eat up this dick. Eat it up good with that pussy. Hmmm.'

Junior Dehasset already knew he was going to be glad to be back home after seventeen long years of exile. There was nothing hornier than a country gal.

3   The House at 3 o'clock

Gemma Rickers sat at the scrubbed pine table in her kitchen as a morning fire crackled behind her inside the iron cookstove, a speckled blue tin coffee pot bubbling, filling the room with its rich aroma, and the sun rising beyond a copse of poplar trees, lighting the sky from dull pewter to a robin's egg blue.

Wearing a print cotton dress, and her black hair neatly arranged for the day in a handsome roll around her youthful face, Gemma sipped her first cup of milky coffee and worried about her daughter.

Emmaline had come home a different person from the excited girl who had gone to New Orleans ten months ago. Gemma remembered how troubled she had been when Emmaline had announced that she wanted to work in New Orleans. But Gemma had once been a strong-minded girl herself, and so she had finally agreed with Warren to allow their daughter to work with Punkin Bluedaw at the home of a wealthy White family in New Orleans, the Shiptons, who had placed an advertisement in the *Longchamp Monthly*.

Gemma's thoughts were suddenly disturbed by the sound of familiar footsteps on the wooden stairs leading from the overhead bedrooms. She immediately arose from her chair and moved toward the cookstove to pour a second cup of coffee for her husband.

Warren padded across the kitchen floor in his stocking feet and bent to kiss Gemma on the forehead. 'Morning, bird face.'

'Morning, lover.'

Immediately recognizing the concern on her face, and

37

the sober tone of her voice, he asked, 'Hey, what's wrong?'

Gemma shook her head.

'No keeping secrets, sweetie.'

She shrugged and took another sip of coffee.

He asked, 'Is it baby?'

Setting down the cup in the deep saucer, she said, 'Emmaline's no baby any more, Warren.'

'So it *is* her. Well, don't forget she's still our little girl.'

'Emmaline's grown, Warren. She's a young lady.'

Fetching his clumpy brown work boots from behind the cookstove, Warren sat down on his chair at the head of the table. 'Go easy on the kid, honey. It's her first time away from home.'

Gemma gave a deep sigh. 'She seems so different, Warren. So cold. So distant. She never was a girl you could get close to. But I can understand that. I lived in my own world, too, as a girl. But Emmy seems more distant that ever. And guarded. Like she's hiding something from us. Like she has some secret she's scared –'

Unable to continue, Gemma looked at Warren stooped over in the chair still lacing the leather strings in his boots.

She asked, 'How did Punkin look?'

Warren grunted. 'You know those Bluedaws. Punkin's just like the rest of them. Hooting and hollering. Clapping and whistling.'

Gemma smiled faintly. She liked Deke and Molly Bluedaw. She approved of how they raised their large family, how they appreciated each other's company, lived for each other's happiness, keeping to themselves on their pretty little farm; Gemma considered the Bluedaw family to be a fine example for the whole neighborhood.

Warren, sitting up in his chair, regarded his wife and asked, 'You're really worried about Fried Eggs, aren't you?'

'Your daughter's name is not "Fried Eggs".'

'Fried Eggs. Friday Night.' Warren shrugged. 'One name's good as the other.'

'And her name isn't "Friday Night". It's Emmaline.'

'Woman, our daughter wouldn't know who the heck you're talking to if you call her . . . Emmaline.'

A small, sleepy voice said in the kitchen doorway, 'Morning, Mama. Morning, Daddy.'

Gemma and Warren both turned in their chairs and saw their daughter – wrapped in a long blue flannel blanket – moving toward the table.

'Hey, what're you doing up so early?' asked Warren.

Gemma held out both hands as Emmaline moved to kiss her, and said, 'Your Daddy and I were going to let you have a nice long sleep, baby.'

'I'm not going to be home very long,' Emmaline said as she next kissed her father on the top of the head and sank down in her chair. 'So why waste my time sleeping?'

Gemma rose from the table. 'Let me start some breakfast.'

Emmaline quickly called, 'Don't fix anything for me, Mama.'

Gemma set a black iron skillet on the stove, saying, 'Your Papa still eats early. You and I can sit and keep him company.'

Warren, cupping one hand over Emmaline's hands clasped together on the table, said, 'So tell us more about New Orleans. Any difference there since the time we all went there to see your Uncle Jay dance on that riverboat?'

At the mention of her uncle, Emmaline's eyes widened and she asked, 'Have you heard from Uncle Jay?'

'Just one letter,' Gemma called as she forked ham into the skillet. 'He's still out in San Francisco.'

'Is he married yet?'

'What do you think?'

Warren said, 'Hey, let's not waste time talking about Jay Greene. Let's hear more about you, cupcake.'

Emmaline had forgotten about the enthusiasm, the physical energy both her parents had so early in the morning.

Shrugging her shoulders, she said, 'Like I told you last night, there's not much to tell.'

'What plans do you have for today?' called Gemma from the stove.

'Not much, Mama. Unless you have work for me to do.'

'Sure we do,' Warren said. 'After you milk the cow, you have to shovel out the horse barn. And when you finish down there, you can start ploughing the south field. That should take you to noon.'

Emmaline smiled at her father; she had also forgotten how much he teased her, and how much she enjoyed all the playful attention from him.

Gemma, poking a fork at the sizzling ham, said, 'Sabrine and Cramer invited us to Belrose tomorrow. They're giving one of their big Sunday afternoon parties and they particularly want you to be there. Isn't that sweet of them, baby?'

Emmaline's heart sank at the idea of going to Belrose Plantation.

Warren saw the change of expression on her face and he said, 'What's the matter, cupcake? You don't look too excited about the idea of going to a party. What happened? Big city turn you into a home body?'

Emmaline pulled the blanket around her. 'I like Aunt Sabrine and Uncle Cramer. They're always so sweet to me. But a party, especially a big party –' She wrinkled her upper lip.

Gemma warned sternly, 'Now there's no way you can get out of going with us to Belrose, young lady, so don't even try. They treat you like family. We treat them like family. So don't go upsetting the applecart, understand?'

Warren glanced at Gemma, surprised to hear her speaking so sharply to Emmaline.

Gemma, realizing immediately how curtly she had spoken, softened her tone as she relented. 'Wait and see how you feel. But you know how Sabrine and Cramer love you. It would be nice if they could at least catch a glimpse of you.'

Moving back to the table, Gemma set a plate of eggs, ham, and grits in front of Warren, saying more gravely, 'But, sugar, I do have to warn you about one thing.'

Emmaline jerked her head; she had recognized her mother's quiet, unspoken displeasure last night during supper, and she could not help but notice the sharp outbreak a few moments ago; Emmaline knew her mother was a bright, intelligent woman, a person not easily duped, and

40

she dreaded any confrontation with her.

Gemma, resting her hand on Warren's shoulder, looked down at Emmaline in the chair, saying, 'This man here is going to try to talk you into not going back to that job you've got in New Orleans.'

'My . . . job?' Emmaline knew this was probably only another playful joke but the words stuck in her throat. 'What about my . . . job?'

Gemma nodded. 'This here man's going to try to keep you at home, to be his maid. So stand warned, sugar pie.'

Emmaline forced a sweet smile, saying, 'Oh, Daddy.'

Warren still lingered at the breakfast table after Emmaline had gone upstairs, washed and dressed, and come back downstairs to announce that she was going to stop at the milk barn to see the new litter of kittens. Warren waited until Emmaine had gone out of the kitchen door and crossed the back porch before he complimented Gemma on her sudden change of attitude with their daughter, saying, 'Thanks for being more yourself.'

Gemma's small oval face resumed its troubled expression. 'I just wish I didn't have this awful feeling that she's hiding something from us.'

'Hiding? What could she be hiding?'

'I can't explain the feeling I've got. But it's there, Warren, and I don't like it.'

'Do you want me to have a little talk with her?'

Gemma shook her head. 'Not yet. She might have to get used to being back here with us. Yes, we brought her into the world. But when we gave her life, we were supposed to do just that – *give* it to her. Not hold onto it like some fishline. So wait, Warren. Let's just bide our time.'

Warren, standing behind Gemma's chair, crossed his arms over her breasts and lowered his face to her lemon-scented hair.

He whispered, 'Coffee Cup, I love you.'

'Oh, get to work, you dirty old man!'

Less than twelve hours had passed since Emmaline had arrived home and already she felt like an awkward outsider,

41

like some stranger sent to visit Warren Rickers, a sweet man with a wonderful sense of humor who loved to tease people, and Gemma Rickers, a handsome woman, neat and orderly, who looked young enough to be her own sister and possessed all the wisdom of the world in those sharp, flashing eyes, and a temper to go with it.

Moving away from the house along a mossy path skirting the farm's outbuildings, Emmaline carried a stick in one hand and thought how far away she was from Smoky Row, from the world of Jocasta Liddle, from the prostitutes who stood in the doorways of cribs and shouted at passersby and at one another, from men who paid money to clean her room, from customers who masturbated as they watched her cupping her breasts, fingering the lips of her vagina, listened to her telling them about the size of another man's penis.

Emmaline felt strangely dirty. She felt as if she might contaminate her mother's spotlessly clean house, leave a trace of some man on the lace-edged sheets, the musty aroma of . . . sin.

Then, with a sudden surge of defiance, Emmaline swatted her stick at the lush ferns drooping across the path and thought that she was a person who possessed her own free will, a person who had rebelled against being a lowly housemaid, another person's lackey, a slave.

Thinking about slavery, Emmaline remembered Jocasta Liddle sitting on the edge of her bed two days ago in Smoky Row, asking her why she had become a prostitute, trying to compare her to Luba and Peaches and Cassy.

Emmaline never thought of herself as a prostitute. She never considered herself to be one of the foul-mouthed women working Smoky Row. She was there trying to have a good time. To see something of life. The world. What other people did.

Nor would she stay there forever, not like Cassy and Luba and Peaches, or even Big Jocasta Liddle herself.

But was she really having a good time? Or was she working for Jocasta Liddle because she wanted the money men paid for her company? Or the independence she got?

42

Proving she could make her own way in the world? Or did she just enjoy hearing the compliments men lavished on her? Enjoy her superiority over the other women on the street? She knew she was the youngest, prettiest, most desirable girl in Jocasta's house – probably in all the bordellos on Smoky Row. Certainly the cribs. And it was fun being the best.

But was that why she stayed at Jocasta's house instead of trying one of the other, more respectable, less rundown bordellos in New Orleans which also employed colored girls? Places like Kate Gilmore's on Basin Street? Mattie Field's on St Louis Street? Was she frightened of being outshone by girls as pretty, as young, as desirable as herself? The woman who had originally spotted her and Punkin on Canal Street, Mrs Franklin, had even tried to persuade Emmaline to go to a bigger, more flashy establishment when she had first described them. Mrs Franklin received twenty dollars from each madam for every girl she supplied and Emmaline had told her that Jocasta Liddle's twenty dollars sounded as good as Kate Gilmore's, Mrs Mattie Field's or Laura Wren's. Emmaline had wanted to find her own stride, even if Mrs Franklin had snidely implied that Emmaline might just want to be a big fish in a squalid little pond.

No, Emmaline told herself stubbornly as she walked through the woods with her stick. She was at Jocasta's because it was the safest place in New Orleans for her to be at the moment, the last place where anybody would ever think of seeing the daughter of fine, self-respecting, upright Gemma and Warren Rickers.

Not being a crib whore, or a street-walker, Emmaline thought that Smoky Row fulfilled her needs fine. Just fine. At least for the moment. Basin Street tempted her, of course. Opulence tempted everybody. But sex was sex.

Sex did not repel Emmaline. Nor the sex games men wanted to play. Sometimes she even enjoyed the games. And considering the fact of enjoying sex, Emmaline wondered if she really was one of those females whom people called 'nymphomaniacs'? A woman who needed sex as if it were water, air, some kind of food?

When Emmaline did not enjoy making love with a

customer, she could easily forget about him and think about a pretty room she might want to live in, the room's furniture and curtains and pretty carpets. Or imagine a dress she could buy, feathers or ribbons she could choose for a bonnet she would be able to afford from the money the man was paying her.

Thinking about bonnets and dresses she realized that she had not brought home a suitable dress to wear to the party at Belrose Plantation tomorrow.

Emmaline suddenly stopped on the path. What if somebody at the party recognized her from New Orleans? Deliberately, she never stood on the bordello's front porch in fear of being seen by somebody from Longchamp Parish. But what if a man at tomorrow's party had seen her entering Jocasta Liddle's house and knew that it was a brothel? Smoky Row was a notorious place. Sometimes people just went there to gawk. Or what if one of the guests at the party was a man who had been one of her customers?

A sudden noise, a sound like a pine cone falling from a branch, disturbed Emmaline and she glanced to the left of the path.

She dropped her stick and stared at the young man standing on a small, grassy knoll.

Alain Summers, handsome with honey-colored skin and fashionably cut clothes hugging his athletic body, smiled at Emmaline as one hand worked the crotch of his twill trousers.

'Why, if it isn't little Emmaline Rickers,' said Alain Summers as he stepped over a fallen log and moved onto the path. 'If this ain't my lucky day!'

Emmaline stammered, 'I . . . I . . . I . . . just got home last night, Alain.'

'Yes, I heard you were down in New Orleans doing something awful.'

'Awful?' She felt her heart beating faster. 'What did you hear about me, Alain?'

'That you were being somebody's maid or something awful like that.' He lowered his eyes to appraise her body, saying disapprovingly, 'What a waste.'

Emmaline kept staring at him, mesmerized, realizing he

was even more handsome, more confident, more desirable than she had remembered.

He said, 'I've been away myself, you know. I just got back from Natchez. But look at you! I still think you're the prettiest girl in Longchamp Parish.'

Alain Summers had always awakened something mysterious in her, Emmaline remembered. Made her say things improper, brazen, made her behave differently than she did around other people.

She flared jealously. 'But Natchez girls are a lot prettier than me, are they?'

Alan laughed, his white teeth gleaming under his thin black moustache; his White Créole blood made his Black features exotic, almost too handsome for a man, a trait which would have induced slave-dealers before the War to dub him a 'Fancy'.

Stepping closer to Emmaline, Alain put one arm around her thin waist and looked down into her eyes, saying, 'You are prettier than any girl I've seen any place. That's why I want to kiss you. Right now.'

He lifted a crooked forefinger to her chin, closing his eyelids with their long, curling black lashes, and lowered his mouth to her lips.

Emmaline stepped back, protesting, 'No, Alain. Not here.'

'Not here? But this place used to be good enough for you!'

'Not now. Not today.'

'I see. You're a city girl and too good for me any more. People tell lies when they say girls always remember the boys who first made love to you.'

'Alain, you know I remember . . . everything!'

'Everything?' He moved his hand back around her waist, asking, 'What all do you remember, my little Emmaline?'

'I . . . I . . . I . . . remember lots of things.'

'Do you remember our kisses?'

Emmaline felt her cheeks flush.

'Do you remember my hands touching you, feeling you, caressing you?'

'Alain . . . please.'

'We did everything, Emmaline. Everything. I remember you being wild with me. Very wild and abandoned and wonderful. Do you remember all the wild and wonderful things we did making love here on a blanket?'

'Alain, can't you talk about anything else?'

Laughing, he said more brightly, 'My tutor used to tell me that the world spins on an axis. And do you know what I said to him, Emmaline? I said that the axis of my world would always be my prick. And my prick's big enough for that, isn't it? Or have you forgotten that, too?'

Emmaline felt as light-hearted as a very young girl, as if she had never been touched by a man before in her life, as if she had never made love, as if she had come home from a convent, not a brothel.

He continued, 'My prick is the axis and the world is right here between your legs . . .'

Moving his hand toward Emmaline's skirt, Alain lowered his voice, saying, 'The axis is my prick spinning, spinning, spinning right here to this very spot . . .'

The firm press of his large fingers between her legs awakened an immediate excitement in Emmaline. But again, she stepped back, saying, 'Alain Summers, you are the most outrageous man I ever met.'

His laugh was deep, mocking, obscene.

He said, 'My Mama tells me I take after my Daddy. And Mama should know, shouldn't she? She's one of those White women who's an authority on men darker than herself.'

'Alain, don't speak so disrespectfully about your very own mother.'

'Why not? Mama doesn't hesitate to tell me I was an accident she had with a field slave.' Alain reached for Emmaline's hand and, kissing it, he paused to study the soft skin.

He said, 'These hands don't look like they've been working too hard, cherie.'

Emmaline quickly pulled her hands away from him, hiding them behind her back, stammering, 'Alain, you are impossible!'

'I'm impossible? Do you know why? Because I need you. My balls ache for you. My prick throbs for you. My prick is so hard at this very moment, Emmaline Rickers, that if you lowered your eyes to my trousers you could see the biggest hard-on you'll ever see in your life!'

Emmaline fought her urge to lower her eyes, instead demanding, 'Stop this talk. Stop this talk right now.'

'Make love to me.'

'No.'

He persisted, 'If you won't make love now, what about tonight?'

Her knees felt weak; the palms of her hands were wet with nervous excitement; but she shook her head, saying, 'No, Alain. It's my first night home. I can't go running out of the house after supper. Mama would have a fit.'

'What about tomorrow.'

'We're going to Belrose tomorrow. There's going to be a big party there in the afternoon. There's no way I can get out of it. None.'

'Belrose Plantation?' Alain was impressed. 'Well, don't look for Mama and me there. The Cramer Crowleys never invite *us* to Belrose. But, then, you're more privileged than us outcasts at High Hill Plantation.'

Emmaline faltered. 'Maybe I can see you tomorrow evening. Before it gets dark –'

'Ah! I knew you couldn't resist me!' Alain reached up to grab her, saying, 'And you won't be sorry. I'm going to make such good love to you, girl, you aren't going to want to go back to New Orleans.'

Lowering his mouth to hers, Alain plunged his tongue between her small lips as he pushed his groin against her, knowing she could feel his size, the hardness of his erection through her dress, remembering that despite Emmaline's childish appearance she was one of the most exciting females he had ever conquered. And he knew she was still weak for him, too.

Emmaline's first day at home was over and, as darkness enshrouded her parents' slope-roofed shingle house, the candle had been snuffed out in Emmaline's room and she was fast asleep. But a pool of silver moonlight cut through the window in Gemma's and Warren's room, lighting them as they lay side by side in their large, carved mahogany bed.

Warren, both hands clasped behind his head as he lay naked under the crisp linen sheets, said, 'You know who gave her that name, don't you?'

'What name?' Gemma asked in the moonlight.

'Friday Night.'

'Broody Hen.'

Warren smiled with the memory. 'The night Broody Hen brought her into the world. Big Spanker was alive then, too. And Paulie was living here with us in the old Slave Quarters. It was right after Junior Dehasset drove Paulie off Belrose Plantation and damned near whipped the life out of him here in our yard.'

He paused, 'Whatever happened to Junior Dehasset? Does Sabrine ever talk about her brother?'

Remembering Sabrine Crowley's older brother, Gemma closed her eyes and said, 'Don't waste good breath talking about . . . trouble.'

The sound of crickets filled the night air; the hoot of a barn owl cut through the darkness and, as squirrels scampered across the cedar shake roof, Warren went back to reminiscing about the old Black midwife, Broody Hen, who had brought their daughter into the world.

'Broody Hen said that sod-breakers like us had to get up before dawn to work every day of the week, and early for church on Sundays, so the only night of the week we had to make love was on Friday, so we should call Emmy "Friday Night".' He laughed. 'Crazy old coot, wasn't she?'

'Broody had her queer ways. But some of the things she said made a strange kind of sense. Like how she saw all the houses and farms in Longchamp Parish laid out like numbers on the face of a clock.'

'She was mighty proud of being able to tell time.'

'Bossburg is twelve noon. Belrose is two. And we're the house at three o'clock. Funny old woman.'

Warren curled up around Gemma, saying, 'We've seen a

lot together on this piece of land of ours, haven't we, Coffee Cup?'

'Hopefully, we're going to see a lot more.'

Putting his arm across the flat of Gemma's stomach, Warren pushed back her freshly brushed hair with his other hand and nibbled at her ear, asking, 'Have I ever thanked you for being so perfect.'

'Hmmm. Every day.'

'Then why don't you let me call you "Perfection"?'

'Because it sounds like a bottle of penny perfume.'

Gently, Warren moved on top of Gemma, positioning his knees on both sides of her legs, kissing her cheeks, her forehead, moving one hand under her nightdress, putting the other hand over her hair spreading on the pillow.

Responding to Warren's overtures, Gemma relaxed her body, allowing him to raise the hem of her nightdress and lift it over her head.

Soon, Warren had locked Gemma's trim body in his arms, his penis thickening into erection, his tongue tracing a pattern between her full breasts; he gently chewed on one nipple, then touching the other nipple's aureola, moistened the raspberry bud with the tip of his tongue.

She whispered, 'We got spoiled, haven't we?'

'Spoiled?'

'Not worrying about making noise.'

'You mean without Emmy here?'

'Hmmm.'

'She must have guessed by now we do more in this room than snore and pull the blankets off each other in our sleep.'

'You know what I mean –'

Gemma stopped talking as Warren knelt between her spread legs, lifting her thighs in his hands, moving his mouth toward her furry patch.

Eagerly, he began poking his tongue in and out, in and out of Gemma's vagina; he worked her feminine lips with his persistent mouth, chewing, eating, licking, tasting, probing his long tongue deeper inside her.

The sensation made Gemma squirm, pump her hips,

crease her vagina tightly like a flower, then blossom into moist fullness.

Soon, she sat forward, her legs wrapped around Warren's buttocks, hugging him around the neck, kissing him, feeling the length of his penis pushing hard against her, pressing, waiting to pierce the furry slit.

Before Gemma allowed him entry, though, she pulled back and lowered her mouth, stretching her mouth to accommodate his erect thickness, savoring the sexual organ as he himself had enjoyed tasting her femininity.

Then, again, they sat clutching one another in the moonlight, exchanging the taste from one another's mouth and, slowly, lovingly, Warren's penis forced its way into Gemma, as she squirmed, twisted, moved for him to sink deeper, keeping alive the physical flame of their many years of love.

By the light of the same moon, Junior Dehasset rode from Ivy Bravo's house on the outskirts of Palmetto Landing, galloping westward through the night, deeper into Longchamp Parish.

He stopped at a stretch of railroad tracks east of Bossburg, remaining mounted on his horse in the bushes as he took out a gold pocket watch from his waistcoat.

Finally hearing the distant chug of the Mississippi-Dixie on its way south from Kettley to Junctionville, Junior Dehasset snapped open the watch's engraved cover and saw that the time was past ten o'clock.

Waiting, listening to the train's locomotive grow louder in the night's distance, Junior Dehasset kept an eye on the watch until the three-car train rumbled directly in front of him, making his horse shy and dance in the rush of steam and the clang of iron pistons.

The time was 10:20.

Satisfied, Junior Dehasset clicked shut the gold watch, put it back into the pocket of his waistcoat, and smiled.

He was glad to be home again, to be doing his God-given duty. And if his plans went as he hoped, his forthcoming duties included gaining his rightful control of Belrose Plantation.

50

But, first, he had to help his friends – brothers by oath – before he claimed the land meant to be his. He had to help rid the countryside of Arky dirt-farmers before he set out to claim Belrose Plantation.

4   Belrose Plantation

Sabrine and Cramer Crowley received their guests on the sloping lawn fronting the big house of Belrose Plantation, a large white neo-classical mansion which had been the home of Sabrine's family, the Dehassets, for five generations, and a gift to her and Cramer Crowley on their wedding day.

A steady stream of buggies, wagons and people on horseback had begun arriving at Belrose shortly after midday: parish families named the Lintotts, the Merrieres, the Rowans, the Tanets. Cramer Crowley had also invited men whom he had known in the Civil War, officers who had served in both the Confederate and Union armies and now tried to work in harmony, helping Louisiana continue its position as one of the South's leading states.

Cramer Crowley, unlike his deceased father-in-law, Senator Dehasset, did not involve himself directly in politics. He talked behind closed doors to his friends from the Senate, Legislature, and Congress, giving them opinions and advice, helping to solve political differences but never attracting public attention to himself. He also kept in the background in the running of Belrose Plantation, allowing his petite but dynamic wife to be the figurehead of the land which had belonged to her forebears - fertile fields, orchards, and forests which had remained unravaged by the Civil War because of its remote isolation in Longchamp Parish.

Sabrine Crowley, wearing an apple-green silk dress and with a crown of fresh violets encircling her blonde hair knotted at the nape of her neck, welcomed Gemma, Warren and Emmaline Rickers in front of the six Doric columns lining the big house of Belrose Plantation.

Kissing young Emmaline on both cheeks, Sabrine Crowley stepped back to admire her, saying, 'How charming you look! And what a pretty pink dress! I heard that bell sleeves were the latest fashion again in New Orleans!'

Emmaline dipped her head, modestly confessing, 'Mama made this dress for me especially to wear to your party, Aunt Sabrine.'

Sabrine, having known that Gemma was sewing a new party dress for Emmaline and planning to give it to her as a surprise only this morning, surreptitiously winked at Gemma, then said to Emmaline, 'Aren't you the lucky young lady.'

Turning to greet Gemma with a kiss on both cheeks, Sabrine said, 'And I still can't believe you're old enough to have an eighteen-year-old daughter.'

'I am,' Gemma said, teasing, 'And don't you forget, dear, you made Emmaline her first doll!'

'I did, didn't I?'

Cramer Crowley, tall, lanky, his curly black hair laced with silver, joined his wife and the Rickers family, bussing Gemma and Emmaline on both cheeks, shaking hands with Warren, then saying, 'Would you ladies please forgive me, but there's a little matter I'd like to discuss with Warren and I'd like to do it before everybody arrives.'

Sabrine chastised him mildly. 'Darling, you promised me you wouldn't talk business!'

'Only for a moment,' Cramer said, then walked with Warren across the sloping lawn.

His hands clasped behind the back of his twill frockcoat, Cramer Crowley began, 'Warren, sorry to drag you away like this but it's about Deke Bluedaw.'

'And Willow Creek?' Warren looked youthfully handsome today, wearing a beige gaberdine suit and a red tie knotted around a crisp white cotton shirt, his black hair shiny and clinging to his head in short, tight curls.

Cramer said, 'Willow Creek and Gus Hankley's argument with Bluedaw about damming it.'

'Foolishness.'

53

Cramer turned to bow graciously to a pair of elderly women with lavender tinted hair alighting from their carriage, then continued strolling down the slope with Warren, saying, 'It's getting all out of proportion, I agree. But what's worse, people are starting to take sides in the matter. Men like Dave Cooper, Dwight Pine, Ron Wilkie. They're saying around Bossburg that Bluedaw barged in here from Arkansas and is trying to make too many changes.'

Warren knew the men whom Cramer had mentioned; he also had been victim of their selfish prejudices.

He said, 'Cramer, if sides are being taken, I'd go with Deke Bluedaw. Heck, he's only damming the creek to irrigate a vegetable patch. There's plenty of water for everybody. It's not as if Willow Creek is going to stop flowing at his place once that dam's there.'

Warren became angry when he thought about the men in Bossburg who tried to run local affairs from the general store; he shook his head in frustration, saying, 'Not all folks hereabouts are as liberal or broad-minded as you, Cramer. I can't come right out and express my opinion in public like other people do. Three-quarters of the population in Longchamp Parish is Black. But we're still what's called the "minority". It's been that way a long time. And I have the feeling it's not going to change overnight.'

Cramer said, 'That's one of the reasons I wanted to talk to you, Warren. About the fact of your so-called "free colored minority".'

Warren frowned, repeating, ' " Free colored minority". Slavery's been over nearly twenty years and they still call us "free" like they might be ready to forget about the Thirteenth Amendment and thinking about putting four million people back into chains.'

Cramer let Warren fume. He understood the frustrations of being a Black person in the South. Every day he saw the prejudices, not only in towns and on farms, but also the lack of jobs, schools, hospitals, day-to-day privileges which White people took for granted, but which Black people were not even allowed to dream about.

He said, 'I thought you should know something else, Warren.'

Warren waited.

'There's talk about the Knights coming back.'

'The Knights of the . . . Camellia?'

Cramer gravely nodded. 'Or as they are now known throughout most of the South – the Ku Klux Klan. Practically all of the small vigilante groups joined into one big one.'

'If that doesn't take the cake!'

'What?' Cramer looked at Warren.

'Gemma and I were just talking last night about Sabrine's brother. I asked Gemma if there's been any word from Junior Dehasset.'

Cramer frowned at the mention of his brother-in-law's name. 'I have army friends who still keep an eye on him. He's more dangerous than ever, I'm sorry to say. Remember Colonel Fenton? The reb officer from Montgomery who dubbed himself the "Grand Cyclops" at the end of the War and tried to organize that underground railroad?'

Warren nodded. He remembered the clandestine venture which had tried to entrap Black people back into slavery to transport them to western states after the War, a plan which Cramer Crowley himself had helped to abort.

Cramer continued to explain, 'Well, Fenton was the power behind the Klan but he died a few months ago and Sabrine's brother has been working his butt off to inherit the mantle of power. Junior Dehasset's been travelling back and forth from Montgomery and Tallahasse, and I hear he's stirring up a lot of old trouble about "out-siders" and "God's Chosen White People" and "Protecting our women".'

Warren thought of the possible consequences which could result from an organization like the Ku Klux Klan if it gained a powerful hold on the South. He himself was now farming five hundred acres. He hired more than two dozen workers during harvest, Black men and women to whom he paid wages, trying to start a local precedent for an honest sum to be paid to Negroes, to prevent the spread of the share-cropper system, a stranglehold which kept Negroes powerless and poor, while at the same time lining the pockets of White landowners. Organizations like the Ku Klux Klan saw share-cropping as their last chance of keeping Negroes in a yoke, of being masters to people technically no longer slaves yet who lived no differently from the old days before Emancipation.

Strolling past a pergola built at the edge of a small lake located at the bottom of the sloping lawn, Cramer Crowley continued, 'Warren, what you tell Gemma about this matter is your business. But I'd prefer for Sabrine not to know about her brother's recent activities in the Klan. Not yet. She's been worried for too long about Junior trying to seek revenge for their father cutting him out of the will. This just might be the moment to bring Junior Dehasset back to Longchamp Parish and cause trouble for more people than Deke Bluedaw.

Warren quickly agreed to help protect Sabrine Crowley from any unnecessary worry.

Behind the two men, the orchestra began playing a lively polka on the upper gallery in the big house; waiters in white jackets circulated with silver trays of a non-alcoholic punch called 'strawberry shrub', but many male guests gathered at the end of a long table, waiting for glasses of bourbon, the favorite label being 'Southern Lightning.'

A wooden dance floor had been laid out across flagstones running the length of the lower gallery and, after the guests had enjoyed luncheon, they began dancing to a violin, a piano and a cello playing on the upper gallery.

Warren, leading Emmaline in a waltz, said, 'You made your Mama very happy by coming to this shindig, sugar pie.'

Emmaline's eyes still darted across the other guests, looking for someone whom she might know from Smoky Row, or someone who might recognize her; she tried to sound calm, relaxed, saying, 'Oh Daddy, you knew I'd come.'

'Sometimes you and your Mama lock horns.'

'Maybe we used to have our differences. But not any more. And why should we? I'm only home for a little while.'

'A little while is right! It seems you just got here. Now you're leaving in four, five days' time.'

'I'll be back.'

'If you aren't, your Mama and me will just have to come down there to New Orleans.' Warren took a deep breath, moving to a three-quarter time music, saying, 'Christmas was no fun without you home, dumpling.'

Emmaline stiffened.

'What's the matter?' asked Warren. 'I say something wrong?'

Emmaline affected a sad voice, asking, 'Don't you think *I* want us all to be together, too, Daddy?'

'Course you do, sugar. Course you do.'

'But there's nothing for me to do in Longchamp Parish.'

'I know, baby. I know you got itchy feet.'

'I may not say so, Daddy, but I cry. I do. I cry because I miss home as much as anybody else.' She sniffed. 'But I wouldn't even be here now if the Shiptons hadn't gone to Baton Rouge.'

'Shhh.' He looked down at her lowered head, whispering, 'Want my hanky? It's clean.'

Emmaline shook her head.

She no longer felt guilty when she lied to her father. And silently following his smooth dance steps, she wondered if her lies meant that she did not love her parents any more, that she no longer had true feelings for that handsome lady who looked young enough to be her sister, for this big sweet man with the easy-going style? She could make up stories for them just as easily as she invented fantasies for Charley the Oysterman, or Henry Peele, the man who paid three dollars to scrub her floor.

Sabrine and Cramer Crowley's last guests left shortly before sundown; the servants worked quickly to put the house, the galleries, the gardens back into order while Sabrine and Cramer retired to their bedroom.

Sabrine sat at her dressing table, brushing her hair by candlelight while Cramer lay on the large tester bed, his hands folded across the chest of his beige silk pajamas.

He said, 'Little Emmaline seemed distant.'

'I noticed the same thing,' Sabrine said, sitting in front of the ormolu mirror. 'She kept looking at all the guests as if she was expecting somebody to arrive.'

'Maybe Alain Summers.'

'Alain Summers?' Sabrine stared into the mirror at the reflection of her husband on the bed behind her. 'From High Hill?'

'I heard they used to see each other.'

Brushing her hair in long, steady strokes, Sabrine said, 'Honestly! Sometimes men are worse gossips than women!'

'Don't forget you married an Army Intelligence Officer. So don't blame me for being a gossip. That was part of my job.'

'The War's well over. And don't spy on our friends! Oh, dear, I don't know what dear Gemma would say if she even suspected Emmaline had ever seen . . . Alain Summers. He's so bold!'

'And how, pray, do you know that?'

'I hear stories, too. Just look at his background! Not only is the poor thing illegitimate – which is no fault of his, I must admit – but his mother does carry on up there at High Hill like some yard dog. Do you really truly think Gemma wants her daughter seeing a boy from an ambience like that?'

'Parents have little control over their children these days. Nor did they when we were young. Do you think your parents wanted you to marry an Irish pedlar?'

'Pooh! You were no pedlar! You just told me that to make me think you were romantic!'

'But there's no denying I'm Irish. And your mother could never forgive you for marrying a shanty Irishman.'

'Poor Mama,' Sabrine said, lowering the ivory-backed brush. 'The Lord rest her soul. And Daddy, too. I guess our marriage was a bit difficult for her to accept.'

Rising from the dressing table, she snuffed out the pair of candles and moved toward the bed.

Untying the white satin ribbons on her peignoir of broderie anglaise, she said, 'Talking about Emmaline, I must confess I have difficulty picturing her working as a housemaid.'

'Why? New Orlean's full of pretty maids.'

As if she had not heard her husband's remark, Sabrine climbed into bed alongside him, saying, 'I think, too, Gemma's troubled about Emmaline. I know Gemma well enough to recognize that. I saw how she kept watching Emmaline, as if she were waiting for her to do something wrong.'

'See what I miss when I keep an eye on you!' Cramer reached for his wife's slim hand and kissed it.

Rolling against him, Sabrine asked, 'What did you talk to Warren about, dear?'

He reached to turn down the wick on the cutglass kerosene lamp, answering, 'The Bluedaws.'

'We must start inviting the Bluedaws to our Sunday parties,' Sabrine said, nestling her head on Cramer's shoulder in the darkness. 'We could even start having a separate party table for children.'

Cramer liked the idea. 'We could have Miss Reba supervise them,' he suggested. 'It's hard for a nurse to grow old with no children around her. Miss Reba would love to have something to do at the parties.'

As Sabrine lay alongside Cramer in the bedroom's darkness, she asked, 'Darling, are you terribly sorry we don't have children?'

'Sometimes love must be shared only between two people.' He kissed her on the forehead, murmuring, 'Now go to sleep thinking how much I love you.'

'Sweet dreams,' she whispered.

He wished he could dream peacefully, but feared he would only have nightmares about Sabrine's brother returning to make trouble for her, for him, for Belrose Plantation.

Warren had evening chores to do when he, Gemma, and Emmaline reached home well before sunset; Gemma went upstairs with Warren, and as he changed into his work clothes she began urging him to hire a man to help full time on the farm.

'You got a good price for the cotton we sold last year,' she reminded him. 'That could well pay for a man to milk the cows and feed the pigs.'

'Money don't grow in cotton bolls. I've got to pay a big work crew soon enough to come back and help.'

'So you'll have money from this harvest, too.'

Emmaline remembered hearing this argument since she was a child, her mother urging her father to hire someone to help him on a full-time basis, and her father always making excuses.

Neither Gemma nor Warren objected when Emmaline called from downstairs that she was taking an evening stroll to walk off some of the rich cream cakes she had eaten at Belrose.

Warren called, 'Sugar pie, don't walk out toward the parish road. Not this time of evening. Keep on our land.'

'And take a shawl,' said Gemma.

Emmaline agreed and hurried out of the back door, first stopping at the coach house to grab a blanket from a saddle rail inside the door, then rushed along the path to where she was supposed to meet Alain Summers.

Emerging in the forest opening, Emmaline looked around at the trees but saw no sign of Alain. Although she was early, she had hoped he would be there waiting for her. They would not have much time before it got dark and her parents came looking for her.

Suddenly, a hand grabbed her from behind and, as another hand clamped over her mouth, a voice whispered into her ear, 'Are you horny?'

Struggling, Emmaline turned her head and saw Alain out of the corner of her eye.

Lowering his hand from her mouth, he began chewing her neck as he pulled at the small pearl buttons on her dress.

'Alain,' she whispered. 'Please. Don't rip my dress. Mama just made it for me.'

He continued working to free her breasts, saying, 'I'll buy you a new dress. I'll buy you all the dresses in the world.'

With his other hand, he grabbed at the long skirt, working to feel between her legs.

Finally, grasping the warmth between her thighs, he felt moisture with his fingertips, and said, 'Ah, you're good and wet, you horny little bitch.'

Emmaline indeed was already sexually excited for Alain; she had never been able to hide her physical response to his domineering ways when she had lived at home, and now she still longed for him more than ever; she began to quiver with excitement as his strong fingers prodded her, again feeling like a young girl about to make love for the first time in her life.

Soon, Emmaline and Alain lay naked on the blanket, Emmaline's clothes heaped alongside them, her brown legs wrapped around the dark golden skin of his buttocks, anxiously working her hips against his erect penis.

'Easy, girl. Slow. Don't rush things.'

Lying on her back, Emmaline looked adoringly up at Alain as she ran her hands over the muscle capping his broad shoulders, studying his handsome chiselled features, admiring the soft curl of his long eyelashes, his thin moustache, following the line of his upper lip, the deep cleft of his strong chin.

He said, 'Go ahead. Enjoy yourself. Look at me. I like being appreciated.'

Holding his erect penis inside Emmaline, Alain remained kneeling between her spread legs but moved his chest, his shoulders, his head farther back, saying 'There! Get a better look!'

'You're confident.'

'Why not? I know what I've got. I know who wants it.'

He lowered his gaze, looking down at the root of his penis, watching himself as he pulled himself out from Emmaline's soft oval, seeing the head of his penis emerge large and bloodfilled, a fine crown for the large size of his penis.

Pushing back inside the soft moisture of Emmaline's vaginal lips, he said, 'You feel hot in there, you . . . bitch.'

Why? Emmaline did not know why but the name – bitch – strangely excited her. Alain said the word sarcastically, with cruelty, as if he wanted to humiliate her. But she enjoyed hearing it. At least from him. But why?

Suddenly, he slapped her face.

Emmaline stared up at him.

Alain, slowly nodding his head as he looked down at her, smiled thinly and said, 'That made you come didn't it? I felt you. You got nice and juicy over that. Ah, so you like being slapped around, do you?'

He slapped her again.

It was true: Alain's slaps did thrill her, and she exploded again with sexual excitement. His physical abuse was as exciting as his words.

'Bitch!' He slapped her again, driving his penis into her this time as he proceeded to humiliate her.

'Little no good cock-hungry slut.'

The words excited him, too, and he pumped faster against her as he taunted her, debased her.

'You're nothing but a slut, aren't you? A no-good slut.'

He slapped her again, ordering, 'Answer me!'

Emmaline nodded.

'Say it! Talk! Say you're nothing but a . . . whore! Say you're a bitch whore!'

Emmaline stared at him, her eyes wide with excitement as well as fear.

'Say you're a . . . whore.' He slapped her again.

Emmaline's heart was beating quickly; she had never felt so alive, so close to a man.

'I'm a . . . whore.'

'That's what I like to hear. That's how I like my women to talk. To tell me what they are! Whores!'

He plunged harder, more voraciously into Emmaline as she now repeatedly submitted to his demands; she did not know what he was doing to her, but she submitted her mind to him as well as her body, not regretting it, loving him for being so strong with her, for making her do what he wanted.

It was late the same night, the indigo sky glittering with stars. A hooded rider sat on horseback in front of the Bluedaw cabin nestling in the forest of cottonwood trees.

Wearing a long white gown and peaked hood and with slit eyes, the rider called, 'Deke Bluedaw.'

There was no light inside the small windows, no sign of activity within the log cabin.

The hooded rider shouted louder, 'Come out, Deke Bluedaw, if you value your family and home.'

The sound of shattering glass suddenly filled the night; the barrels of a shotgun poked out through a broken window pane and a man's voice called, 'Who are you?'

The rider called, 'Put down the gun, Bluedaw. Don't be a fool. Your house is surrounded. We'll burn you out like the bunch of Arky rats you are!'

All around the small log cabin, other hooded men emerged on horseback from the cottonwood trees, more than a dozen men carrying sputtering torches, armed with a variety of guns, new Sharp rifles, old Fisher muzzle-loading long rangers, Ballard off-hands.

Deke Bluedaw called from the house, 'Hankley, is that you?'

'Bluedaw!' shouted the rider. 'This is your last warning to come out!'

The cabin door opened and Deke Bluedaw, wearing trousers but no shirt, stepped out onto the porch, holding his Remington shotgun in his hand, demanding, 'Which one of you sons-of-bitches is Hankley?'

The masked leader called, 'Throw down your gun, Bluedaw. You're coming with us.'

Bluedaw moved to the edge of the porch, calling, 'I know one of you chicken shit bastards is Gus Hankley. So why don't we settle our feud between us like men? Just you and me, Hankley.'

The leader repeated, 'Throw down your gun, Bluedaw, or we'll burn down your house!'

Two men carrying torches danced their horses toward the long cabin.

A woman cried from inside the cabin. Deke Bluedaw waved her to stay inside and, with a thud, he dropped his shotgun to the dirt.

Two more horsemen quickly galloped forward, grabbed

Bluedaw by both arms and lifted him from the ground as Molly Bluedaw ran to the door with a Smith and Wesson .44 pistol in her hand.

The masked leader fired a shot toward Molly Bluedaw, missing her but calling, 'Woman, you and your kids stay inside if you ever want to see him again.'

The locomotive on the Mississippi-Dixie Line chugged in the far distance as the hooded riders halted alongside the railroad tracks northeast of Bossburg. Two men pulled Deke Bluedaw from the rump of a horse and dragged him to the iron tracks; two more men brought rope from their saddles and knotted it around Bluedaw's hands and feet; the men shoved Bluedaw's face down between the tracks, lashing his wrists and ankles across the iron rails.

As the sound of the train grew nearer, the hooded leader dismounted from his horse and lifted a bullwhip from his saddle horn; he unfurled it with a loud snap as he approached Deke Bluedaw spread-eagled between the tracks.

He said, 'Bluedaw, we're just going to have enough time to warm you up before your train gets here.'

Laughing, the hooded man snapped the whip, landing his first strike across Bluedaw's naked back.

He struck the whip a second, a third time, and when the train whistled at the far side of the bend, a ladder of blood already flowed from Deke Bluedaw's back, running down over his ribs.

As the train chugged closer, the hooded riders began mounting their horses; one man called anxiously, 'If you don't hurry, Junior, that train's going to get you, too!'

Junior Dehasset, taking one last strike at Deke Bluedaw's body tied between the railings, quickly ran the whip between his thumb and forefinger, wiped off the blood and the bits of torn flesh between his fingertips, flicked the coagulation to the ground and turned toward his horse.

The hooded riders had already galloped off into the

night when the coal-stoked engine of the Mississippi-Dixie charged over the track, the heavy gauge iron wheels acting like a chopper on the wrists and ankles of Deke Bluedaw lying screaming beneath the locomotive's roar.

5   Ku Klux Klan

Deke Bluedaw did not die. But rumors spread rapidly in Longchamp Parish about his condition as he lay in the Friends of Robert E. Lee Hospital in Palmetto Landing, reports that both arms and legs had to be amputated completely from his body, stories that he was near death, and whispered information about the true identities of the masked riders who had tied him to the railroad tracks, whipped him and left him to die in the path of the Mississippi-Dixie Line.

Molly Bluedaw and the seven children moved temporarily from their farm to a small house in Palmetto Landing to be near Deke in the Lee Hospital; Punkin Bluedaw felt that her mother needed extra help at home at this critical moment and decided to postpone her return to work for the Shiptons in New Orleans.

Two days remained before Punkin and Emmaline had meant to catch the stagecoach from Bossburg. And Emmaline, sitting in the kitchen with her mother and father at the breakfast table, insisted, 'Mama, I can take the stage by myself. Nothing will go wrong. I know the way.'

Gemma was both distressed and confused by recent events; she said, 'I can't think straight. I can't make up my mind yet what we should do. But, young lady, if you do go back to New Orleans, you must not breathe a word about masked riders to the Shiptons.'

Warren agreed. 'No! It's wrong for Black people to spread stories about vigilante gangs. Our worries fuel the wrong fires.'

Emmaline, more anxious to leave home than she was

worried about hooded vigilante gangs, said, 'Mrs Shipton will understand that Punkin had to stay home. She knows Punkin comes from a big family.'

Gemma said, 'Emmy, I have a half a mind not to let you go back at all.'

'Mama, the trouble's here in Longchamp Parish. Not in New Orleans.'

'The girl's right, Gemma.'

'But you can't travel alone, Emmy. I won't have it.'

'Mama, everything is going to be fine. I'm not a little baby.'

Th clip-clop of a single horse on the driveway distracted their attention; Gemma quickly rose from her chair and, peering out of a window said, 'Don't tell me it's more bad news.'

Warren rose to look, too, asking, 'Who is it, honey?'

Gemma finally recognized the driver of a bright yellow and red carriage halting in front of the house. 'Now what does *he* want?'

'Who is it, Mama?' asked Emmaline from the table.

'That boy from High Hill. Alain Summers.'

Emmaline froze on her chair.

'Let me talk to him,' said Warren.

Glancing down at his stocking feet, Gemma said, 'First put on your boots. There was a touch of frost last night and all we need is you catching a late cold.'

Waiting to hear footsteps on the back porch, Gemma was surprised when, instead, she heard a knock on the front door.

She said, 'At least he shows *some* good breeding.'

Moving from the kitchen, she passed through the arch-way into the parlor.

Alain Summers, holding a grey felt hat in his hands, stood politely on the bricked doorstep, saying, 'Mrs Rickers, sorry to disturb you so early in the morning, mam. But I heard the bad news about Mr Bluedaw and I knew he was a good friend of yours.'

'How very thoughtful of you to stop by, Alain. But

shouldn't our concern be directed toward Mr Bluedaw and his family?' Gemma had to admit to herself that Alain Summers had certainly grown into a handsome young man, that his clothes were not only neat and clean but very well tailored, and his manners seemed impeccable.

He continued, 'You're absolutely right, Mrs Rickers. Yet when something like this strikes in the neighborhood, people must try to show some unity – if you take my meaning, mam.'

Gemma nodded, feeling corrected. The Knights of the Camellia had almost run them out of the state. And she knew that Alain and his mother had always been vulnerable to vigilante attacks themselves, Marisse Summers being a White woman who had given birth to a child sired by a Black slave, Alain being that half-caste offspring.

She said, 'You are very good to stop by, Alain. I didn't even know you were in the Parish.'

'I came home last week from Natchez, Mrs Rickers,' he said, gripping the brim of his hat and looking Gemma straight in the eye as he continued, 'Word travels fast here in Longchamp Parish and I heard that your daughter, Miss Emmaline, had also come home with the oldest Bluedaw girl for a visit. And, so, naturally, after Mr Bluedaw's tragedy, I imagined that his daughter would not be returning to New Orleans, and that Miss Emmaline might be faced with the prospect of travelling alone.'

'Ah! So he's here because of Emmaline!' Gemma felt ever-so-slightly relieved that at least she knew the motive for Alain's surprise visit.

She said, 'You're right, Alain. In fact, Emmaline's father and I were just discussing whether we should allow Emmaline to go back to New Orleans at all.'

'I can understand you thinking along those lines,' Alain said considerately, 'but as I am driving to New Orleans, I wondered if you and Mr Rickers would feel safer if Miss Emmaline travelled with me rather than take the public stage.'

'Why, Alain, that is very thoughtful of you. But New Orleans is a long way away, and, well, you're both young people, and –'

'I understand your concern about – shall we call it "propriety", Mrs Rickers? The matter does pose a problem, too, because I plan to drive as far as Junctionville the first night. But I only have a place there to stay myself. I'm afraid I don't know any place where Miss Emmaline can stay.'

'Junctionville? Why that's where Emmaline and Punkin spend the night.'

'What a coincidence! So she already has a place? That's one problem solved. I stay with a school friend from Natchez. But his parents barely have room to put me up for the night.'

Warren came to stand alongside Gemma; he shook hands with Alain and, after hearing the proposal, he said, 'That's very neighborly of you, Alain.'

Gemma took a cue from Warren's warmth to the young man and said, 'Forgive me, Alain. Please do come inside and let me pour you a cup of coffee. Or maybe a bite to eat.'

'Thank you, Mrs Rickers, but I have chores to do for my mother in Ketley. Mama always takes advantage of my brief visit home.'

'She's lucky to have such a fine, capable son as you.'

'Thank you, mam. You flatter me, I'm afraid.'

Warren asked, 'What do you do in Natchez, young man?'

'I was at the Business Academy, sir. I took a course in book-keeping. That's why I'm going to New Orleans. I've got a letter of introduction to a law firm.'

'How very impressive,' Gemma said. 'May you have the best of luck.'

'Thank you, mam. I'll need it.' Then shifting his weight from one boot to another, Alain Summers said more brightly, 'Why don't we leave things like this? I leave for New Orleans the day after tomorrow. I'll stop around here and, if Miss Emmaline can ride with me, there'll be room for her in the buggy. If not, I'll only lose a few minutes from my travelling time.'

'That seems to be a very civil, sensible solution,' said Warren.

Gemma agreed.

Alain said, 'And who knows? Maybe your daughter doesn't even want to ride with me! I don't know if you folks remember but the last time I was here I was a ten-year-old and you sent me home with a switch, Mrs Rickers.'

Gemma grinned, 'Oh, I remember all right, Alain, you were a handful of trouble! You emptied a basin of wet mud all over Emmy's head, you devil, and I almost used that willow switch on your little . . . bottom!'

Laughing, Alain said, 'So you better ask Miss Emmaline. Maybe she's never forgiven me.'

Shaking hands with Gemma and Warren, Alain centered the gray pork-pie hat back on his head and turned back toward the gate in the white picket fence.

Gemma called, 'What a smart buggy you have, Alain.'

'Thank you. I bought it with money I made from the first job I had in Natchez.'

'Not a bad paycheck!' shouted Warren.

'I hope to see more.'

Alain waved goodbye from his buggy, calling, 'Give my regards to Miss Emmaline.'

Emmaline, standing beyond the parlor archway, had been listening to the entire conversation between Alain and her parents, and she smiled to herself at the way he had charmed them both.

People change, both Gemma and Warren agreed. Alain Summers had grown up into a very friendly, very personable young man. By midday, though, they decided that he still had the touch of the devil in him and it would be foolish to allow Emmaline to travel alone with him on an overnight trip. By suppertime, Gemma and Warren had both considered the consequences of Emmaline taking the stagecoach alone, perhaps having to sit on the roof alongside the driver if she was the only Black person on the journey, and so they again thought more positively about Alain's offer of a ride. By the next morning, both Gemma and Warren were convinced that Alain had spoken honestly and straightforwardly to them, and when Emmaline offered no objection to riding with him, in fact, kept her mouth shut about the entire matter, except for saying that she had to get back to New Orleans for her job, Warren and Gemma decided that, yes, people do change and that Emmaline would be perfectly safe travelling to New Orleans with Alain Summers. And their revised opinion about the young man from High Hill was fortified by the hand-drawn map he thoughtfully brought to them, showing the route he planned to follow south from Longchamp Parish.

Packed and dressed for the long trip, Emmaline tried to hide her excitement about her parents' decision to allow her to ride with Alain.

Alain took Emmaline's bags from Warren, and the food packets which Gemma had prepared for them; he said, 'It's too bad Palmetto Landing is so far out of the way. We could stop and pay a call on the Bluedaws.'

Warren, standing alongside the carriage, said, 'You just concentrate on yourselves. And don't forget we're holding you responsible for our girl, young man.'

Smiling as he delivered the words, Warren's eyes none the less twinkled with a fortitude which told he meant what he was saying.

Topping his jacket, Alain bragged, 'I've got a 7-shot Knuckler right here, plus a Winchester repeater rifle under the buggy floor.'

Gemma still did not know if she had made the right decision but she tried to act brave. 'What's the name of the people you stay with in Junctionville, Alain?'

'The Bennetts,' he answered as he sat on the buggy's button red leather seats. 'Before I go there, I'll see Miss Emmaline gets delivered safely to Miss Spooner's home.'

'Keep to the main roads,' Warren instructed. 'It's best to lose a few hours rather than risk getting lost – or to wander into the wrong people's back yards. There's a lot of men who'd like to take that buggy away from you.'

Emmaline, seated alongside Alain in the buggy, leaned to kiss her mother and father farewell one last time, promising to write, saying, 'But don't write till you hear from me. The Lord only knows what changes there'll be without Punkin.'

'Emmy, you need us for anything, you just say!' called Gemma, clinging onto Warren with one arm, dabbing at tears with the other hand.

Warren shouted, 'And don't let them work you too hard, baby girl!'

Emmaline waved as the buggy moved away from the yard, 'I love you, Mama. I love you, Daddy.'

The bright red and yellow buggy had not yet reached the end of the driveway - Emmaline still waving goodbye to her parents - when Alain mimicked, '*I love you, Mama! I love you, Daddy!*'

Emmaline whispered, 'Alain don't!'

'Why not? Do you think they can hear?'

'No, but –'

'You're a real little bitch. You know that, don't you. A real little bitch.' He reached to stroke her thigh.

'Alain!' She pushed away his hand.

'You better be ready for me tonight, pussy. I know a roadhouse a few miles south of Junctionville. You and I are going to get a room there with the biggest bed you ever saw.'

'Alan! A roadhouse! Dare we?'

'It's not "dare we". It's "can we". They won't be worried about us not being married. But not all roadhouses allow colored people to spend the night. But for an extra dollar I know a place where we can get a whopping big bed.'

The idea thrilled Emmaline. 'I never expected a . . . roadhouse!'

'You don't think I'd let you stay with some old withered-up parson's sister, do you?'

'You mean that was all a lie?'

'You told me about the parson's sister, don't you remember?'

'But you staying with a school friend? Was that a lie?'

'You'll see what's a lie tonight, pussy. I'm so horny I'm about to shoot my load in my trousers. I couldn't think of anything all last night except you sucking me, you down on your hands and knees in front of me, chewing on my dick, when I'm driving.'

'Stop it!'

'You think I'm joking?'

'Alain! We barely left home!'

Reaching to the front of his trousers, Alain freed his penis, strong with an erection, and ordered, 'Suck it, bitch. Suck or I'll stop right here and use this buggy whip on your little brown ass!'

The idea thrilled Emmaline to make love with Alain in a moving buggy. But she asked, 'What if somebody sees us?'

'They'd be so lucky?' He grabbed for her neck.

Soon Emmaline crouched on the buggy floor, kneeling between Alain's tall black leather boots, holding his penis with both hands and sucking his hardness as the horse clip-clopped, clip-clopped through the leafy Louisiana country-side.

'You're nothing but a slut.'

'You're so handsome, like a god.'

'Horny bitch talk, that's what you give me.'

'I can't believe we're here, Alain. All alone by ourselves. A bed for the night in a roadhouse.'

'A man and his slut.'

'You feel so good in me.'

'I am good. You're good, too, when you act like you're supposed to act. Now let's see you play with your titties while I'm screwing you.'

'Do I feel good for you, Alain?'

'Good enough.'

'Good enough? You told me back home I was the best, the best gal you've ever had.'

'That was back home.'

'Stop teasing.'

'Spread your legs and grab my balls. Play with my balls while I'm screwing you. I like to feel your hands on my balls.'

'I like doing what makes you feel good.'

'Because you're my whore.'

'Alain . . .'

'Play with those balls, whore.'

'Alain . . .'

'Shut up and hold those balls and watch me screw you. Watch me own you. Look down there and see how big I am. Look down there and see how I fill that pussy of yours, whore.'

'Alain . . .'

'You're my little whore.'

'Alain, there's something I have to tell you.'

'You already told me. You adore me, whore. And I already knew that before you told me. I can always tell by the eyes. I can tell every whore who adores me. All you whores are the same. I'm a god to you whores.'

'Alain, what if I told you you were speaking the truth?'

'That I'm your god?'

'That I *am* a whore. That I don't work as a maid in New Orleans but go with men for money.'

There was a momentary silence in the candlelit room upstairs in the beamed road-house; Alain Summers momentarily paused the drives of his penis, looking down at Emmaline lying on the white sheets, studying her as if he re-evaluated her, and, then, slowly, he began nodding his head, saying, 'It makes sense. A lot of sense. A lot more sense than you even know.'

Without saying another word, Alain resumed driving his penis deeper into her teasing vagina, holding his eyes on her. And, suddenly, without any warning, he spat on her face, not breaking the strokes of his penis, curling his upper lip with disgust as he kept looking at her, feeling her excitement surrounding his manhood; he spat on her again, then slapped her, rubbing the saliva around her face.

Cramer Crowley had gone to Palmetto Landing to pay another call on Deke Bluedaw in the hospital. Before leaving Belrose Plantation, he had given his wife a pistol as protection for when he was away. Although Cramer had not told Sabrine anything specific about the hooded riders who had attacked Deke Bluedaw, except that they might be local farmers who resented Bluedaw making changes, Sabrine had also heard that a hooded vigilante group had come back to Longchamp Parish, men called the Ku Klux Klan.

Keeping her eyes on the gravel driveway which rose gently from the parish road toward the big house of Belrose Plantation, Sabrine sat by a draped table in her bedroom, wondering if her brother, Junior Dehasset, had come back to Louisiana and was part of the Ku Klux Klan. Sabrine remembered her brother with fear because she knew he remembered her with hatred, a deep burning hatred which would make him do far worse to her – and Cramer – than those hooded men had done to Deke Bluedaw. She wondered if she could use the pistol, shoot her own brother.

Less than ten miles away from Belrose Plantation, a stout, balding man stood in front of a small frame house, pounding on the front plank door, a yellow dog barking behind him on the porch as he shouted through the door, 'Marjorie! Let me in! Don't lose your senses!'

A woman's voice shouted back, 'Gus Hankley, you try to break in that door and I'll set fire to this house, believe me! Set fire to this house just like you did that awful thing to Deke Bluedaw!'

'Believe me, Marjorie! It wasn't me!'

'Lies only make your sin worse, Gus Hankley. I found that piece of sheet and your peaked hood. I saw you sneak off that night. Oh, Gus, Gus, Gus! How do you expect me to show my face in church on Sunday with everybody knowing a man's been crippled for life just because you got hot-headed over some . . . water!'

'Marjorie, don't make me pay more than I am!' Gus Hankley called, the dog still yelping behind him.

Unrelenting, she called, 'It's between you and the Lord now, Gus Hankley – I don't want nothing more to do with you. Clear away from that door. Stay away from this house. Just leave me a horse and a saddle. I can't stay around here no more. Not knowing what you are!'

'Don't leave me, Marjorie,' he begged. 'Please don't leave me! We've been married twenty-five long years!'

'Eternity's a lot longer,' Marjorie Hankley called adamantly, the kerosene lamp burning threateningly inside the small window. 'And the Good Lord won't let you hide behind no white sheet and peaked hood. You're damned, Gus Hankley! You and all you Ku Kluxers are . . . damned!'

6 Willy the Whip

Emmaline was awakened by a jolt of Alain's buggy and, recognizing the row of brick storefronts on Julia Street, she realized with a start that they had reached New Orleans while she had been napping. Last night in the road-house, Emmaline had slept little with Alain; instead they had made love, discovering, exploring, inventing, following the ways of domination and submission between lovers that she had never known existed. Alain had made no further mention about her admission to being a prostitute in New Orleans but he had remained silent, even petulant throughout the day's journey, ignoring Emmaline when she tried to talk to him in the bouncing buggy, and she had begun to learn that he was temperamental, someone as moody, as secretive as she was herself.

The horse and buggy moved quickly in the evening traffic, cutting from Julia Street, to Broad Street, to Canal Street, bouncing over the New Orleans and Carollton Railroad tracks for the horse-drawn street cars, and then on to Rampart Street, dodging in and out between other buggies, wagons and carriages.

Passing a tall wooden fence papered with advertisements – Chero Cola 5c, Chieftain Cigars, Dr Billingay's Elixir Pads for Rheumatic Aches and Pains – Alain finally spoke, keeping his eyes straight ahead as he asked, 'Where you want to go?'

'How well do you know the streets?'

Emmaline longed to put her hand through the crook of his arm, to snuggle up to him on the buggy seat, but she dared not risk his temper; Alain gave the definite impression of not wanting to be touched.

'I was here last year,' he answered.

'Do you know the French Quarter?'

'Vieux Carré.'

She was not surprised to hear him use the Créole word for the oldest part of New Orleans; his mother came from a privileged background, a fashionable way of life, and had bloodlines to the city's early settlers, those people called Créoles.

She asked, 'Do you know Burgundy Street?'

'Smoky Row?'

'Yes.'

'You weren't joking, were you?'

'Did you think I was?'

'Why, why, *why* Smoky Row?'

'Why not?'

'It's nothing but a cesspool.'

She angrily asked, 'Where else am I to go?'

'Good God, Emmaline. Working Smoky Row, that's as bad, even worse than being somebody's . . . damned maid! The whores there are nothing but old hags!'

'Am I an old hag?'

'That's exactly what I mean.' He looked at her with exasperation, shaking his head, saying, 'Well, I guess we're just going to have to do something about it, aren't we?'

Emmaline did not ask Alain what he meant; she did not want to argue with him, to part company with a fight and the risk of never seeing him again. She had grown close to him in the last few days and he made her feel excited, sexually alive, hungry to explore new ways of love-making, dark corners of her personality, hidden desires.

Trying not to sound too concerned, she asked, 'Where are you staying in New Orleans, Alain?'

Sulkily, he answered, 'I don't know yet.'

'Do you really have a job at a law firm? A letter of recommendation from a business school in Natchez? Or was that another lie like the story about the family you know in Junctionville?'

He admitted, 'I've never seen the inside of a business school.'

78

Emmaline quietly asked, 'Will I see you again?'

His laugh was empty, mocking her again. 'I'm certainly not paying for the privilege, thank you very much, Miss Rickers.'

Angered by his words, and seeing they were approaching the corner of Rampart and Iberville Streets, she said, 'You can let me out right here by the drug store.'

'I'll drop you on the corner.'

'Don't trouble yourself to do more than you have to,' she said frostily.

Reining the dappled horse at the corner of Iberville and Burgundy Streets, Alain sat motionless, holding the leather reins, as Emmaline stepped to the kerb. She lifted bags and parcels from the buggy as he gazed down Burgundy, staring at the double row of rundown shacks, looking at the windowless hutches called the 'cribs', watching the Black women dressed in ragged smocks clustered in front of a two-storey house on the corner of Burgundy and Bienville Streets, shouting obscenities at the house.

Shaking his head with disgust, Alain said, 'The old girls are having a bit of a demonstration today.'

Emmaline ignored him.

He asked, 'You in a house?'

Angrily lifting her possessions from the boardwalk, Emmaline answered, 'I'm certainly not on the street!'

'Who's your old man?'

'A woman owns the house.'

'What's her name?'

'Jocasta Liddle – if it's any concern of yours.'

Looking down at her, Alain suddenly gripped her wrist, saying, 'Hey!'

Emmaline stared at him, her big brown doe eyes eager, waiting for him to say one word of warmth to her, to give her one speck of hope she'd see him again.

He winked, saying, 'You'll hear from me, babe.' He then released her wrist, almost tossing it back to her like an old bone.

Emmaline stood on the street corner, holding her wrist and watching Alain Summers drive toward Rampart Street;

he did not turn around to wave goodbye to her, a man she had less than twenty-four hours earlier worshipped like a god, a man to whom she had surrendered herself, told her innermost secrets, and he did not even turn to wave goodbye to her. The bastard!

Jocasta Liddle opened the kitchen door, holding a coffee mug in one hand, a bottle of Raleigh Rye Whisky in the other.

Emmaline, struggling up the back steps with her luggage, her straw hat sitting slightly askew on her head, edged her way through the screen door and dropped the bags and packages down on the kitchen floor.

Untying the blue ribbon on her straw bonnet with one hand and fanning her face with the other, she asked, 'What's all the ruckus out front?'

Jocasta kicked the back door shut. 'Business is slow. So those bitches across the street decided to liven things up by jawing about Lizzie.'

Emmaline looked around the kitchen, 'Lizzie?'

The thin Black woman, Peaches, perched on a stool next to the cookstove, raised one hand to her mouth as she sniggered, lowering her eyes to avoid Emmaline's stare.

Emmaline remembered who Lizzie was.

She asked, 'That White girl still in my room?'

Luba, a short, stout woman with braids crossing her head from ear to ear, sat by a small table covered with green oilcloth and said, 'She's in there okay – on her back.'

'Well, she better get out.' Emmaline began unbuttoning her coat, already feeling curiously at home, more at home than she had in the house where she had been raised in Longchamp Parish.

'Honey, you look tired,' said Jocasta as she splashed Raleigh Rye into her cup of strong black coffee.

Luba shook her head, saying disparagingly, 'Country air. Home cooking. It'll get a girl every time.'

Emmaline glanced from Luba to a man sitting in a far corner of the dark kitchen, a thin, sharply-featured White man wearing a neat grey suit, celluloid collar, maroon tie, and expensive button boots.

80

Jocasta nodded her marcelled head at the White man, saying, 'You remember Willy, don't you, Em honey?'

Willy the Whip nodded at Emmaline, his eyes dark and motionless like water at night.

Emmaline dipped her head, feeling uncomfortable under his stare; she remembered the whip which Jocasta was going to buy from him for her, but Willy the Whip strangely frightened her, and she did not mention the purchase.

Willy finished his cup of coffee with a gulp, rose from his chair and lifted a crocodile bag from the floor.

As soon as he left the room, Luba and Peaches began gossiping with Jocasta, telling Emmaline what had happened in her absence, stories about the crib prostitutes complaining about Lizzie the White girl being on Smoky Row, telling about a police raid nabbing seven girls three houses away on Saturday night because their madam had not paid her weekly bribe to Alderman Bates, and, finally, telling about Cassy waking up from a bad nightmare, a dream she had about Baby Jesus giving her penance to do for being a whore, which was why Cassy had sent for Willy the Whip to pay a professional visit with his crocodile bag of whips, lashes, and straps.

As the women talked in the kitchen, Willy climbed the rickety stairs of the two-floor bordello and knocked on the door of the small room where Cassy lay face down on the bed.

'Come in,' she called, her voice muffled by the pillow.

Willy entered the floral-papered room, closed the door behind him, set down his large crocodile bag on the mattress of the double bed, and said in a soft drawl, 'Afternoon, Cassy.'

'Afternoon, Will.'

Opening the bag with a click, he asked, 'Say, who's the young lady working here? Young colored gal?'

Cassy lay dressed in a soiled kimono. Not raising her head from the pillow she asked, 'Country stuff?'

'She's the one. Just been home.'

'Called Emmy.'

'Emmy.' Willy nodded, thinking how he had not seen

81

such an attractive young girl in a long time, a girl who had that look in her eye, a need for a man, a strong man to take her in hand and keep her within the boundaries of some good, strong discipline. He also thought how he might even get a house on Basin Street where she could work for him, be one of his own girls.

'Emmy,' he repeated, saying, 'You fix me a meeting with that Emmy, and I'll give you a nice, long free visit. How about that for a fair trade, Cassy?'

Willy removed a buggy whip from the crocodile bag; he bent it back and forth to feel for pliancy, and, satisfied with the tool, he set it down on the bed, shut the bag, set the bag on the floor, removed his jacket, and said, 'Now, Cassy, why don't you be a good girl and shuck off that robe.'

Not moving on the bed, Cassy complained, 'I ain't feeling good, Will. I feel poorly. Mighty poorly.'

'Sure you do, baby. Sure you do. Work can be a right strain on you. So you let Daddy see that nice black ass of yours. Daddy's come to talk some sense back into you. Daddy's come to get you back up on your feet again. Make you feel good as new.'

'It's my brain, Will. My brain troubles me. I can't shut it off. Not even when I sleep. I see Jesus. I see Jesus too much and He makes me feel bad.'

'Just shuck off that robe,' Will coaxed, 'you've been ignoring yourself. But I'm going to fix you up good as new. You'll let Jesus stay in Heaven and you'll be good as new. So shuck off that robe.'

Slowly, obediently, Cassy moved to lower the kimono from her shoulders, inch it down her back, over her buttocks, then she dropped it to the plank floor in a heap.

The first stroke of the buggy whip made Cassy flinch, gasp with pain.

The second strike was lighter, touching her softly as a feather, as did the third and the fourth strike. But the fifth strike was stronger, harder again, making her gasp, but the pain had changed, had come to her more sweetly.

And gratefully, she murmured, 'Oh, that feels good, Will. That feels real good.'

Willy proceeded with an expertise in varying his strokes of the whip, administering the corporal punishment as if it were medicine, a form of religion, one pain stronger than another, the hand of authority.

Emmaline looked up from sorting through the heap of clothing piled on her narrow iron bed and saw a White girl with curly black hair, wearing a shiny fringed Chinese shawl, standing in her doorway; the girl forced a faint smile, saying, 'You must be Emmy. I'm Lizzie.'

Emmaline resumed her work, saying, 'Don't you know how to knock before you enter other people's room?'

Lizzie leaned against the door, saying, 'Don't be mad at me, Emmy. Please . . .'

Emmaline stared at Lizzie, seeing tears suddenly brimming in her large brown eyes; she asked, 'You sick or something?'

Shaking her head, Lizzie hoarsely whispered, 'No.'

'What's the matter? Why the tears?' Emmaline had been back less than two hours but already she heard her words change, the sound of her voice already becoming hard, careless, impatient, back to how she had spoken before she had gone home.

Lowering her head, Lizzie sobbed, 'Oh, I'm so, so much trouble.'

Emmaline nodded toward the street beyond the closed shutters. 'You mean those crib whores?'

Lizzie nodded. 'Part.'

'Then why stay someplace if you know you're not wanted?'

'No other place will have me.'

'Why not? You're not ugly.' Emmaline could feel her strength returning, the strength she had hidden during her visit home when she had tried to pose as her parent's innocent daughter; she felt the return of her energy, too, that she had surrendered to Alain, the control she had given to him to master her as his love slave.

'Looks don't matter,' sniffed Lizzie. 'Not when people find out.'

83

'Find out what?' Emmaline asked impatiently.

'You haven't heard?'

'You aren't making much sense to me,' Emmaline said, absorbed in her own worries.

'Maybe this will make sense.' Lizzie loosened the Chinese shawl from her neck, exposing a tattoo of a six-pointed star etched in blue ink between her collar bones; she said, 'If you know what a Jew is, you'll understand how much sense it makes.'

Emmaline stared at the tattoo, a star about the size of a silver dollar; she remembered her parents talking about Jews and Catholics, people often treated with the same contempt as Black people.

Returning to her work, Emmaline coldheartedly said, 'So keep something over it.'

'People always find out.'

'Keep trying,' Emmaline said. 'Maybe someday they won't.'

Lizzie, seeing she was not going to receive any sympathy from Emmaline, said, 'You're very pretty, Emmaline. So what are *you* doing here?'

'Smoky Row's for Blacks.'

'But there are other places where you can work. There are Black girls on Basin Street. Rampart Street. Parts of St Louis Street. I can name six, eight houses in the French Quarter alone where you can work. You don't have to stay here.'

The words reminded Emmaline of what Alain had told her only a few hours ago, and she said, 'Why don't you leave me alone.'

Lizzie, studying Emmaline, said, 'You're not very well organized, are you?'

Emmaline looked at her with a start. 'Are you looking for an argument?'

Not lowering her eyes, Lizzie challenged, 'You don't know how to make plans, do you? Think out things for yourself. See what your real talents are.'

'Talents? What are you talking about talents for? I'm not some kind of . . . singer.'

'You don't have to be a singer or a dancer or poet to have talents. Everybody has something special. Maybe if you let somebody be your friend, you could start polishing your talents.'

Emmaline narrowed her eyes, saying, 'Don't try to sweet talk me, girl. Coming in here and giving me compliments. Talking big. You're not getting this room no matter what you claim you can do.'

'Rule number one!' Lizzie nodded approvingly. 'Never Trust Anybody. But Rule number two. Play-act like you trust the entire world!'

'Play-act? *Play-act?* That's all I do!' Emmaline sank down onto the bed.

Lizzie, sitting alongside her, put her arm around Emmaline's shoulder, saying, 'Sweetie, you need help! Bad. What's the matter?'

Emmaline looked at the curly-haired White girl, tears now welling in her own eyes; she began to speak, but she stopped, shaking her head.

'You can talk to me,' Lizzie assured her. 'I don't want your old room. I don't want to stay here any more than those women outside want me to stay here. I don't want to spend the rest of my life in a third-rate dump like this. I'm headed for the best street in town. Basin Street. I don't know how I'm going to get there. But I'm going to get there. Sure as shooting. So just relax. I'm going to take nothing away from you.'

Soon the girls, sitting side by side on Emmaline's bed, began exchanging stories. Emmaline poured out her troubles, telling Lizzie about her visit to her parents, how she had been lying to her parents for the last ten months, saying she was a housemaid. She also told Lizzie about Punkin Bluedaw, how she somehow had to tell Punkin's employers that Punkin was not coming back to work. She even confided in Lizzie about Alain, how she was falling in love with Alain, not knowing if it was right because wasn't love supposed to make you feel happy? But all she felt was nervous and irritable and so, so unhappy!

Lizzie, full of authority, said, 'First thing you have to do is send word to those Shipton people. Or stop talking about it. Worry just eats up a person. Like they say, "Piss or get off the pot!" '

Junior Dehasset knew that the golden rule for his survival – at least during these days when he was determined to become Grand Master of the Ku Klux Klan – was to keep moving, to keep one step ahead of any local powers which might try to stop the justice he believed he was spreading in the towns and parishes he visited. The people of Long-champ Parish were still shocked by the action taken against Deke Bluedaw, and Junior Dehasset knew it would be wise to leave the parish, at least temporarily, before local men and women began demanding an investigation. But Junior Dehasset also had work to do in New Orleans, and so he saw his imminent departure as a choice, not a sentence of exile.

Ivy Bravo already knew Junior was leaving for New Orleans, and tonight was meant to be their last evening; Junior Dehasset was not Ivy's idea of a good lover, not even a good companion, but at least he was a male, and he did not stint on money, at least when she humored his whims.

Junior's latest request was to tie Ivy to the bed with leather thongs, and he offered her ten dollars if she consented. Ivy always needed the extra money.

Junior, having gently but firmly lashed her ankles and wrists to the bedstead, said, 'You still haven't made your forty dollars yet from my "whorebreaker".'

Ivy tried to remain calm, not to panic at the idea of being restricted by leather thongs.

'Want to have another go tonight with the "whore-breaker"?' he asked.

Ivy considered the proposal, asking, 'Would that be fifty dollars all told?'

'Cash.'

Soon, Junior sat alongside Ivy on the bed, inching the greased phallus into her vagina, casually inquiring, 'You hear any stories about me, Ivy?'

'Stories? What kind of stories?'

Pressing the phallus deeper, he said, 'Where I go. What I do. Or maybe you snoop in my saddle bags when I'm taking a nap.'

'Snoop? Why'd I snoop?' Ivy took a deep breath; the phallus was hurting her; she urged, 'Easy, Junior . . .'

'You want that forty dollars?'

'Fifty,' she corrected.

He smiled, thinking, 'Greed gets them every time.'

'Go easy,' she begged. 'That's painful now. That dick's thicker at the base, don't forget.'

'So you ain't heard no –' Junior gave the wooden and leather phallus a firm push, '– stories?'

'Junior, take it out! I can't go it!'

'Sure you can, Ivy,' he coaxed.

Working her hands against the wrist-ties, Ivy began to panic, begging louder, 'Junior, please, take it out. *Please!*'

Watching the tissue beneath her pubic hairs stretch wider, making a fuller path he asked, 'You heard what happened to Deke Bluedaw, Ivy?'

Ivy had indeed heard stories about the farmer, Deke Bluedaw. She had suspected that Junior Dehasset might have played a part in the ordeal, but she had not voiced her suspicions. Junior was company for her – at least, he paid regular visits to her house, often staying overnight with her – and she tried to forget about his previous history with the Knights of the White Camellia.

'Ivy, you know too much.' His voice suddenly sounded cold, mean.

'Junior, take that thing out of me!'

He shoved harder.

She screamed. 'Junior, sto-o-o-p!'

Smiling as he saw the phallus eased inside her vagina, the discomfort he was causing her, Junior said, 'You're up to twenty dollars already, Ivy. Let's make it . . . twenty-*two!*'

He gave it another shove.

'Junior!' she cried.

'Ivy, you know way, way too much for your own good. And we can't have that.' He now twisted the phallus inside her, increasing the torture.

'Junior, please! Take anything! Take my money! Take my furniture! Take my Ma's golden wedding band! Take anything but just untie me. Untie me and take, take, *take* that . . . thing out of my pussy!'

Excited by her panic, Junior said, 'Let's *see* if we can go for twenty-four or twenty-six dollars. Or how about shooting for thirty, Ivy? Thirty whole Yankee dollars!'

'*Junior!*'

Laughing, forcing his hand into a fist and beginning to slug the flat base of the leather and wood phallus, Junior ignored Ivy's painful screams, watching it sink deeper between her spread legs.

The bed rattled, banged, shook as Ivy pulled her hands and kicked her feet, but, still, she could not free herself from the leather bondage.

Junior, thrilled by his power over the woman, fell fully-dressed on top of her body; he pressed his groin against the butt-end of the phallus, pumping his hips as if the phallus were attached to his body, as if his own penis were not small but as large as the wood and leather phallus.

Holding onto one of Ivy's arms with one hand and clamping his other hand over her mouth, Junior frantically pumped his hips, making his weight push more heavily against her, causing the phallus to work deeper into her.

Hypnotized by the idea of being endowed with such power and sexual magnificence, Junior continued working his hips, driving his imagined endowment, shouting to Ivy as he pumped against her, 'I'm too much for you. I'm too much for you. I'm too much of a man for you . . . bitch!'

Junior reached for a bed pillow and smothered it over Ivy's face as he increased the wild movements of his hips, beginning to feel a tingle growing inside his groin from thrusting against the phallus.

'Bitch!' he roared as the tingle spread from the roots of his scrotum, quickly building into a shuddering sexual orgasm.

Jerking back his head, closing his eyes, gulping with the rush of pleasure and power, Junior felt his sexuality explode inside his trousers.

Satisfied, sated both in body and mind, Junior rose

sluggishly from the bed; he did not even look at Ivy's body but glanced instead around the room for a rag to rub his trousers.

Ivy Bravo was motionless. Smothered. Dead. Junior knew that without looking at her. He wanted her to be dead. But if he had not already killed her, he would before he got rid of her body. She would not remain alive to tell people stories about him.

Thinking of the road he would take tonight for New Orleans, Junior remembered the settlement of Crowforks, and he quickly thought out a plan to dump Ivy's body near the share-croppers' shacks, letting it be discovered by some passer-by and allowing her murder to be blamed on the Black share-croppers.

Packing away the 'whorebreaker' in his saddle-bag, Junior hurriedly wrapped Ivy's corpse in the bedspread.

7   The Assignation House

A week had passed since Emmaline had returned to New
Orleans, seven days in which summertime humidity had
grown more intense, and sporadic rainfall drenched the city
in heavy downpours, bouncing off cobbled streets like
hailstones, turning dirt streets into quagmires, sending
people on foot in search of refuge under the ornate iron
galleries which covered the boardwalks, called *banquettes*,
in the French Quarter and keeping street vendors close to
doorways with their nosegays of herbs, small sacks of
spices, necklaces of garlic, wreaths of almond bread.

Dismal and oppressive, these rainy days on Smoky Row
kept both prostitutes and customers indoors, except for the
crib whores who eagerly awaited a break in the rain to dash
out into the marshy street in search of a man or boy, or to
start shouting abuse again at Jocasta Liddle's house, complaining about a White girl working their territory.

Lizzie and Emmaline became better friends during these
wet days of early summer. Despite Lizzie's urging,
Emmaline still had not written a note to the Shipton family
and explained the reason why Punkin Bluedaw had not
returned to New Orleans and to work.

Emmaline sat alone in her room, listening to yet another
afternoon downpour, again considering how she should
contact the Shiptons, when she heard a carriage stop on the
street, followed by a barrage of loud, angry shouts.

Looking outside through the peeling green shutters,
Emmaline saw the crib prostitutes gathering like crows
around a horse-drawn cab, the gnarled and often toothless
Black women gripping ragged shawls over their heads in

the rain, holding up the hems of their ragged Mother Hubbards from the mud and shouting, 'Go back home, White girl!' 'We'll pin those pink titties to the fence!' 'What's the matter? Too poxy to work on your own side of town?'

Emmaline, knowing that Lizzie had been trying to find another place to work, suspected the cab was bringing her back to Smoky Row, but wondered why Lizzie was not using the rear door, why she was not coming through the kitchen like everybody else in the house had been doing since the crib prostitutes started their vigil of shouts and angry catcalls.

Watching, listening to the obscene women, Emmaline saw a stranger in a green hooded cape pushing her way through the crowd and hurry down the narrow boardwalk leading to Jocasta's sagging front porch.

Seeing the woman's face, Emmaline gasped and rushed to open the front door.

Punkin Bluedaw, unnerved by the rude, jostling reception she had met outside on Smoky Row a few minutes earlier, sat rigidly on the straight-back chair in Emmaline's room, insisting that the women had not injured, not disturbed her. Nervously untying the black faille ribbons on her cape, she asked shakily, 'Emmy, are *you* well?'

Still dazed at the unexpected appearance of Punkin Bluedaw, Emmaline watched her rearranging her clothing and hair, noticing that her best friend had physically altered since she had last seen her, that Punkin was wearing her hair differently, that she looked more like an adult woman, attractive and feminine, rather than a freckle-faced girl.

She said, 'Punkin, you look different. What is it? You aren't the Punkin I know. You're . . . beautiful!'

Modestly dipping her head, Punkin blushed, the smear of freckles less obtrusive on her creamy-white face. 'Probably all the worry and strain about Daddy took off some of my baby fat!'

At the mention of Punkin's father, Emmaline quickly said, 'Oh, Punkin. I'm sorry about what happened.'

'The doctor says he's going to live. But they've had to

amputate both hands and feet. They might have to operate again, to cut past his elbows and knees. We're praying that that won't happen but everything depends on infection spreading. Oh, Em, I know it sounds gruesome. And it is. We're just grateful that Daddy's still alive. But many changes will have to be made at home. Mama's going to need all the help she can get on the farm. Jeb and Mike are old enough to do their share. And so are the girls, Marianna and Sue. But the others are really nothing but babies, bless their hearts. So, Em, I'm quitting my job at the Shiptons' to go back home and help Mama.'

'You're quitting your . . . job?'

Punkin nodded. 'For good, Emmy.'

The news stunned Emmaline.

Punkin had anticipated Emmaline's reaction; she said, 'That's why I came to see you, Em. I don't know how this is going to affect the stories you tell your folks.'

'You're never coming back? *Never?*'

Shaking her head, Punkin looked down at her slim white hands twisting nervously in her lap. 'There's also something else to tell you, Em.'

'What?'

Without raising her eyes, Punkin said, 'Cramer Crowley's in New Orleans, Em.'

'Cramer Crowley? From Belrose?'

Punkin nodded. 'He brought me to town to collect my things from the Shiptons.'

'Cramer's been to the Shiptons' house?'

'Now, don't panic, Em. Mr Crowley doesn't know a thing about you. I didn't tell him one word. Not a single word. Believe me.'

'Why did *he* bring you to New Orleans?'

'It was Mr Crowley who found the best doctor for Daddy, a surgeon who saved hundreds of lives in the War. Thousands, they say. And since Daddy's accident, Mr Crowley's been spending hour after hour at the hospital talking to him, trying to come up with some clues to those men who did that awful thing to Daddy. Oh, Em, Mr and Mrs Crowley have both been so wonderful to us -'

Pausing, Punkin forced a faint smile, adding, 'Maybe that's why you think I look different. Mrs Crowley visits the house where we've been living near the hospital. She's showed me how to fix my hair. Pluck my eyebrows. Use little dabs of lip rouge. She even gave me some of her old clothes. Like this cape, these shoes –'

Punkin held out both feet, proudly displaying a pair of buckled calfskin slippers.

Emmaline asked coldly, 'Is she in town, too? Sabrine Crowley?'

Punkin shook her head. 'Just Mr Crowley. We drove as far as Junctionville last night. I stayed with Miss Spooner.'

'Did she say anything? Miss Spooner.'

'About what?'

Emmaline closed her eyes, imagining the repercussions of Cramer Crowley's visit to New Orleans with Punkin.

'Emmy, don't worry! I've dodged all Mr Crowley's questions about you. He's not a nosy man. He's got other things on his mind. He stopped asking questions when he didn't see you at the Shiptons'. And I tell you, Em, you're a very lucky girl!'

'Lucky?'

'Yes you are,' Punkin insisted. 'The Shiptons still haven't come back from Baton Rouge. The house is as empty as a tomb, except for Miss Lucy. But she stays in her room at the top of the house the whole live-long day. So Mr Crowley didn't talk to anybody. He thinks you've gone to Baton Rouge, too.'

'Is that what you told him? That I went to Baton Rouge to meet the Shiptons?'

'No. Not exactly. Emmy, you know I wouldn't lie. But I – well – I . . . implied.'

'Oh, Punkin, thank you!' Emmaline was suddenly relieved, falling back onto the bed, holding both hands across her chest, laughing, 'I love how you "imply"! Maybe I should tell fewer lies and do more . . . implying!'

'Emmy, it's not a laughing matter. What are you going to do after I go home?'

Emmaline sat back up on the bed, sobered.

Staring at Emmaline, Punkin said, 'Emmy, will you be terribly angry if I tell you what I think you should do?'

'I can guess.'

'Emmy, leave here. Leave this awful place.'

As if she had not heard Punkin's remark, Emmaline asked, 'Punkin, do you know what good friends the Crowleys are to my parents? How close they are?'

'Emmaline Rickers! You aren't even listening to me! You asked me what you should do. And I said . . . leave . . . Smoky . . . Row!'

Emmaline stared at her.

'Oh, Emmy, you've got to start being realistic. Those women outside are nothing but old witches. And the language they use! The shocking things they said to me! The threats! The vulgarity! Oh, Emmy, you're not like that!'

Emmy thought fleetingly of how she talked obscenely to her customers, whispered lewd words to them in the cover of darkness, telling them tantalizing stories to arouse them. She wondered if Punkin had the vaguest notion that she, too, had a ready store of words, expressions, remarks which she would call 'vulgar'?

Punkin continued, 'Emmy, I love you. I love you like my own sister. Probably even better. And I don't want to go back home knowing you're still here in this . . . house. I don't want to keep telling lies - or *implying* lies - that you're a housemaid at the Shipton's when you're really nothing but a - oh, Emmy, leave this dreadful place! I beg you! Leave it!'

Emmaline testily replied, 'Don't worry, Punkin Bluedaw. You won't have to keep "implying" stories about me much longer.'

'Promise me?'

Emmaline nodded her head, forcing herself to sound more cheerful, asking, 'So what about you? Your own life? And that Black boy you met and love so much? What about him?'

'I'm seeing Ben tonight.'

'Good. I'm glad you finally worked up the courage to meet his family.'

Shaking her head, Punkin said, 'No, Emmy. I'm not going to meet Ben's family. Remember? I told you the Shiptons are still out of town.'

'You're inviting him to the Shiptons'?'

'We can be all alone there.'

'Punkin Bluedaw! You sit there telling me to be careful! What about you?'

'This will probably be the last time I ever see Ben. I love him, Emmy. I love him very much and –'

'And what?'

'Em, can you help me?'

'Help? what can you possibly want from . . . me?'

Timidly, Punkin again looked at her hands nervously wringing in her lap, beginning, 'I suppose this is a subject girls should really discuss with their mothers. But Mama thinks having babies is the best thing in the whole wide world. But Ben and I aren't married. So I was wondering, Em, I was wondering if maybe you could tell me something I – we – could do . . .'

Faltering, Punkin raised her eyes and, seeing the strange expression on Emmaline's face, asked, 'Emmy? Why are you looking at me that way? What's the matter? Am I shocking you?'

'No, you aren't shocking me, Punkin. I was just thinking how many things are changing.'

Rising from the narrow iron bed, Emmaline moved quietly across the plank floor and opened the top drawer of the bureau.

She removed a pasteboard shoe box from the drawer and, rummaging through the contents, she said, 'Funny, isn't it, Punkin, how life can change so fast? How something can happen over-night and make other things happen. First, your Daddy's accident. Now you moving back home. Me having no excuse, no cover-up any more. You and Ben scared about having babies . . .'

Turning, Emmaline held out one hand to Punkin, saying, 'Here's what you need. And whatever happens, Punkin, remember I love you. I love you to ribbons. I really do.'

They embraced, Punkin's eyes red with tears,

Emmaline's eyes dry and staring stonily over Punkin's shoulder.

As the rain had now stopped, Emmaline insisted on walking Punkin to the street and helping her find a cab; they left the brothel through the kitchen door to avoid the crib prostitutes waiting at the front of the house.

The rain began to fall heavily again as Punkin was stepping into the cab; the two girls again embraced, then Emmaline turned and ran back to the house, dashing through the crib whores as they also scrambled for cover, and she bounded up the brothel's front steps.

As Emmaline was drying her hair with a hand-towel, she heard a knock on her door and, turning, she saw Jocasta stick her marcelled head round the door, announcing, 'You must be some hot firecracker, baby doll, to get a man to brave this pissy weather and come see you.'

Jocasta opened the door wider, saying, 'He's kind of wet, baby doll, but the cutest piece of mulatto stuff I've seen in a long time.'

Alain Summers, a brown paper parcel tucked under one arm, stood in the doorway.

Jocasta held out one large hand, wiggling her stubby fingers, saying, 'Three dollars for spring chicken with no trimmings.'

Alain peeled off the bills from a money roll, bowed with mock respect, then quickly shut the door behind Jocasta.

Tossing the brown paper parcel onto the bed, he ordered, 'Get dressed. I got you a job.'

Emmaline stared at him, asking, 'Aren't you even going to say hello?'

'Hello,' he said, then repeated, 'I got you a job. Don't you want to know where it is?'

'Where is it?'

'An assignation house.' He moved to the bureau and, beginning to open and close drawers, he asked, 'Where's that dress your Mama made you? The little pink thing that makes you look so cute and kissable?'

'An assignation house?'

Alain turned to a cluster of clothes hanging on wooden hangers bunched together on a wall peg; he dug through the clothes until he found the pink dress, and a long ruffled white cotton petticoat.

Tossing the garments onto the bed, he yanked the string from the brown paper parcel and removed a fluffy white rabbit scarf and a pair of ivory kidskin gloves.

'Wear these, too,' he ordered. 'I borrowed them. So don't get them dirty.'

Emmaline ignored his instructions, asking, 'Why are you taking me to an . . . assignation house?'

'First of all, I'm not "taking" you. I'm "sending" you. And secondly, why do people usually go to an assignation house? To meet other people! I arranged an appointment for you. So stop all this jawing, get out of that white dish-rag, and start making yourself presentable, gal!'

'An appointment with . . . *whom?*'

'A very rich man, that's who. If you're good to him, he might even want to see you again. Now shake your ass and put on these clothes.'

'You want me to see . . . another man?'

Alain looked blankly at her. 'You're a whore, aren't you?'

She stared at him.

'If you want to be a whore, be a good one.'

Emmaline collapsed on the bed, keeping her eyes on Alain; for the last two weeks she had been thinking about him, hoping to see him again, she had been dreaming about him coming to Jocasta's house, taking her out for a stroll, an evening ride in his bright red and yellow buggy, maybe even out to a meal like Charley the Oysterman used to do. But none of her dreams, her hopes, her wishes had included Alain coming to the house and telling her that he had arranged for her to go to bed with another man.

Standing in front of the bureau mirror and repositioning his pork-pie hat on his head, he said, 'And don't tell your fat lady where we're going. I'll give her a few more bucks when we leave and say I'm taking you out for a meal. The less she knows the better.'

Emmaline's voice was without emotion. 'You want to be my fancy man, don't you?'

'I want you to be a good whore for me, that's what I want. Now if you don't want any more of my dick, sugar, if you don't want any more of the loving I give you, just tell me right now. We can forget the whole thing. There's plenty of pussy in town. You're not the only cat dragging her hind legs down the alley. So what's it going to be? Do things my way? Or wait around in this room, letting Fat Ass out there say who and what you're going to get between your legs?'

Quietly, Emmaline reached for the petticoat.

The assignation house, a small red brick hotel at the corner of Basin and Liberty Street, was called 'The Diana Retreat', and the swarthy young desk clerk, dressed in a brown pin-striped suit, led Emmaline up the frayed blue-and-gold carpeted stairs, knocked on a cream-enamelled door inset with a frosted glass oval, then stepped aside for her to enter the room.

An elderly white man, with long, neatly barbered gray hair and salt-and-pepper goatee, rose from a gilt armchair to greet Emmaline with a gracious bow.

'Champagne?' he asked as he pointed to another chair placed across the round table from him.

'Please.' Emmaline, remembering Alain's instructions, sat down primly on the edge of the chair and hoped the champagne would not tickle her nose and make her sneeze.

'Splendid! Here you are!' He handed her a fluted crystal glass and, sitting back in his chair, he lifted his own glass, toasting, 'Santé!'

The room was musty, the wallpaper peeling in the corners from damp; the few pieces of gilt French furniture were chipped, and grouped around the marble-topped table situated across the room from a divan draped in a fringed cover and heaped with shiny cushions. The furnishing far exceeded the decorations in Emmaline's room on Smoky Row, however, and she was very impressed with the surroundings.

'Excuse me for not introducing myself,' apologized the old man. 'My name is Stéphane. Like Stéphane d'Indy, the great French actor. But, ah! I'm afraid I'm not on the stage. No, nothing so glamorous as that, I'm just a dull, country planter.'

Emmaline smiled, thinking he was a sweet old man, and probably immensely wealthy.

'Do you enjoy the theatre, mademoiselle?'

Remembering the briefing which Alain had given her about the old Southern gentleman, Emmaline ambiguously answered, 'Some of the finest theatre is in New Orleans.'

He asked, 'And the opera?'

Alain had not told Emmaline that the old man might want to talk about the opera. But remembering that Charley the Oysterman had once showed her the pillared French Opera House on Toulouse Street, she nodded, saying, 'The opera is beautiful.'

'Marie loved the theatre,' announced the old man. 'That's the only reason I make any effort to go to the theatre any more. To remember Marie. But even the theatre has changed in New Orleans since the War. Good artistes seldom make the trip here any more. They don't get the audiences, the appreciation they did in the old days.'

Sipping the champagne, Stéphane continued, 'You are lucky, my dear. You are too young to remember the War. So many people suffered and died in the those devastating years. Women as well as men. Oh, especially women. I was at Vicksburg when the Yankees came to Moorlands.'

Pausing, he explained, 'Moorlands is my plantation. Up river. My wife, Isabella, died well before Fort Sumter, and Marie was living with me in the big house. I could not allow a woman with Marie's charm, her culture, her grace to live in the slave quarters. Such a thing would have been an outrage. An affront to all civilized ways. But even when my regiment was routed to Vicksburg, I felt safe knowing Marie was ensconced in the big house, in comfortable surroundings, protected by a warm, caring staff.'

Staring at the champagne flute in his liver-spotted hands, he asked, 'Who knew what was going to happen in the following months? Who knew exactly how far South the Union Army would march? That Northerners would behave like such . . . vandals? Northern men are intrigued with colored women, you know. Obsessed with them. And they all wanted Marie. Every last one of them. Even . . . even . . . even after she was dead.'

Tears welling in his eyes, the old man repeated, 'Even after the lovely thing was dead. After her tiny body was cold . . . or so my people told me.'

Stopping, he dabbed at the corners of his eyes, saying, 'Enough of my memories, cherie. People must not dwell in the past. The present holds too many surprises.'

He smiled, 'Forgive me, I forgot your name.'

Emmaline spoke exactly – word for word – as Alain had told her.

She looked directly into the old man's watery gray eyes saying, 'But I am . . . Marie!'

He stared at her; a sudden look of astonishment covered his face, followed by a slight flicker of recognition.

Finally, he said, 'Marie . . . yes! I thought it was you when you came through that door. I couldn't be certain. I didn't want to make a fool of myself. But, yes, I thought it was you –'

Rising to his feet as if he were in a dream, the old man stood in front of Emmaline's chair, smiling down at her, then he slowly sank to his knees, burying his face in the skirt of her pink dress.

Covering her small hands with grateful kisses, he said, 'Thank God. Oh, thank God those rumors were false. I knew I'd come home and find you waiting for me, Marie. I knew you'd be safe, unharmed, waiting –'

The old Créole planter, Stéphane, had been enacting this charade of a reunion with his mistress, Marie, for the last twenty years. Alain had told Emmaline the story of how the old man paid Black prostitutes to pretend to be Marie, to take part in the fantasy that his Negress lover was alive, unmolested, living and waiting for him to come home from the Civil War.

*   *   *

That same night Punkin Bluedaw also sipped champagne, seated with Ben Hopper in the front parlor of the Shipton home on Carondelet Street; Punkin had taken a dusty green bottle of Moet and Chandon from the wine cellar, iced it as she had seen the Shiptons do, carried the silver champagne bucket and two glasses into the parlor, and returned to the kitchen to wait excitedly for Ben to arrive at the back door.

Less than an hour later, as night-time enveloped the magnolia bushes behind the iron spear fence which surrounded the Shipton house, Punkin sat alongside Ben on a deep oak-and-tapestry settee; two candles flickered on a table in front of them, the glow illuminating the bouquet of pink roses which Ben had brought her as a gift.

Ben complimented, 'You look so beautiful tonight, Punkin.'

Trying to control her nerves not only about being alone with Ben but also about acting so bold by commandeering the use of the Shipton house, Punkin nervously fingered the sprigged silk dress Sabrine Crowley had given her, saying, 'Funny, but Emmy told me the same thing this afternoon.'

Ben also was frightened, both at being alone with Punkin, and at sitting in somebody else's house; he glanced around at the tall-ceilinged room, at the swagged velvet curtains, the ornately carved chairs, the bulky Bechstein piano, the oil paintings in heavy gold frames hanging on the green-and-yellow striped wallpaper.

He asked, 'And everybody's away?'

'Everybody but Miss Lucy the cook. She's up at the top of the house. She takes a big dose of laudanum each night. I don't know what ails her but the laudanum knocks her out cold.'

'We shouldn't complain about that, I guess!' Ben joked, reaching for Punkin's hand. 'Not if she's going to sleep till morning.'

'I guess not.' Punkin giggled, feeling awkward and clumsy.

She looked back to the cut-glass vase of pink roses and

101

said, 'Nobody's given me roses before. Not any kind of bouquet.'

Squeezing her hand, Ben said, 'Because nobody's loved you like I do, Punkin.'

'This is supposed to be a party,' Punkin said nervously. 'I hope I don't cry.'

'Why should you cry?'

'Oh, all the things on my mind.'

Ben looked at her. 'Have you thought about the question I asked you?'

She nodded. 'I want to say yes, Ben. I want to scream and shout yes, yes, yes, yes. But, Ben, do you truly, honestly believe we – you and I, Ben Hopper and Punkin Bluedaw – can really get . . . married?'

'Because of our color? Is that why you're worried?'

Punkin nodded.

'And because of what our parents might say?'

'Them,' she answered, 'and other people.'

'You've got to forget about other people, Punkin. And as for your parents, I'm ready to ask their permission. I'm ready to promise them I'm willing for us to move away someplace safe, to start a new life together; someplace faraway like out in California; someplace new and exciting where everybody's trying to make a new start.' His eyes glistened in his mahogany-dark face, full of excitement over the challenge.

'I believe we could make a good start out West,' Punkin said. 'But there's still the problem of Daddy. I can't leave home yet. Mama and Daddy need me too much for the moment.'

'I don't care where we live, Punkin. I'll promise your parents to make you the happiest girl in the world wherever we live.' Ben gripped Punkin's small white hand in his large dark fingers. 'Your folks surely can't argue with that.'

Punkin gave a deep sigh. Sometimes she thought Ben was naive about people and their prejudices, that he was too innocent to realize that promises had so little to do with everyday reality.

Moving closer to Punkin on the settee, Ben wrapped one

arm around her thin shoulder, saying, 'Punkin, I love you so much I ache.'

'Ben, I have the same feeling.'

Reaching forward, he turned Punkin's face toward him, and leaned forward to kiss her.

Immediately responding to his kiss, Punkin wrapped both arms around his neck and pressed her own lips against his, feeling his tongue poke cautiously, to explore the front of her teeth, then prod deeper into her mouth.

The kiss immediately unleashed Punkin's emotions; she stretched her mouth wider, accommodating the full width of Ben's tongue, allowing their breathing to join one another, gasping when she felt the wide palm of his hand against her breast.

Punkin knew that Ben had been raised to be a gentleman; he had not made any previous overtures toward her to compromise or dishonor her. But wanting him to know that she was as anxious, as physically excited, as he was to explore the next step of their loving, she pressed her breasts more firmly against the cup of his hand, and she moved her own hand toward the crotch of his trousers, her heart beating wildly, hoping he would not think she was bold and brazen.

They understood one another, and their next movements were natural and spontaneous. Ben began unbuttoning Punkin's dress as he simultaneously moved to take off his own clothes, his large brown fingers gently working, and, soon, their bodies lay naked together on the commodious settee; Ben cradled Punkin's head against his sinewy shoulder, enjoying the feel of her nakedness against his bare muscle, watching the candle's soft glow enhance the creamy whiteness of her skin, dance in her red hair, make the nipples of her fulsome breasts pink and plump as strawberries. His heart also quickened when he saw the sharp contrast of her fair skin against his darkness.

Punkin, also secretly excited deep inside her by making love with someone whose race she had always heard was taboo for White women, cuddled tightly against Ben's muscular hardness, trying to ignore the enormity of his phallus, confessing, 'I don't even feel . . . embarrassed.'

He kissed the top of her pug nose. 'Why should you?'

The nearness of Ben's phallus inflamed her, and she was surprised that the whispered legends about the size of Black men were true. But she was also frightened by the consequences of love-making, and she asked, 'Can I say something, Ben?'

'You never have to be ashamed or frightened to say anything to me, Punkin.'

'Ben, you and I talked – hinted, I guess – about . . . being like this. I was worried, I must admit. So I did something this afternoon. I went to see a friend of mine, Emmy. She gave me something for us to use so we don't have to be worried about –'

Ben held one finger to Punkin's lips; he said, 'Shhh. I know what you're going to say. But just listen to me for a minute. Please.'

'I'm listening.'

'Punkin, it's my place to take care of things like that. But for the moment, we aren't going to use anything but self control. *My* self control. We have a long, long time ahead of us. We have forever. So for the moment we aren't going to use anything but control. And don't worry your pretty little head about us getting in trouble. I love you, Punkin. *I love you!*'

Melting with the gentleness of his assurance, Punkin pressed more tightly against his nakedness, wanting to be closer to him, saying, 'Oh, Ben, you're so wonderful.'

Clenching her tightly in his arms, Ben said, 'Love's to be enjoyed. Not worried about. Right?'

'I'm going to miss you so much.'

'And I told you, Punkin-head, not to say that. You're going to see me again. I promise you that.'

'Hold me, Ben. Just keep holding me tight.'

'I'm never going to let you go, Punkin. And don't you forget that either.'

Ben began kissing Punkin again, but his kisses became more passionate, and he moved one knee between Punkin's legs, his penis hard, aching, a firm bend of skin and cord crowned with a large throbbing head.

Punkin, feeling the enormous penis press against her groin, whispered, 'Ben, I want you. But I'm scared. I'm so scared.'

'Anytime you want to stop, just tell me and we'll stop.'

Ben went on feeding his kisses to Punkin as she lay quivering on the settee; he again pressed one hand against her breast, feeling the nipple taut, and he stroked his other hand across her silky red hair, and all the while the crown of his penis pressed closer toward the lips of her vagina, probing toward her thatch of fair hair, the feminine slit moist with anticipation.

'Honey,' whispered Ben. 'This is the first time for me, too. We're together. You and me. Never forget that. We're together in every way. And we'll always be together, Punkin, always –'

He pushed a bit more; Punkin gasped, clinging onto his shoulders as she bit back her scream.

Lavishing his kisses onto her cheeks, her neck, against her verbena scented hair, Ben whispered, 'We're there . . . we're there . . . we're there . . .'

Waiting for Punkin's body to relax, Ben slowly resumed moving ever so gently, pushing deeper, inching his penis further into her warmth, slowly, not wanting to hurt her with his bigness, soon enjoying his longer strokes into the heat, a sensation exciting his penis, a thrill so different, so much more fulfilling than boyhood games of masturbation with brothers and neighborhood friends.

Punkin, the shock of her broken hymen past, discovered her own passion, joining Ben's rhythms, beginning to feel the penis give pleasure, and she understood the enjoyment of physical love, of a man and woman being together.

Ben, holding Punkin securely in his arms, moved to sit on the edge of the settee, securing Punkin's naked legs around his waist, allowing his penis to plumb even more deeply inside her, stirring, listening to her groan with excitement, proud of his newly-discovered prowess, thrilled with the sensation engulfing his own body, pleased to be giving pleasure to the person he loved.

'Hold tight,' he whispered as he reached to hold both her legs locked around his waist.

Cautiously, Ben rose to his feet and, cradling his hands behind Punkin's buttocks, he moved her up and down on his penis, smiling as he gave them both pleasure in a different way.

Punkin instantly responded to the variation Ben created for them, tossing back her head as she felt his penis create what felt like fireworks inside her body.

He next whispered, 'Now don't be afraid. I won't let go. Just lock your hands around my neck so I can . . .'

Punkin obeyed, and as she lowered from Ben's chest, he placed one hand between her shoulder blades and worked the other hand on her breasts, remembering how his previous manipulations of her nipples had excited her, now wanting to give her excitement between her legs as well as gentle pinches, quick tweaks, a friction on her breasts that also aroused her.

Suddenly, Punkin tensed.

Ben whispered, 'What's wrong?'

She clung to him, staring into the darkness over his shoulder.

He turned to look, too.

Punkin raised one hand, pointing.

Still gripping onto her back, Ben did not at first see anything but, soon, by the candlelight, he saw a naked Black man standing with a White woman, her pale legs wrapped around his dark waist, her ivory feet crossed over his round black buttocks, her strawberry-red nipples pinched by his big thumb and forefinger – their contrasting bodies reflected in a tall parlor mirror.

Ben turned farther, allowing both him and Punkin to enjoy the sight of their reflected love-making.

Smiling, he asked, 'Now what could be wrong with something as beautiful as that?'

Punkin smothered his face in kisses, whispering, 'I love you, Ben Hopper. I love you, love you, love you so much.'

He promised, 'Punkin-head, I'm not going to give you up for the world.'

*   *   *

Alain Summers knew that the old Créole planter had paid the desk clerk at 'The Diana Retreat' an entire night's rent on the room; Alain assured the desk clerk that he would be bringing more business to the assignation house, and the desk clerk allowed him to join Emmaline in the room after the old man had dressed and departed.

The old man had not been a demanding lover, wanting only to undress Emmaline and cover her body with adoring kisses, masturbating as he relived old memories about his dead mistress, using Emmaline as a touchstone for sentimental fantasies.

Relaxed by the champagne, Emmaline quickly forgave Alain for arranging the meeting with another man and she was waiting longingly for him when he joined her on the divan.

Alain had developed a simple formula for making women fall in love with him. First, a young lady would become addicted to his appearance, his brusque attitude, his domineering ways. Next, he would ignore her, allowing her to become desperate for him, to think she might never see him again. The subsequent step was to make some outrageous demand on her, using the withdrawal of his love-making as a threat. And when she surrendered, he would surprisingly pamper her, spoil her, make love to her as if she were a soft, helpless little feminine creature, not the woman whom he had slapped, abused, debased, humiliated. And, then, he would make the next move, the ultimate demand.

The time was not right for Alain to make the ultimate demand on Emmaline. She had been malleable to his masculine advances, yes. She had been deprived of his companionship for two weeks, and she had missed him. Also, she had obediently come to the assignation house as he had ordered her, to be another man's whore. And now she was responding to his soft touch, his sweet words, his tender kisses.

'Look at my sweet little girl,' Alain teased, kneeling naked between her legs. 'You like your man loving you don't you, pussy?'

107

Emmaline twisted, moved, clutched her vagina on his penis deep inside her, responding to his words, adoringly kissing his cleft chin.

'That's my pussy. Be a pretty pussy for your man. Be a sweet helpless woman for me. Be a sweet, little, loving woman. Show your man this is how you want to be for him.'

'Alain . . . *Alain!*'

'Who says I don't take care of my woman? Who says I don't give you the loving you need?'

He stirred his penis inside her, watching her eyes roll as he worked to give her enjoyment, to bring her to her peak of ecstasy, to make her his devoted, grateful slave.

He said, 'That's the only cock you want, isn't it, baby? That's the only cock you want, the one you adore.'

'Alain, I adore you . . . I adore you, Alain. Don't ever leave me again. I need you.'

'You need this cock, do you, pussy?'

'Alain, I was so scared. I thought I had lost you. I need you, Alain.'

'Sure you do, baby. Sure you need me. That's how it's supposed to be. You need me.'

Alain knew that he could have turned Emmaline into a prostitute even if she had not already been one. But now it was his challenge to decide when and how to get her away from the bordello, to have her working solely for him, to get her to support him as other women - other prostitutes - had done only a few short months ago in Natchez.

8 Citizens of White

Lizzie left her suitcase outside Emmaline's room, knocked on the door, then stepped inside to bid her farewell. 'I'll only be a few blocks away on Basin Street. But those few blocks make the difference of Heaven and Hell in this town.'

Lizzie, wearing a wide-brimmed hat decorated with a stuffed ptarmigan and a black feather boa thrown casually around the shoulders of a long burgundy coat, bragged, 'Emmy, I told you that girls have to think with their heads and not with their twats. So I started thinking – how am I going to get out of this dump? What sells big in this town? They like French champagne. Italian opera. German beer. Spanish lace. Chinese shawls. So I thought, why not English . . . whores? Why, being English is so high class in New Orleans, they'll forget all about me being a Jew!'

'Lizzie, how can you say you're English? You told me you were born in New York!'

Airily, Lizzie fluffed her long boa, saying, 'Sure I was born in New York – when my mother, the Duchess of Raleigh, was on a tour of the Colonies!'

'How did you dream that one up?' Emmaline felt brighter these days herself.

'From a whisky bottle. Raleigh Rye. Who knows? I might even say my family owns the distillery.'

'Will people really believe you're English?'

'Henrietta Gibson did.'

Emmaline gasped. 'Henrietta Gibson?'

Lizzie nodded. 'None other. I thought, what the heck? A fine English lady would want to start at the top, right? So I marched up the front steps of her big house on Basin Street.

I pulled that brass bell chain. I handed my card to the maid and said I desired to be received by Miss Gibson.'

Digging in her beaded reticule, Lizzie produced a small white engraved calling card, saying, 'This is the only investment I had to make.'

Emmaline read, '*Lady Elizabeth Louise - London, England.*'

'Pretty classy, isn't it?'

Handing back the card to Lizzy, Emmaline said, 'If you'd thought of this before, you would've saved yourself a lot of misery.'

Lizzie waved for Emmaline to keep the card, saying, 'I never thought of it before, Em, because I never got so low. Nothing against you, but Smoky Row is the bottom of the barrel. Except for street-walking and working those miserable cribs. But I had to do something or just . . . die here.'

'Well, you did it. You're on Basin Street. That's what you wanted.'

'Oh, I'm not stopping there! I made it out of New York's Lower East side. I tricked my way down to New Orleans. But I'm not stopping till I get to San Francisco! Where the beds are paved with gold! Nob Hill!'

'Lizzie, you even sound different. Not English. But a lot different from the gal who came sniffing and sobbing in here just about a month ago.'

'Because I *am* different!' Lizzie affected what she believed to be a British accent, announcing, 'I'm Lady Elizabeth Louise!'

'You've got so much nerve, Lizzie, I know you're going to make it - to San Francisco or wherever you want to go.'

Lizzie sobered, asking, 'Now what about you?'

Emmaline had not yet told anyone about the plans which Alain had been making for them over the past weeks, that Alain had been arranging dates for her with men in parlor houses in the French Quarter, keeping the money the men paid, saving it toward a room into which they would move when he had enough money saved for Emmaline to leave Smoky Row.

Lizzie looked around the small room, saying, 'You know

110

Emmy, you've got to set your sights a little higher than this chicken coop.'

'Lizzie, don't worry. You've been a good influence on me.'

'I hope so. Because Smoky Row's no place for a pretty girl like you. Especially now, with that new bunch of old biddies parading back and forth on the corners with those signs. Have you seen them? I thought those bitches in the cribs across the street were bad enough! But this new bunch even shut them up!'

A new collection of women had arrived on Smoky Row last Thursday, veiled matrons who stood with signs and placards denouncing Smoky Row and the Black prostitutes working there, women whose signs proclaimed them to be respectable citizens, the 'Citizens of White'.

' "Citizens of White", indeed!' Lizzie snorted, 'It sounds more like the Ku Klux Klan to me.'

Emmy took a deep breath; she had heard Luba and Peaches mention the same fact; she said, 'At least you don't have to worry. You're White – and you're leaving!'

'But you're Black and you're staying!' Lizzie hugged her, saying, 'I love you, Em. I love all you girls in this house, for better or worse. And I don't like the idea of old hens making trouble for you.'

'Don't worry. It's not as bad as you think,' Emmy said. 'The Ku Klux Klan's just for men. And why would the Klan be here, in Smoky Row?'

'Because this little street is notorious! It gives New Orleans a bad name. At least the houses on Basin Street, Customhouse Street, places in the rest of the Quarter, make some show of glamor and wealth. But the broads screw right on the street here. The houses are sure no picture-card showplaces. And nobody really important comes here except – excuse me, honey – but horny niggers and perverted old White men. It's a sitting target for do-gooders and the Klansmen. They can clean out the whores, Black people, and White freaks all at the same time.'

Stopping, Lizzie said, 'Listen to me! Telling *you* about Smoky Row!'

Leaning forward, Lizzie again kissed Emmaline on the cheek saying, 'I wish I could stay longer but, la dee da, my carriage is waiting!'

Emmaline followed Lizzie to the hallway, helped her carry her bags through the kitchen and out the back door, hoping to escape the scrutiny of the white-veiled women on the corner of Burgundy and Conti Street, the Citizens of White.

Cramer Crowley was a considerate and patient man, but, also, he was a methodical man; he had driven Punkin Bluedaw back home to Longchamp Parish, leaving her at her parents' farm with her younger brothers and sisters, and he continued home to Belrose to enjoy a few days with his wife before returning to New Orleans to verify his suspicions – without raising the suspicions of other people – that Emmaline Rickers was working as a prostitute on Smoky Row.

At Belrose Plantation, Cramer Crowley spent three happy days with Sabrine, listening to her reports about the plantation overseer, Melvin Hanks, and the fine prospects of the first harvest; the old slave quarters had been completely restored as a small community for migrant workers, and both Cramer and Sabrine believed that Belrose was on its way to providing steady work for free slaves; they both realized that twenty years was very little time to secure work and homes in the world for four million people freed from bondage, as well as a new generation of Black offspring already grown into young people, ready to bring yet another generation into the world.

Sabrine had little time for entertaining and Sunday Socials these days, and she welcomed the quiet suppers with Cramer when they could enjoy each other's company, evenings which culminated in strolls down to the lakeside pergola, then back up the grassy slope to the big house, upstairs, and to bed.

Sabrine spoke mostly about Belrose, her belief in Mr Hanks as a conscientious overseer, the attitude of this season's work crew; she had little social talk to report to her husband except good news about Deke Bluedaw's progress in the hospital, and about one delightful afternoon she had spent with Gemma and Warren Rickers.

She confessed, 'I always know when Gemma's worried about something. She avoids it in conversation. And, Cramer, do you believe she never once mentioned Emmaline. Not *once* during the entire luncheon!'

'Gemma is a strong woman,' Cramer said, satisfied after a good supper and an invigorating walk. 'Emmaline favors her mother in that way.'

'Strength is a fine quality . . . when it's not destructive. But it can be. The same goes for independence. I don't know if I would have allowed a daughter of mine to ride back to New Orleans with Alain Summers.'

'Would you want a daughter of yours to ride on top of a stagecoach with the driver? Because some White people didn't want to sit with her? Or perhaps put her off the stagecoach in the middle of nowhere?'

Sabrine nodded. 'I know. I know. Gemma and Warren - all Black people - have troubles, problems to face we don't even consider. But Alain Summers still bothers me.'

Cramer did not tell Sabrine - nor had he told Punkin - that he had questioned Miss Lillibelle Spooner about Emmaline, and that Miss Spooner had confided that she had not seen Emmaline since the night she and Punkin had stayed with her on their way home from New Orleans.

Waiting for Sabrine to climb into bed, Cramer blew out the kerosene lamp on his bedside table and, pulling Sabrine toward him, he asked, 'You're certain you don't mind me leaving you again for a few more days?'

'If you have work to do in New Orleans, it must be done. I only hope you can put together a few more pieces of information about those men who attacked Deke Bluedaw. They must be brought to some kind of justice.'

Neither Cramer nor Sabrine had mentioned Junior Dehasset, or the Ku Klux Klan, since Cramer had been home.

Cramer, thinking it was time to mention in passing the Federal Government's new concern in New Orleans, said,

113

'There's another group that's sprung up in New Orleans. A group of women this time.'

'Women? Doing what?'

'Picketing prostitutes.'

'But isn't that normal for New Orleans? Aren't citizens continually objecting about vice in that city? And rightly so?'

'These women are different, Sabrine. They wear strange veils over their hats. White gauze you can't see through but, presumably, they can see out of. They look like an odd kind of . . . bee-keeper. They call themselves "Citizens of White" and the Federal Bureau wants to know if they might be connected in some way to recent disturbances in rural areas, if they might be part of the White vigilance sweeping through the Southern states, like some kind of woman's auxiliary.'

'Cramer, do be careful.'

'Of the bee-keepers or the prostitutes?'

'If you want to visit a prostitute you obviously have a need for the call.' She added, 'I was talking about the . . . bee-keepers.'

'Sweetheart, that was a joke about the prostitutes. And obviously a very feeble one.' He rolled against her, saying, 'I miss you, Sabrine. I miss you more than you know.'

'I miss you, too, darling. But I try to keep busy.'

'I worry about you, too,' he confessed. 'Alone on these country roads in your buggy. Driving back and forth from here to the Landing, then over to the Rickers', and down to the Bluedaw place. I wish you wouldn't be such a brave little thing. I wish you'd allow somebody to drive you.'

Secretly enjoying Cramer's concern for her, Sabrine assured him, 'The hospital's letting Deke move home next week. So you don't have to worry about me making that trip any longer. Oh! You didn't tell me how Punkin looks. Is she still keeping herself pretty?'

'You really fixed that girl up! In fact, you might have done too good a job. I swear she was mooning all the way home over a beau she had to leave behind in New Orleans.'

'Punkin? A beau? I don't think so. Not yet. She was probably sad about leaving Emmaline.'

114

'Hmmm.' Cramer still wanted to avoid all mention of Emmaline Rickers, that he had not seen her at the Shipton House, that he doubted if she had ever worked there. He had not even told Punkin that he had followed her from the Shipton house, had seen her get out of the cab in front of a rundown brothel on Smoky Row, had waited and seen her come out of the back door with Emmaline, that he had watched Emmaline help Punkin find a cab, then seen Emmaline dash back alone through the rain, running into the brothel, going inside as if it were her home, as if she lived there, and most likely did.

'You're tired, darling.'

Sabrine's voice jolted Cramer from his drowsiness; he was tired but, also, he felt a desire to make love to his wife. He knew, too, that Sabrine was a physical woman, and that it had been a long time, too long, since they had made love.

He whispered, 'I'm just catching my second wind.'

'You catch some sleep,' she said, turning her head to kiss him goodnight in the darkness.

Cramer's kiss was more than a light brush of the lips; he wrapped his arms around Sabrine, pulling her closer to him.

Instantly responding to his embrace, Sabrine rolled on top of him, accepting his kisses, feeling his sexual hardness against her midsection.

Long ago Cramer and Sabrine had discovered the joy of Sabrine lying on top of him during love-making, that there were no set rules of positions, and that her being in the position normally attributed to the aggressive male could be exciting, especially when she pressed down on her womanhood, opening her vagina to take her husband's penis in close, slow-moving drives.

Also, Cramer enjoyed mounting Sabrine from behind, prodding the tips of his fingers against the lips of her vagina as he drove into it, working the tissue as he increased the friction of his penis, teasing, tapping, rubbing her sensitive vaginal lips as he drove his penis deeper, more quickly, or slower, teasing her walls, receiving his own satisfaction, excited by the sensations he was giving to her.

Sabrine, undressed and kneeling on the deep feather mattress of their bed, groaned pleasurably as Cramer balanced himself naked on his haunches behind her, pressing his wife's shoulders down into the mattress as he probed her vagina from behind her, working to satisfying her with his penis, his quickly working fingers.

Apart from the moans, gasps, quickening of breath, a silence always accompanied their love-making: Sabrine and Cramer seldom spoke as they moved, changed positions, assumed different poses on the bed to enjoy one another. Years of love had brought them closer together, allowing their minds to share their passions as well as their bodies, almost becoming like mind-readers, responding by touch and thought.

Cramer Crowley had no reason to visit a prostitute; he believed Sabrine understood this, especially in moments such as now when they moved - silently - on the bed, Cramer again on his back, Sabrine lying on top of him, her breasts brushing against his smooth chest as she received the plunges of his penis, the pressure of Cramer's long legs wrapped around her calves, his legs becoming tighter and tighter as he thrust upwards, listening to her breathing, feeling her clutch, finally enjoying his own jet of excitement pour from the roots of his scrotum to join the flood she had waiting for him.

As Sabrine collapsed against him, Cramer finally spoke, whispering, 'I love you, Mrs Crowley.'

9   The Egg Roll

Jocasta Liddle lay on her brass bed at this mid-morning hour, studying Emmaline standing next to the bed, Emmaline's nubile body covered by the thin white cotton shift showing the firm rise of her nipples, and cutting across the soft, silky skin of her brown thighs.

'How long you been working for me, baby doll?' Jocasta asked, propped up by her bed pillows. 'Little over a year now?'

'A year last month, Miss Jocasta.' Emmaline set down the tin mug of coffee on the bedside table.

'A year last month! Lands! And I ain't seen you in my bedroom the whole time. Well, if you ain't a sight for sore eyes. And, gal, if I had a pecker, it would be so big as I lie here looking at you that you'd think there was a tent pole under this crochet bedspread!'

Laughing, patting her marcelled hair which had only been ever-so-slightly disturbed by sleep, Jocasta beckoned Emmaline to step closer to the bed, saying, 'I ain't going to ruin a good thing by asking why I get the pleasure of your company. But I hope it was more than to bring me some morning coffee. I sure do hope.'

Emmaline tried to act genuine, to sound sincere but, also, to come right out with the reason she was visiting the bedroom; she said, 'I remember what you told me, Miss Jocasta.'

'What I tell you, honey? I say so many darned things I can't remember all I say.'

'About a woman needing the feel of another woman's body - when a man's not enough . . . or too much.'

'You had enough of men already, gal?'

Emmaline shrugged, wondering if Alain's advice was right about going to bed with Jocasta, about trying to get extra favors.

Jocasta said, 'I say something else, too, baby doll. I say when a rat sniffs a nice big chunk of cheese, that rat better watch out or a trap's going to snap right down on his snout! But, oh, baby doll, let this big Mama Rat get a nice big nibble of some of your cheese.'

Pulling Emmaline closer, Jocasta felt Emmaline's nipples through the thin white cotton shift, then moved her mouth closer, chewing the cotton as she worked her fingers to feel between Emmaline's thighs.

Motioning for Emmaline to lift the flimsy garment over her head, Jocasta said, 'Your heart's beating fast, honey. Why's you little heart beating so fast? You scared? What you scared for?'

'I've never done this before.'

'Then hop right into bed and let Jocasta show you what the fuss's all about. And I think for being such a good little doll this morning, I'm going to give you some nice . . . egg roll!'

Jocasta threw back the covers and moved to sit on the edge of the bed as Emmaline lifted the white garment over her head, then hesitantly climbed into the deep, warm hollow made in the mattress.

Reaching toward the bedside table, Jocasta ignored the mug of coffee and reached for a small tin box. She picked up a wooden match stick from the table, stuck one tip of the match into powdery white cocaine inside the tin box, held the tip of the match toward each nostril, sniffed deeply, then set the box back down on the table.

Pulling off her wrinkled red kimono, Jocasta stretched out her arms wide as if she were about to plunge naked into a pool of cold water; she shivered, then moved quickly back into the bed, her breasts, buttocks, thighs, stomach, large and rotund, but firm for her size.

Hoisting Emmaline's shapely brown legs in the air, Jocasta lowered her marcelled head between them and began darting her tongue back and forth into Emmaline's furry vagina. After enjoying the first taste, a fresh sweetness she savoured, she enveloped Emmaline's entire vagina with her mouth and sucked in her cheeks.

Emmaline gasped, an instant sensation shooting through her groin, and she bolted upright on the bed.

Jocasta, relaxing her mouth grip, chuckled, and ordered, 'Lie back down, gal. Lie back down and let me get that egg rolling good and proper for you.'

Again, her mouth positioned between Emmaline's knees, Jocasta suctioned her lips around Emmaline's vagina, but instead of a swift intake of breath, she blew, shaking her head back and forth as she puffed, using her lips to vibrate Emmaline's outer tissue, her vulva, the entirety of her feminine mound.

Emmaline had hated the idea of coming into Jocasta's bedroom, of being in bed with another female; Alain had ordered her to do it – and she was addicted to Alain's orders, his commands, his domination. Nevertheless there was something which Jocasta was doing to her, something new and completely different, that made her momentarily forget about Alain, about being his love slave, and she enjoyed the pure physical pleasure of Jocasta's love-making.

Jocasta, exhilarated by the cocaine, allowed Emmaline to be totally passive, and she moved from her vagina to her anus, tonguing the tightness of the rosebud sphincter.

Also, Jocasta had a fondness for breasts, sweet, young, tender breasts crowned with plump nipples: she sucked, chewed, worked on Emmaline's nipples while fingering Emmaline's vagina, then sucking the sweetness from her fingers as if the taste were the sugary, sweet residue from sticky candy.

Finally, after the drug's rush had waned, and after Jocasta had satisfied her curiosity about Emmaline's body, she reached for her red kimono, moved to the edge of the bed and put her arms into the kimono saying, 'Don't get too comfortable, gal. Pretty soon that fancy buck of yours is going to come calling. You've only got him and the Oysterman booked for today.'

Emmaline groaned, relaxed, stunned into euphoria by Jocasta's ardent chewing and puffing.

Smiling, Jocasta reached toward the bedside table and, lifting the piece of lead pipe attached to the leather thong, she slipped it over her head, letting the pipe fall down into her cleavage, nodding as she watched Emmaline stumble from the bed.

She joked, 'You're acting a little pie-eyed, gal.'

'I . . . I . . .' Emmaline shook her head, confessing, 'I don't know what to say.'

Jocasta settled back into the hollow of her mattress, asking, 'It wasn't what you expected?'

Emmaline lingered by the door. 'Two women . . . people always say two women have nothing to use –'

'Baby doll, you listen to what people say and you're going to have a pretty dull life. Now get your ass out of here. It ain't noon yet and I still need my beauty sleep.'

Emmaline was dressed in a white organdy dress and straw bonnet when Alain arrived by late morning; he paid Jocasta ten dollars, pursuing the charade of taking Emmaline out for a midday meal, even asking Jocasta for the name of a new saloon or café they might enjoy.

Jocasta had not yet warned Emmaline about seeing Alain as she had warned her about Charley the Oysterman. For one reason, Alain was giving money to Jocasta. And, secondly, Jocasta still had not decided what the handsome young mulatto truly had in mind.

She said, 'A smart man like you should know his way around town pretty good.'

Alain reminded her, 'Around Natchez, yes, mam. But New Orleans is your town.'

'You're working hard to turn it into your town, sonny boy. You're working mighty hard.'

After Emmaline and Alain had departed, Jocasta sat alone in the kitchen, holding a tin mug of coffee in one hand, the bottle of Raleigh Rye whisky in the other; the other women had not yet risen for the day – Effie, Luba, Cassy and Peaches still asleep upstairs; Eva and Claire snoring on cots in the parlor.

Enjoying the solitude of the kitchen, Jocasta sipped her spiked coffee and considered the good and bad things happening in her life at the moment.

Strangely, the 'Citizens of White' were having a profitable effect on business: men were frightened to go to the cribs; they would rather spend an extra seventy-five cents, dollar, two dollars to get quick sexual satisfaction in the privacy of a brothel than be under the nearby scrutiny of respectable matrons holding placards and signs.

Thinking how more and more customers were beginning to use the brothel's back door in recent weeks, Jocasta suddenly heard a knock on the front door and guessed it must be a Black man, a regular customer who did not care who saw him going into a bordello on Smoky Row.

Jocasta, wondering whom she would wake to entertain the early day caller, was surprised to see a White man standing on the porch, a tall, neatly-dressed White man with curly black hair streaked with white.

Leading him into the kitchen, Jocasta began her usual speech to newcomers; she said, 'I got no professor on a piano. I got on eats and champagne. The towels might not always be fresh. But the girls are clean and guaranteed not to give you the gleet.'

The man nodded, watching Jocasta's high-riding buttocks chew back and forth under her purple dress as he followed her into the kitchen; he replied, 'I'm not looking for music and a banquet or champagne. I've got my mind set on a sweet little colored girl, about eighteen, nineteen years old. Not too spoiled by the ways of the big city.'

Jocasta pointed at the chair across the table from her. 'I got just the little lady you describe, mister. But at the moment she's out for a stroll.'

'Do you advise me to wait?' Cramer Crowley had decided to come directly to Jocasta Liddle's bordello as soon as he had come back to New Orleans, anxious to talk to Emmaline.

Jocasta asked, 'Want some coffee? Plain, it's free. A quarter if you want a grizzly bear to pee in it. That's the limits of extras in this place.'

121

Putting a silver dollar on the table's blue oilcloth, Cramer Crowley said, 'Give us both a double.'

'Thanks,' she said, pocketing the dollar. 'I'll take mine later.'

Leaning back on the hind legs of his chair, Cramer asked, 'Those ladies bother business? Those women holding signs on the corner?'

'Mister, I've been in this business some thirty-odd years. The only thing that's bad for my line of work is a wife who knows how to please her old man at home.'

Cramer smiled, thinking of Sabrine.

Jocasta asked, 'No use you sitting here wasting your time. I got a nice country gal named Peaches. She can show you a real good time. For just five little dollars.'

Cramer still didn't know what name Emmaline used as a prostitute. Could it be 'Peaches'? He asked, 'She a young thing, too?'

'Peaches ain't exactly spring chicken. But –'

'I'll wait for –' He looked at Jocasta, asking, 'What did you say the girl's name is?'

'I didn't.'

'But you did say she's gone out with a young gentleman.'

'I didn't mention her going with nobody.' Jocasta took a sip of coffee, asking, 'You ain't the law, are you, mister? Some sheriff or Pinkerton detective?'

Cramer shook his head. 'No, and you probably have to pay the law so much in bribes you know them all by first name.'

'You can never pay enough in this racket. The worse the dump, the bigger the graft.'

'How much *do* you pay?'

She studied him more closely. 'And you ain't some reporter? Some guy with a pencil from the newspapers? Or from that *Mascot* rag, that little shit-sheet making smart talk about fancy ladies and sporting men. Because if you are, mister, you can get out of my house right now. You ain't going to buy me or my talk for no dollar.'

'How much does it cost to buy you?'

'Buy me? *Buy me?* Mister White Man, I've been bought

122

and sold since I was eight years old. I was eight years old when I was sold off a farm to a travelling slave pedlar on a mule. Two months later I was sold from the back of a barber shop here in New Orleans. Down on Levee Street. Barber Bill cut hair, did abortions, and sold pickaninnies all in the same shop. I was eight years old when Barber Bill sold me for ten dollars. That was a lot of money in those days, especially for a pickaninny gal who was no shining rose.

'A sailor with breath like an alligator and pecker like a horse took my cherry. I'd rather let him screw me than kiss me his breath was so danged bad. The sailor set me loose in a house on Gallatin Street. Betty Blue's place. I slopped shit buckets for Betty Blue from then on. Oh, Gallatin Street was the big whore strip back in them years. Before Basin Street and all these other fancy-ass places uptown. And the whores on Gallatin Street were tough, mean. They fought with each other and spat in a man's eye. They'd make Smoky Row look a Sunday School picnic.

'Betty Blue got knifed by her old man in a brawl on a pool table in the Crescent City Bar and Grill. I next went to Girod Street which never had been no better than Gallatin Street. Probably worse. I was twelve years old which was old enough to suck dick and play with men's balls. I soon started sprouting little titties, and was ready to do my first screwing for dimes and quarters in a proper whorehouse – or "bagnio" as they were starting to call them in those days. I still was no beauty. But I gave a man what he paid for. I threw in a few laughs to boot. Sure, I've been bought. I've been bought, sold, and bought again. As a slave and a whore. But I always give what the man – or the lady – bargained for, and so don't look to me for some big story about goings on around here just because you lay down a silver dollar on the table. For a little hopped-up coffee.'

Cramer Crowley, impressed by the fat woman's honesty, said, 'Somehow I have the feeling that even a hundred silver dollars wouldn't get some facts out of you.'

Looking at him, Jocasta narrowed her eyes and asked, 'You some father looking for his kid? Your kid run away from home, mister, and you think she's hiding out here on Smoky Row?'

'You're close.'

'This kid of yours colored?'

'Pretty, too.'

'Mister, this town's full of folks looking for pretty colored kids. They're lucky if they find them in places good as this. If they find them alive. If they don't find corpses. Their throats slit. Skeletons eaten up by VD. Mutilated in some fancy orgy.'

'That's what I want to avoid.'

'A girl old enough to screw, mister, is old enough to know her own mind. No way you're going to keep her home. Not even if you tie her to the barnyard fence. She's going to chew her way through the rope and run right back to New Orleans.'

'Why do they run away in the first place? What's the attraction of towns like New Orleans?'

'Find the answer to that and tell me.' Jocasta shook her head. 'What gives a man his first taste for some titty? To go dipping dick in a nice fuzzy dish? What gives a gal her first tooth for sweet pecker? To want it up her hot pussy? Maybe crave it day and night up her ass?

'Mister, answer those questions for me, too. All I know, all I seen over the years is that when a gal gets a wild notion to take off for the city and be some high-stepping slut, there's nothing going to drag her back home if she's got her mind made up. Especially if she gets some fancy man sitting in her saddle, holding the reins nice and tight, shouting orders to do this, do that. Then she's really a goner.'

Cramer Crowley stared at the plump brothel keeper. 'And that's what's happened to Emmaline Rickers? She's got a "fancy man" now?'

'Mister, your silver dollar just run out of time.'

Cramer Crowley left the bordello; Jocasta sat alone in the kitchen, knowing that the tall White man had come purposely to see Emmaline. But she also knew that the White man – or anybody else – could not get Emmaline to go home.

Earlier this morning, Jocasta had finally discovered why Emmaline was a prostitute.

Emmaline was a pretty girl. And she knew it. Emmaline also knew she was sexually attractive to many people, that she could buy - trade - her body for money, for favors. She did not desperately need the money. She always had more than pin money to spend. She needed the attention. And the special favors. To be spoiled. Pampered. Jocasta had learned all about Emmaline this morning in bed. Jocasta knew when a woman wanted to be in bed with her, was hungry for love-making. But Emmaline had gone to bed with Jocasta - using her body - to get a special favor. Jocasta did not yet know what that favor was. Nor if Emmaline had come of her own free will or if somebody - like her new mulatto dandy - had told her to do it. But she had done it. And Jocasta now knew for certain that Emmaline was a born whore, a whore through-and-through, using her body like a purse. Jocasta had once heard, 'Whores aren't born bad. They just get mean if you don't pay them enough.' That was Emmaline. Looking for, expecting, wanting something in return for being pretty, cute, a baby doll beauty. To Jocasta, Emmaline was nothing but another brown purse.

Sitting in the kitchen, remembering that it was a tradition in this business for brothel-keepers and pimps to work hand-in-hand, Jocasta wondered if she should propose to the mulatto, Alain, that they work together, not only working Emmaline, but to work more girls. Alain was flashy, good-looking, had the cruel, heartless ruthlessness which whores flocked to, and he was greedy himself. Jocasta had not seen such a pimp of a man since she had first seen Willy the Whip, the White man who pimped for the Indian woman, Kuda, on Basin Street as well as making a fine living by flogging prostitutes.

Considering all these facts as she sipped her spiked coffee, Jocasta also weighed the fact that - like Gallatin Street, Girod Street, the Swamp, any of the other down-trodden districts for cheap prostitutes which had once scandalized New Orleans - the days of Smoky Row were also numbered.

125

She had to do something to survive this phase of her life as she had survived all the others.

Alain found a furnished room above Basin Street, on Liberty Street, two blocks away from the assignation house called 'The Diana Retreat'. Emmaline stood in the furnished room looking out of the second floor window at the back wall of St Louis Cemetery, staring down at the oddly shaped vaults, and she said, 'I don't like it.'

'Why not?' demanded Alain. 'It's ours for fifteen dollars a week – with a kitchen!'

Emmaline turned away from the window. 'That bone yard down there gives me shivers.'

'Listen, there's more corpses wandering around Smoky Row than in that cemetery.'

Emmaline wished that she felt better so that she could work at the brothel as well as help Alain look for a decent room; she had been feeling nauseous the last few weeks, depressed, and had little energy.

She looked at the dingy wallpaper, the faded curtains hanging limp at the windows. 'When could we move in?'

'I'll move in right away. Today.'

'You?' She looked quizzically at him.

'Sure. You don't think you're ready to move out of Smoky Row yet, do you? It's going to take time to build up a bigger nest egg. Do you know how many regular johns you've got, baby? None! Zero!'

'But last week I made seventy-five dollars around town!'

'And I had to pay Jocasta forty dollars to take you to those houses!' He turned away from her, puffing on a thin cheroot cigar, saying, 'No, you can't even think about leaving Smoky Row. Not yet.'

'I *want* to leave.'

He turned, suspiciously eyeing her. 'Did you do what I told you to do? Let Fatty pull down your pants?'

Emmaline nodded. 'I heard Cassy and Eva say that Jocasta likes it in the morning. So I waited until I knew she was awake and took in some coffee.'

He smiled. 'And my little whore jumped right in the sack along with big mama!'

'Well, you told me to,' she pouted.

'Hey, I'm not scolding you, sugar. I'm just saying it would be stupid for you to leave that dump. She'll let you do anything the next few weeks. I probably won't even have to pay her a penny to stroll you.'

'But I don't *want* to go to bed with her again,' Emmaline protested. 'I just want to be with you!'

Moving closer to her, Alain pulled her against his crotch, murmuring, 'I know what you need. You need your man's cock. And maybe to be slapped around a little, huh?'

Emmaline was in no mood for crude, sadistic love-making; she wanted soft, gentle attention; she wanted to hear Alain tell her she was pretty, that he loved her.

He put his forefinger under her chin, asking, 'How many johns have you got tonight?'

'One. So far.'

'Who?'

'Charley.'

'Charley?'

'Oysterman.'

Alain remembered. 'The guy who likes to hear about my prick.'

She frowned. 'Charley doesn't know it's you I describe.' She sometimes wished she didn't tell Alain everything she did in bed, that she didn't repeat stories she told customers.

Alain laughed. 'Well, you feed him a real good story tonight, baby, and you tell him pretty soon he's going to come visiting you at your own private address.'

'Charley's no problem,' she said. 'He'll follow me.'

'Follow you? What do you mean?'

'Like a friend.' Emmaline looked around the dismal room one last time, saying, 'I'd better get back to Jocasta's. After-noons can get busy.'

'Hold on a minute. What's this about you and this Charley the Oysterman guy being friends? You don't need friends, understand? *I'm* your friend.'

127

Emmaline began, 'Charley used to take me out, for walks, to eat –'

Alain decided not to pursue the matter of Charley the Oysterman any further for the moment; he said in a lighter voice, 'Baby, why don't you take a street-car back? I want to see the landlord. Tell him I'm taking the place.'

'Suit yourself.'

He held out his hand.

Emmaline looked from his hand, to his face.

'The money,' he said. 'Let's have it. Why do you think I brought you here?'

'You brought me here to give you . . . money? What happened to the other money I gave you? The money you've been keeping for us?'

'Baby, your man's got to live!'

'You brought me here for money? Not to show me what this room looks like? To get my approval?'

'Your approval?' He laughed. 'Oh, gal! There's some things you still don't understand. I run this show. You just lie in bed on your back or your belly or however those guys want you, bitch. That's what you do, understand? But I run the show!'

Emmalne felt fury rise in her, her small hands tightening into fists.

Alain, seeing the anger in her eyes, grabbed one of her hands, and pressing it against his crotch, he ordered, 'Feel that, woman!'

She glared at him.

'*Feel* that!'

His penis swelled – jerked – under the twill fabric of his trousers.

He said, 'You love that cock, don't you? You wouldn't know how to live without it, would you?'

Emmaline's hand weakened, feeling the penis lengthen down Alain's leg; she pictured in her mind how the penis looked, how it tasted, how it felt when Alain made love to her, how it bobbed with excitement as he spat on her, how she trembled with excitement.

'Your world revolves around that cock, slut, and don't

128

you forget it! Understand?' He threw away her hand.

Emmaline silently reached in her purse for money which Jocasta had given her, her share from the brothel.

Alain, counting the green banknotes, ordered, 'Catch the street-car on the corner. I don't want you walking.'

Her voice was soft. 'I want to walk. I want to try and see if I can get in to see Doc Williams.'

His eyes flared. 'Doc Williams? You don't have clap, do you?'

Emmaline, realizing that this was the worst moment to tell Alain she had missed last month's period, lied, 'Jocasta . . . Jocasta wants us all to get check-ups.'

'More money down the drain,' he grumbled. 'She probably gets a kick-back from the doctor as well. Fat bitch.'

Junior Dehasset sat on Iberville Street holding the leather reins to a pair of dappled mares harnessed to a three-seated surrey; he checked the time on his new pinchbeck pocket watch, again cursing the fact that he had lost his gold engraved one.

Twenty-five minutes past noon, and Junior continued to wait to collect the first shift of women, the 'Citizens of White', from the corner of Burgundy Street before bringing the next group of Klansmen's wives to Smoky Row, a stronger, more aggressive group of women who would have different signs, a bolder tone, putting into effect the next attack against the Black prostitutes.

It had taken Junior Dehasset this trip to New Orleans, though, to realize that he did not like women. That he, in fact, hated them. It had been his idea to use the wives of New Orleans Klansmen. He had seen women serve the Klan in auxiliary groups in other states, and he had to admit they were often useful. In Tallahassee, Klansmen's wives had run a Black minister out of town, thereby keeping a powerful group of educated Negroes from uniting in the community. In Mobile, White women had testified before a judge and jury against three Black men, claiming that the men – a school teacher and two men helping him to open a school for young Black children – had attempted to rape

129

them. Here in New Orleans, the women's secret auxiliary were picketing prostitutes, hoping to draw public attention to the fact that Negroes were dirty, lazy, degenerate, and undesirable citizens and neighbors.

What was worse, though? Black people as a race or White women for companions? To Junior's mind, women were very similar to Negroes: they got so bossy and out-of-hand once given a little freedom and power. But for the moment, he urged the Klan to use their wives, sisters and daughters in the struggle to keep the ex-slaves in poverty, in the background, no better than slaves.

The Ku Klux Klan had been organized after the Civil War as a prank among college boys in Tennessee, young men home on holiday who formed a secret social club called *Kuklos* – the Greek work for 'circle'. Junior Dehasset also knew that the original 'Kuklos Klan' had come at a time when other White men in the South were uniting into vigilante groups to protect themselves from the Black people being freed from slavery. A vigilante group in Mississippi had been called 'Liberty Lodge'. In Louisiana, they had dubbed themselves the 'Knights of the Camellia'. Junior had been one of the vigilante ring-leaders in Longchamp Parish, and he might still be powerful there – as well as the master of Belrose Plantation – if it had not been for the damnable Union Army, their Freedom Bureaux after the Civil War, and meddling carpet-baggers like his brother-in-law, Cramer Crowley.

Cramer Crowley had brought many changes with him to Belrose Plantation; Junior's father, Senator Dehasset, had been a liberal, soft-hearted politician who doted on his daughter, Sabrine, leaving Junior and his mother, Noele Dehasset, a weak match against them and their radical ways.

Junior, sitting in the surrey on Iberville Street, thought about his deceased mother and smiled when he tried to imagine the elegant woman here on the street holding a picket sign with these White women who called themselves 'Citizens of White'. Noele Dehasset would never have come here. She had been born of a fine Créole family, the

Bonheurs, and would not even have spoken to such lower-class women as these Klansmen's wives, common house-wives, daughters of farmers and tradesmen and sailors.

Despite his disregard for them, the 'Citizens of White' were none the less serving Junior's purpose, helping to sow racial discord in the city, and he had been forcing himself to be gentlemanly toward them. They would become increasingly influential too, spreading hatred in communities, preventing Negro schools and hospitals from opening, keeping Black people uneducated, frustrated, helpless, poor, and powerless. The 'Citizens of White' were useful in their way to Junior, as the country whore, Ivy Bravo, had been useful in her way. But, secretly, Junior felt the same contempt for these women that he had felt for Ivy Bravo, and he would as quickly, as guiltlessly, kill them as the woman who had greedily wanted his 'whorebreaker'. Junior's 'whorebreaker' had become more important to him than any woman.

Junior put the cheap pinchbeck watch back into the pocket of his waistcoat and, knowing it was approaching the time to bring the stronger group of Klan women to Smoky Row, he suddenly saw a tall White man leaving Jocasta Liddle's brothel, a well-dressed White man bravely, confidently walking out of the brothel's front door.

'Well, I'll be damned!' Junior thought. 'I'll be God-damned to hell! Isn't that my lily-assed brother-in-law? Why, yes indeed! Cramer Crowley! And he's coming out of that coon house! So that's what he likes! A little black meat!'

The germ of a new idea slowly sprouted in Junior Dehasset's brain as he sat in the surrey and watched Cramer Crowley amble down Burgundy Street toward Toulouse Street.

10   Shame

Peaches, Luba, Eva, Effie, Cassy and Claire sat around the kitchen table, and on stools in the corner, drinking coffee with Jocasta after Cramer Crowley had left the bordello; they were discussing prostitutes who had been arrested in the house on the far corner of the block when they heard a trumpet blast outside the front of the house. The blast of the trumpet sounded again and Luba said, 'The Waffle Man!'

The Waffle Man was a street vendor in New Orleans who blew a trumpet to announce his arrival, a man who made waffles on a cast-iron stove in the back of his wagon, sprinkled them with powdered sugar, and sold them for five cents. Burgundy Street was not on the Waffle Man's route through the French Quarter, but the women quickly crowded with Jocasta to the front door to see if there might be a little joy in their lives, to see if they could rush with their nickels and buy a waffle from the Waffle Man.

The women stopped short in the doorway, staring angrily at the women on the corner, the 'Citizens of White'. One woman was blowing a trumpet, another woman pointing a large white wooden hand at Jocasta's house, a large silhouette of a hand stencilled with the word – SHAME.

Slamming shut the front door, Jocasta fumed, 'That's disgusting!'

'Cruel!' muttered Eva, a tall woman with eyes like fried eggs.

'It's also disturbing the peace!' proclaimed Cassy.

Peaches wailed, 'And I wanted a waffle! I ain't had a waffle from the Waffle Man in years!'

Then came the stones.

'God damn them to hell!' roared Jocasta, looking through the slats of the front shutters. 'They're throwing rocks now!'

Another stream of stones pelted the front of the board house.

Jocasta said, 'We might not be able to do nothing about screaching trumpets, and pointing hands! But I sure in hell can stop them bitches from throwing rocks at my house!'

'Miss Jocasta, you be careful of them women,' begged Cassy.

More stones hit the outside wall, clattering across the front porch.

Jocasta, lifting the leather thong over her marcelled hair, quickly removed the roll of money from the lead pipe, stuffed the money into a brass Chinese vase and reached for the door handle.

Luba warned, 'Miss Jocasta, we can't fight all them women!'

'I ain't asking you to fight!'

'Neither can you, Miss Jocasta!'

'Who the hell says?'

'You can't, Miss Jocasta! There's nothing meaner than White ladies in big hats!'

'I've never backed down from a fight in my life, and I ain't backing down now.' Jocasta threw open the front door.

'But they got the Law on their side!' cried Peaches. 'They're . . . White!'

Jocasta, standing in the doorway, gripping the lead pipe in her hand, asked, 'What do you think this is? A licorice stick? They might get me. But, my God, I'll take six of them bitches with me!'

She charged down the front walk.

A volley of stones flew from alongside the house at Jocasta, from the boardwalk on Bienville Street, striking her on the buttocks and legs; she glowered and started running toward the front gate, her breasts shaking, her jowls trembling, shouting, 'That does it, ladies! That does it!'

A group of five women rushed Jocasta with their signs,

using the poles as pikes. But Jocasta swiped wildly at them, with her lead pipe, knocking signs and women to the ground, grabbing with her other hand to rip at gauze veils, to slug women on the chins, to push them down to the ground, then kick them.

Across the street, the crib whores gathered and began cheering; more prostitutes appeared in doorways and windows in bordellos lining Smoky Row; Peaches and Luba ran down the front walk to join Jocasta. But as soon as they reached the gate, a loud bell clanged down Burgundy Street, and a team of horses charged toward Iberville Street, pulling a police wagon.

'Shit!' muttered Luba, stopping by the gate. 'It's a set up! Quick! Get back inside the house!'

The brothel women, the crib prostitutes, everybody disappeared from the street, except the 'Citizens of White' who surrounded Jocasta as the Police Wagon stopped alongside them.

The police wagon took Jocasta to the St Charles Street Police House, where she was booked on disorderly conduct, and on two accounts of attempted murder; Jocasta was locked in a barred cell until all the complaints could be filed against her. Luba and Peaches, returning home from the Police House, reported this news to the other women as they again gathered in the kitchen, debating what they should do now as the police were refusing to allow Jocasta free on bail.

'Everybody's entitled to bail,' said Luba. 'Even Black people.'

'Least it was that way when my Daddy kicked holy shit out of Ma,' said Eva, sipping at her coffee. 'And he was Black.'

'Should we put all our money together and hire some slick lawyer?'

Luba reminded them, 'Miss Jolly got herself a slick lawyer to defend her, and her place down the street's still closed.'

Cassy asked, 'So we shouldn't feel they're just picking on Jocasta? On us here?'

'They're picking on all Smoky Row, honey,' said Peaches. 'We're just one of the first houses they're hitting. They got – what? Ten, twelve places to go.'

'But Miss Jocasta pays the Alderman good money,' said Claire. 'Every Monday noon.'

Peaches nodded. 'And I paint my snatch with voodoo grease. Does that keep me from catching crabs?'

Footsteps on the back porch disturbed them and, turning, they saw Emmaline come through the kitchen door.

'Jocasta's been arrested!' said Peaches.

'Arrested?' Emmaline looked at the six women gathered around the table and on corner stools. 'What for?'

'Those White lady citizens started blowing a trumpet –'

'Like the Waffle Man!' said Eva.

'But it wasn't no Waffle Man,' said Peaches.

'And they were pointing a cut-out wooden hand, the finger pointing at this house with the word "shame" painted on it.'

Luba said, 'Then they started throwing rocks at the house. Jocasta went on the rampage with her lead pipe and got hauled into the Police House for disturbing the peace and attempted murder.'

'Attempted murder?' Emmaline looked at the worried faces.

'It was some set-up sure as shooting,' said Luba. 'The police won't let her out on bail until all complaints have been filed. Tell me that ain't a set-up!'

Emmaline moved toward the archway leading toward her room. Then she stopped.

Cassy leaned forward on her stool, reaching for the coffee-pot on the stove. 'You might as well have a mouthful of this mud, honey. Park your ass and help us hatch some kind of plan.'

Peaches, studying Emmaline, said, 'You don't look too good yourself, honey. Your new man giving you hell?'

Emmaline looked back at the six women sitting around the room; she thought about Jocasta being locked in jail; she knew business would get slower, if not stop completely once word spread about Jocasta.

'Hey, Emmy? Where you going?' called Luba.

Emmaline was already halfway across the back porch.

'Alain!'

Emmaline stood on the second floor landing of the gray board building where Alain had found them the room; she called louder, 'It's me! Emmy! I'm back!'

Looking up at the glass transom over the door, she again tried the door but it was locked. She had left here just a few hours ago after looking at the room with Alain. Was he still with the landlord?

'Alain?' she called louder, then beat on the door with a fist.

The door opened a crack.

Alain, staring out at Emmaline, said, 'I thought you had to work.'

'Jocasta's been arrested. She got in a fight. The police took her –'

Emmaline stopped; she asked, 'Why don't you open the door?'

'Is that what you're doing back here? Telling me . . . that?'

'Alain, why don't you open the door?'

He frowned at her.

'Alain, have you got a woman in there?'

'Emmy, don't be stupid. Now why don't you –'

'Alain, you *do* have a woman in there.' She pushed at the door and then saw the girl on the bed, a Black girl with bushy hair, a pretty girl holding a sheet over her naked breasts.

Alain, grabbing for his trousers, ordered, 'Emmy, go back downstairs.'

Emmaline, staring at the girl, said, 'I thought you had to see the landlord, Alain.'

'Emmy, I said go downstairs.'

'This bitch? She our new landlord?'

'Emmy, I said –'

Ignoring him, Emmaline moved closer to the bed, asking, 'Who are you, honey? You our new landlord?'

The girl, trying to be brave, asked, 'And who are *you?*'

'I'm his woman, that's who I am!' Emmaline snatched for the sheet. 'I'm his *whore*, that's who I am! I pay for this room with my ass! Now get the hell out of here, understand, or I'll pull that frizzy mop off your head!'

Alain moved behind Emmaline, grabbing her arms before she could attack the girl; he ordered, 'Emmaline, calm down! Just go downstairs and calm down!'

'Calm down!' she repeated. '*Calm down?* I pay for this room! I gave you money for this room! I go to the doctor. He tells me I'm pregnant. I go back to Jocasta's. They tell me she's in jail. I come back here. I find you in bed with another woman. You tell me –'

Releasing her hands, Alain spun her around and asked, 'You went to the doctor and he . . . what?'

'I'm pregnant!'

The other girl, seizing the moment, grabbed her clothes from the chair, sneaking out of the room as the pretty-boy pimp was slapping his whore, thinking, *'I don't need this bullshit.'*

The same night, two horse-drawn fire wagons circled the block on Canal Street between Burgundy and Dauphine Street three times before finally going to the fire on the corner of Burgundy Street and Bienville Street; the flames by then had spread too far for the firemen to save Jocasta Liddle's brothel from destruction, the sparks spreading, setting the nearby cribs into a small inferno which flared into a momentary brightness, then left no more than a heap of ashes, a few tell-tale frames and charred arches, and a lingering cloud which made an Irish fireman joke, 'Holy Mary, this filthy place now be looking like its name – Smoky Row.'

Part Two

Basin Street

11 Playing the Hambone

'Gemma, you hear that?' Warren Rickers halted the buggy in the dirt yard in front of the Bluedaws' log cabin. Gemma Rickers listened and heard whistling and the sound of hands clapping, hands slapping against bare skin, the Southern music known as 'playing the hambone', a pastime developed over the years by Negroes in slave quarters, and White farmers on small plots of rocky ground.

Warren, listening to the slap-and-whistle, said, 'Deke Bluedaw's the only guy around these parts who remembers how to play hambone. But Deke's hands –'

Still holding the reins, Warren said, 'Honey, do you think we could be imagining this?'

Gemma frowned. Deke Bluedaw had been out of the hospital for two weeks. His hands and feet, and large sections of his arms and legs had been amputated. Gemma and Warren had seized this evening's balmy air as an excuse to come and pay their first call on him and his family since the tragedy.

Laughter suddenly exploded inside the log cabin, applause followed by voices begging, pleading for more, more, more.

Warren shrugged. 'Seems like nothing's changed around this place since I was last here with Emmy.'

Gemma, gathering her gingham skirt, stepped down from the buggy and said, 'There's only one way to find out. So why don't you give me a hand with these things I brought Molly.'

'Gemma! Warren!' called a cheerful voice from the cabin.

Turning, Gemma and Warren saw Molly Bluedaw, looking thinner than when they had last seen her, but still cheerful and rosy-cheeked.

'Molly!' Gemma held out both arms to embrace her.

Warren called, 'Sounds like we're disturbing some big shindig.'

Molly Bluedaw, suddenly embarrassed, said, 'Why, that's just . . . Ben, Ben Hopper, a boy from New Orleans who's helping out here till we get settled.'

Warren lowered his voice, saying, 'Between us, Molly, it kind of spooked me hearing that sound. Deke was the only fellow I knew in our parish to play hambone.'

'Oh, this young man can play just as good as Deke!' Molly said. 'Deke claims the boy even plays better.'

Punkin appeared in the cabin doorway and, seeing her mother with the Rickers, called, 'Papa! It's Mr and Mrs Rickers!'

The Bluedaw cabin was cramped for space inside and, as the evening air was pleasant and the sky a soft lavender, the party moved to the front porch; the two older Bluedaw boys, Jeb and Mike, carried their father in a litter they had lashed together from poles, a wooden frame stretched with canvas which could be rested between four chairs and enable Deke to sit upright.

Deke, comfortable in the special litter, joked, 'I can't shake hands with you, Warren, but thanks for dropping by to say howdy.'

Warren patted Deke on the shoulder, saying, 'Good to see you smiling, my friend.'

Gemma fought back tears at the sight of a man bravely trying to make a joke out of the four stumps he had been left with for arms and legs.

She stepped forward, saying, 'Deke, you don't know how good it is to see you. I just want you to know that we've all been praying for you.'

Deke recognized the compassion in Gemma's eyes. 'Thank you, Mrs Rickers. I knew you, of all people would have a prayer to say.'

Molly, busily rearranging chairs and stools, said, 'Now

everybody make themselves comfortable out here while I put on some fresh coffee.'

'No, please!' Gemma begged. 'We've just finished supper.'

Warren nodded. 'And coffee's starting to keep me awake at night. A sure sign I'm getting old.'

Seeing a tall, broad-shouldered young Black boy idling alongside the house, Warren held out his hand, saying, 'Evening, son. My name's Warren Rickers. This here is my wife, Gemma. We're neighbors from down the road.'

Smiling, the young man reached to shake Warren's hand.

'Oh, excuse me!' said Molly. 'This is Ben Hopper!'

Young Jeb Bluedaw excitedly added, 'Ben's from New Orleans! He's come to help us with the crops! Ben can lift two bales of hay at the same time – one in each hand! Honest! And he's going to teach me how to do the same thing!'

Eleven-year-old Mike Bluedaw said, 'Ben told us that if you lift a calf every day from the time it's born, you can lift it when it's a full grown cow!'

Eleven-year-old Marianna Bluedaw giggled, 'Ben's sweet on Punkin!'

A momentary embarrassment filled the air.

Warren said, 'So I understand it was you playing hambone, son.'

Ben, modestly dipping his head, said, 'That's was me, all right, making a fool out of myself.'

Deke disagreed. 'No more fool than I used to do. Fact is, Ben plays a lot better than I could.'

'Punkin,' said Gemma, 'I brought your Mama a few things for the kitchen. Mind you, nothing as good as she bakes or puts up. Just something to tide you over till you all get settled back in home. So maybe I can get you to help me find a place for things on the shelves.'

'Oh, Gemma, that wasn't necessary!' Molly quickly protested.

'And neither is it necessary for you to stuff all those delicious fresh cinnamon rolls and raisin cookies down our

143

throats every time we come over here. So hush. Sit down. It's been too long since I've had a little visit with Punkin.'

Gemma lifted the package she had brought and moved toward the cabin door.

Producing jars of golden apple butter and dark red strawberry jam, a tin pan of vanilla frosted flat-cake and a honey-cured ham, Gemma said to Punkin as she worked, 'That young man, Ben Hopper, seems like a nice enough person.'

'I –' Punkin paused to correct herself. '– *We* were all so surprised when Ben showed up, Mrs Rickers.'

'You met him in New Orleans?'

'Yes, mam.'

'At the Shiptons'?'

'Ben and his father drive a vegetable wagon in New Orleans.'

'What does Ben's father think about him leaving New Orleans to come all the way up here?'

Punkin shrugged. 'Not too happy, I guess.'

'Families are odd, Punkin. Sometimes they're blind, so blind and can't see what their children want.'

Gemma did not look at Punkin as she next asked, 'Are *you* happy Ben's here?'

'Yes, mam. Very much.'

'And what do your Mama and Daddy say about it?'

'They're trying to be nice to Ben. But he's no trouble. In fact, Ben's a big help. He sleeps in the barn and you heard how he helps with the work. That's why he came. To help Daddy.'

'But your Daddy didn't know him before this visit.'

'No, mam.'

'And what do your brothers say?'

'Jeb and Mike are crazy for Ben. And the others – you know, they love anybody who tickles them, makes them willow whistles, plays cat's cradle with them.'

'Then that's one of the battles won right there, Punkin, isn't it?' Gemma said. 'Having your family approve of him.'

'I guess so,' agreed Punkin, not realizing that Gemma

144

had artfully led her into admitting that Ben Hopper had indeed come from New Orleans because of his intentions for her.

Gemma next said, 'Now tell me about Emmy.'

'Emmy?'

Gemma was lining jars side-by-side on a narrow overhead shelf. 'What's Emmy really doing in New Orleans, Punkin?'

Punkin stared at her.

Continuing with her work, Gemma said, 'Punkin, I've known you since your family moved to the parish goodness knows how long ago. You and Emmy used to play rag dolls together for hours and hours on end. You went to school hand-in-hand at Mrs Rootes'. Remember that? And you learned to dance together in our parlor. I'll never forget sitting at the upright, playing "The Silver Moon Waltz", listening to you and Emmy slide your little brown lace-up shoes across the floor, taking turns playing lady, playing gentleman. So, please, Punkin, don't insult me with stories. I know Emmy's up to something in New Orleans and I don't want her to end up in trouble. Now I think you should tell me everything you know about it, don't you?'

Punkin was silent.

'Is it bad?' Gemma asked.

Punkin began to speak, then hesitated.

'Very bad?'

'Emmy would kill me if –'

Gemma turned her eyes – hard, black, penetrating – onto Punkin; she said, 'Emmaline's not working at the Shiptons', is she? She never was?'

Slowly, Punkin shook her head.

'What has she been doing, Punkin?'

'I can't – I don't want to – oh, Mrs Rickers . . .'

'Tell me this, Punkin. Do you approve of what Emmy's doing?'

'Oh, Mrs Rickers, of course not!'

'So it's bad.'

Punkin lowered her head.

'Is she going to get in trouble? Is she *already* in trouble?'

'Mrs Rickers, please –'

'Punkin, if you don't tell me the truth, I'm going to imagine the worst. I'm going to think my baby's gone to New Orleans and she's . . . dead!'

'Oh, she's not dead, Mrs Rickers!'

'Then what is she, Punkin?' Gemma quickly demanded. Punkin took a deep breath.

'Punkin, what is she? What is Emmaline doing in New Orleans?'

Punkin's voice was almost a whisper. 'I can't tell you, Mrs Rickers. Please don't make me tell you.'

'Why? Because it's that bad?'

Punkin nodded her head.

'Emmaline's a whore.' Gemma's words were not a question.

Punkin flung her arms around Gemma, saying, 'Oh, Mrs Rickers, please don't tell Emmy I told you. Please don't tell her it was me.'

Gemma, standing sternly in the darkening cabin, said, 'Punkin, mothers have a strange intuition. I knew Emmaline was doing something wrong. Something very wrong. I just needed to be certain. Thank you. You did the right thing.'

Warren had not driven the buggy past the Bluedaws' plank bridge when he said, 'Gemma Mae Rickers, you may be able to fool other people but not me. You came out that cabin a changed woman. What did Punkin tell you to make you come over all sober?'

Trying to sound happy, Gemma asked, 'What do you think about Ben?'

Warren humored the question. 'He seems like a nice kid. But if my suspicions are true, Ben Hopper is doing a lot more at the Bluedaws' than lifting bales of hay and playing hambone.'

Snapping the buggy reins, Warren said, 'But that's not what I asked you, Gemma.'

Gemma turned away her head, not able to look at Warren.

'Gemma, talk to me.'

The words caught in her throat. 'I . . . can't, Warren.'

'Why not?'

She tried not to cry. 'It's Emmy.'

'What about Emmy? Is she sick?'

'No . . .'

'What about her?'

'The feeling I had. I talked to Punkin and –'

'What did Punkin tell you?'

'Nothing I didn't know.'

'Punkin must have told you something new, Gemma, or you wouldn't be acting so damned queer!'

Gemma took a deep breath, pleading, 'Warren, please can't we wait till we get home?'

Warren stopped the buggy in the middle of the parish road; he grabbed Gemma's wrist, turning her to look at him, saying, 'You're a good woman, Gemma Mae. A wonderful woman. I couldn't ask for a better wife. But sometimes you are the most headstrong, the most stubborn, the orneriest woman I ever met. Now tell . . . me . . . about . . . our . . . daughter!'

'She's a *whore!*' Gemma screamed at him. 'Our Emmy's a whore in New Orleans!'

Warren stared at her.

'Well, you wanted to know!' Gemma said, throwing off his hand from her wrist and gulping back her tears.

He continued staring at her, stunned.

'Oh, I knew something was wrong, Warren. I knew Emmy was keeping something from us. That something had changed since she left home. But we let it pass. It was such a short time she had back home, we didn't want to make a fuss. And we let her go back to New Orleans, to go back being . . .'

'Punkin said that? About Emmy?'

'Punkin only confirmed my suspicions, Warren. I knew something was wrong. Something was very wrong. Punkin only confirmed it.'

'Punkin's lying.' Warren nodded his head. 'Punkin's telling lies.'

'Warren Rickers, why should Punkin Bluedaw lie about

147

Emmy? She loves her! She didn't even want to tell me. Did you see Punkin's face when she came out of the cabin?'

'Emmy? Our baby?' Warren still could not comprehend what Gemma had told him.

'Our baby.' Tears streamed down Gemma's cheeks.

Warren, sitting motionless in the buggy, stared at the horse standing in the middle of the parish road.

'Our baby,' he repeated. 'Fried Eggs . . . Little Friday . . .'

Ben Hopper helped the two oldest Bluedaw boys, Jeb and Mike, carry their father's litter into the cabin's one bedroom and, as Molly changed the dressings on Deke's arms and legs, preparing him for sleep, Ben left the cabin to milk the cow while Punkin put the children to bed upstairs in the cabin's loft.

It was late night, the cabin hushed, the children all asleep; Ben sat outside in front of the hay barn before he climbed up the ladder to sleep. Punkin sat alongside him in the moonlight, enjoying the new status she had been given in the family since returning home from working in New Orleans, more like an aunt than an older sister, someone above the discipline imposed on her brothers and sisters.

Ben said, 'Those Rickers are nice people.'

'I'm afraid I did something awful,' Punkin confessed.

'What?'

'I told Mrs Rickers something about Emmy. Something I haven't even told you.'

'Probably because it's none of my business.' Ben chewed on a piece of straw, holding one arm around Punkin's shoulder.

'But I hate keeping secrets from you.'

'You feel guilty about telling her mother?'

'Very.'

'Don't. You must have thought it was important or you wouldn't have told her.'

'Mrs Rickers is such a smart lady. She got the words out of me without even asking.'

'See! You have nothing to worry about.' Ben tossed away the straw.

148

'Oh, Ben. You're so good and considerate to me.' Punkin snuggled against his warm body.

'I've got my selfish side, Punkin. Like I know every time your folks look at me, they can see selfishness in my eyes.'

'What kind of selfishness?'

'For you. I want you all for myself.'

'If that's selfishness, I'm guilty, too.'

'But I hate deceiving your parents. I don't want them thinking I'm taking advantage of them.'

'You're not!' Punkin insisted. 'Oh, you're not. Every time I think about that night at the Shiptons' house, I get goose bumps.'

'Don't talk about that night. I get bigger than goose bumps. Right down here!' He pointed comically at his groin.

Punkin laughed, and snuggled closer.

Soon, their laughter sobered and they were embracing on the ground, Ben holding Punkin tightly in his arms, plunging his tongue into her mouth.

'Make love to me,' she whispered.

'I feel like such a traitor. Accepting your parents' hospitality, then –'

'I'm asking you.'

'Punkin, please –'

'Please?'

Soon, they lay naked, their arms around each other, Ben kneeling between Punkin's legs, driving his penis into her femininity, his trousers and shirt rolled into a cushion and placed under her buttocks to give them both fuller enjoyment.

'Marry me, Punkin,' Ben whispered as he felt the sensation tingle in his penis, 'please marry me.'

'Ben, I'm scared.'

'Let me ask your Pa, please? I want to have babies with you, Punkin.'

'Ben, not yet. Please not yet.'

'But some night I might not be able to stop in time. To pull out. To keep from exploding.'

'Stop now, Ben – stop now if you want to.'

149

'No, Punkin. I want you to get your enjoyment. I want you to get all your enjoyment.'

Ben pulled Punkin toward him, sinking deeper into her warmth, reaching to knead the tautness of her breasts, concentrating with his working finger tips, his penis, determined to make her enjoy full sensation, an orgasm that made her squirm, toss, break out in small pearls of perspiration all over her skin.

Tossing her head back and forth on the ground, Punkin finally began taking deeper breaths, grabbing for Ben's forearms, to cling onto his muscle as her entire body seemed to clutch his deep penis.

Quickly, Ben ejected his penis, shooting a high, white arc of sperm over Punkin's stomach, gasping, taking deep gulps of air, smiling as he said, 'Punkin, oh, Punkin-head, we're playing it too close. You better marry me soon, honey, or else shoo me off this place with a broom. One of these times I'm going to get you in trouble.'

He hurried to wipe the chilling sperm from her skin, shaking the last of it from the knob of his penis.

Marjorie Hankley, after moving out off the farm where she had lived with her husband, Gus Hankley, stayed temporarily with Euba Stone, an old Black woman who lived with three grown daughters, two sons, and one grandson in a small one-room share-croppers' shack on the boundary of the settlement called Crowforks. The Stone family worked ten acres of a fourteen-hundred acre farm, and, presumably, 'shared' in the profits of the farm's annual crops with the owner – and eight hundred and seventy three other Black men, women and children who worked and lived there.

Sitting at night in the poor cabin with Euba and the young grandson, Marjorie Hankley stared at a sputtering candle and again thought about where she would go from Crowforks, and again thanked Euba for the temporary home.

'Mama Euba, you're the only good thing that ever happened in my entire life.'

'You ain't getting much here, Miss Marjorie, mam.' The old woman tucked a wad of tobacco into her mouth, making a bump under her lower lip.

'I'm leaving pretty soon. But I promise to find some way to repay you.'

'For what? A mat on the floor? A couple withered spuds and a tin cup of squirrel stew?'

Marjorie, looking across the dirt floor at the fat boy wearing the grimy felt slouch hat he never seemed to take off his head, said, 'Maybe I can do something good for your grandchild.'

'Washtub's just like his Pa and older brothers. Snoopy as a bedbug and bound to end up like his kin – "Louisiana fruit", black and dangling from a tree.' She cackled.

Marjorie disliked racial jokes about Black people, especially jokes about Black people being lynched. She had heard enough of that kind of humor from her husband and his friends who rode in vigilante groups.

She asked, 'Why do you say the boy's snoopy? What's he done wrong?'

'Washtub found the dead body of a White woman, that's what he's done. I had to bury the poor critter deep in the ground.'

'The dead body of a . . . White woman? Near here?'

'Just near the shack. Butchered like a pig and dumped here.'

'Oh, what is this parish coming to?' Marjorie held both hands to her face.

Old Euba held out her gnarled fist. 'This fell out of the sheet wrapped around her body.'

Marjorie took a pocket watch from Euba's hand; she saw that it was gold, that the case was engraved – *Junior Dehasset, Belrose, 1862.*

'Mama Euba, can I borrow this?'

'Do more than borrow it, Miss Marjorie. Sell it if you can. No use niggers trying to sell gold. White folks just say we stole it and take it away from us. Sell it, Miss Marjorie, and maybe we can get a little bit more food. And maybe Washtub there can get a nice sack of candy. Oh, does that fat boy love his chocolate drops! And while you're shopping, Miss Marjorie, I wouldn't say no to a little box or two of Favorite Tobacco. Do you know how much they charge for Favorite Tobacco at the company store?'

Mama Euba then embarked on complaints about the local general store where share-croppers in Crowforks had to buy food, clothes and hardware, a store run by the same White man, Leroy Don Struthers, who owned the cotton fields, a store which never accepted cash but kept a running account for each family of workers, charging inflated prices, deducting the charges from people's 'profits', never allowing the Black families to get out of debt and claim an annual income. Mama Euba's three daughters and two sons had to work for the next seven years to pay for bills up to a year ago.

Marjorie Hankley listened to the old lady's complaints, commiserating with her, and at the same time secretly planning where she was going to take the gold pocket watch.

12 The Pearl in the Oyster

Emmaline's long skirt clung to her legs in the night's sticky heat; the perspiration flowed in rivulets over the naked groin, drenching the fine hairs of her mound, and she flicked the long skirt as she walked along the boardwalk, trying to create some circulation between her naked thighs.

The night was still young, but Emmaline's head ached, her feet were sore from tightly laced boots, and how much had she earned so far? One buck! One measly dollar! For a hand-job on a toothless old man!

Also, Emmaline was angry because somebody was following her in a buggy, a man who could not work up enough courage to approach her, who kept trailing two blocks behind in his buggy.

The sound of footsteps on the boardwalk attracted Emmaline's attention; she lowered the flimsy shawl from her bare shoulders and stepped into the doorway of an apothecary shop, able to see a man coming closer to her on foot; she watched in the yellow glow of the gaslight and saw he was barely older than a boy, a White boy probably even one or two years younger than herself.

Remembering the advice Alain had given her about letting men know immediately she was working for money and not looking to share companionship, Emmaline waited until the boy drew nearer and she called, 'Got a little spending money?'

The boy stopped, his eyes widening under the brim of his cap as he studied Emmaline's body - ripe, almost visible beneath the thin blouse, the long cotton skirt clinging to her legs, the yellow fringed shawl pulled back from her breasts.

Emmaline smiled, her dainty brown fingers toying with the top buttons of the blouse, not wanting to frighten away the White boy, wanting him to know she was available for him.

The boy was neatly dressed, and Emmaline judged that he was definitely no older than seventeen. Alain had told her that White boys had more pocket money to spend than Black boys, that most White boys also had little sexual freedom with girls in their neighborhoods, were better targets than Black boys for prostitutes.

Emmaline, thinking how she was barely older than this boy in the cap, quickly tried to imagine how she would have seduced a boy her own age back home, somebody at school, or a barn dance. But home seemed so far, far away, and she felt so much older than eighteen, and certainly not innocent.

She asked, 'Want to feel me? A little feel won't cost you much.'

'How much?' The boy's voice cracked; he cleared his throat, asking in a deeper voice, 'How much?'

Stepping toward him Emmaline suggested, 'Or maybe you want more than a feel. Maybe you want the real thing?'

He smiled nervously, soft down now visible on his upper lip.

'Flatter the little bastard,' she told herself. 'Make him think he's a big man. Get five bucks out of him for a screw and he'll shoot his load before you even pull up your skirt.'

The sound of footsteps sounded on the boardwalk; the boy nervously looked over his shoulder.

Emmaline, eager not to lose this easy mark, quickly soothed, 'Don't worry. We're not doing anything wrong. We're just two friends standing here on the street talking.'

The footsteps grew louder. The boy looked at the approaching man; he looked back at Emmaline; he pulled down the peak of his cap; he muttered, 'Sorry, Miss, but -'

He was gone.

Emmaline, sinking back against the locked door of the apothecary shop, felt her headache throb and, although

154

she was only three months pregnant, she was certain she felt something kick inside her womb.

The buggy continued to follow Emmaline as she proceeded down Ursulines Street. She haughtily ignored it, as she also ignored other women lingering on the street, swishing her skirt back and forth, circulating the air between her naked thighs, keeping her eyes peeled for customers in this lower section of the French Quarter considered to be open territory for street-walking prostitutes.

The idea of walking the streets had repelled Emmaline when Alain had first told her to do it; she had sobbed and screamed, but Alain had asked her what choice she had. Jocasta's house had burnt down. The other brothels left on Smoky Row weren't hiring new girls. She was pregnant and would get kicked-out of a big house uptown – if a big brothel would hire a Black girl in the first place – when they discovered she was pregnant. And it was senseless to pay the price to rent a crib when they already had the room on Liberty Street. Alain had also reminded her that not many customers were even coming to the room, and so he again assured her that working the streets was the only logical thing to do, at least for the moment. And when she had angrily asked about his original promises, his boasts about making her a good whore, about white fur pieces and fine kidskin gloves, he slapped her, saying she had ruined those plans for the moment by having a kid in her belly. The blame was on her. He told her she was still lucky to have him. She did not argue with that.

'How much, honey?'

The sudden voice in the night frightened Emmaline.

'Hey, I made you jump!' A round face smiled at Emmaline from alongside a red and white barber pole, a Black man chewing on a cigar and wearing a white homburg hat, a gold chain swagged across his pin-striped waistcoat stretched over his fat belly.

He repeated, 'How much, sugar pie?'

Regaining her composure, Emmaline announced, 'Depends what you want.'

'I want my dick sucked. A lay. To sleep cuddled up with you all night on a fine feather mattress. Eat ham and grits for breakfast in bed. Get my back scrubbed with lots of hot soapy water. But, sugar baby, all that's going to cost me a boatload of dollars and I ain't no sailor fresh in town from some foreign port.'

'How much did you steal from your old lady's sugar bowl, Daddy?'

In the last weeks since working the streets, Emmaline had quickly learned that the glib, tough-sounding words she had once hated hearing women use on Smoky Row were not so bad after all. She had learned that a fast remark, along with a painted smile, a shake of the hip, attracted as much attention to herself as the long shiny fringes on her buttercup yellow Chinese shawl.

The man chewed his cigar. 'Two dollars.'

She frowned. 'Two dollars?' You save your two dollars, Daddy, and buy a kiss next year at Mardi Gras.'

She turned to continue down the street.

Grabbing her arm, he said, 'Plus I got some loose change in the other pocket. All comes to three-fifty, four dollars, honey.'

'Make it come to five, Daddy, and you come all over me.'

'Well, listen to the little girl talk! You may be a sweet country honey, but you've got one big bad city mouth on you!'

Emmaline held out her hand, palm-upward. 'Let's see the five, mister, and this mouth will take your balls and dick at the same time.'

'Don't promise till you see what you'll be chewing,' he said, chuckling at her.

'Don't brag till you pay.'

Still chuckling, the man in the white homburg hat produced the money and, soon, Emmaline had unbuttoned the fly on his baggy striped trousers and was kneeling in the deep doorway, sucking his pendulous testicles, holding the fat head of his thick, soft penis in one hand, working to squeeze it into a firmness as she sucked on his large, hairless brown sac.

'Chew, baby,' he coaxed, holding the cigar delicately up in the air with one hand, looking down at her. 'Chew the nice man's big meat!'

Emmaline, remembering from Jocasta's house that men liked to talk dirty when they had sex, pulled back her head, saying, 'You got a fair pair of nuts on you. Now I'm going to taste a little bit of the other . . .'

She sucked on the penis, wondering how she was ever going to make it hard, to make him explode so she could continue down the street; her hands and jaws were already aching; she felt her headache returning.

Again, pulling back her head, she said, 'I should have another gal helping me do a fine set up like you've got.'

'Another gal?' the idea instantly excited him. 'Two sugar pies?'

Emmaline, feeling the sudden jump in his penis, realized the idea appealed to him.

She said, 'Why not? My twin sister and me both suck dick together lots of times. One mouth on each side.'

'Two girls on one dick, and both . . . sisters?'

'Twins. And both talking dirty as . . . hell!'

His penis swelled harder.

Emmaline, both hands working as she spoke, said, 'One of us sucks balls while the other one sucks dick. My sister, she usually takes the balls. But me, this is what I like!'

She moved her mouth forward, finding the penis much fatter, longer, the crown so large she could barely stretch her mouth around it.

Instead of kissing it, she began licking it, wetting it with her tongue, working it with both hands as the man stood looking down at her, asking questions, eager to have two girls both sucking his genitals.

He asked, 'Do you think you could keep it up all night, you and your sis?'

'Hmmm.' Emmaline squeezed his scrotum gently, rhythmically as she watched his penis now bob with excitement.

'Do you think I could watch, you know, tonguing each other's little pussies?'

157

'Oh, we like that . . . .'

Moving her mouth back to his penis, she began to suck harder, suspecting he would soon begin to explode.

'Do you think I could eat both your pussies myself? Bury my face, my face, my mouth, my nose between your two little pussies while you . . . suck me . . . suck me . . . oh, suck me, you sweet little whore!'

Walking up Ursulines Street to Rampart Street, Emmaline tucked the six dollars down the front of the blouse – the man in the white homburg hat had tipped her an extra dollar – and she again began fanning the hem of her skirt back and forth, trying to ignore the man following her in the buggy, tossing her head at a pair of White prostitutes lingering by a bakery shop, continuing home to sponge off some perspiration before she went out again for the night.

The phosphorescent moon, helped by the yellow glow of the gas street lamp, was the only lighting at night in the hallway of the greyboard building on Liberty Street where Emmaline and Alain rented their furnished room.

Slowly making her way up the wooden stairway in the near darkness, Emmaline silently cursed the landlord for his stinginess but finally reached the second-floor landing.

Seeing the lamp was off behind the glass transom over the door of their room, Emmalined tried the handle and was surprised to find it turn with her grip. But before she stepped into the room, she heard voices whispering from the darkness in front of her; she remained outside in the hall, slowly pushing the door wider so she would not be seen nor heard.

One voice whispered, 'Forget about Emmy . . .'

Her heart began to beat; she recognized Alain's voice coming from across the dark room; he was obviously in bed with somebody and they were whispering about her.

Carefully opening the door a little bit wider, she edged farther into the room and strained to hear more.

The other voice protested, 'I've never done this before.'

Why had Alain left the door unlocked? Emmaline wondered as she stood listening.

In the room's darkness, Alain whispered, 'You like getting

a look and a feel at what Emmy's been telling you about?'

The other voice answered, 'Emmy's talked about a big prick screwing her.'

'That was me, Charley. That was my prick. The pecker Emmy gets up her hole is the same pecker you're getting up yours.'

Charley! Emmaline remained silent, listening.

Alain continued, 'You like this prick, don't you, Charley? You like it as much as Emmy likes it.'

'I hope Emmy don't get mad at me.'

Alain assured him, 'Emmy gets mad and she won't get your money.'

There was a pause and Alain asked, 'You *are* leaving the money for Emmy, aren't you, Charley?'

'Then Emmy would know I was here.'

'She was expecting you tonight.'

'Why wasn't she here waiting?'

The bedsprings squeaked and, finally, Alain answered, 'I had to send her out. But you leave the money and I'll tell her you were here and couldn't stay. But you wanted her to have the money just the same. She'll like that.'

Emmaline stood in the darkness by the door, able to see Alain's sinewy body rising and dipping on the bed, the glow from the street lamp catching the gleam of Charley's muscled body on the thin mattress beneath Alain, Charley's round buttocks raised in the air.

Alain asked, 'You enjoying this, Charley?'

'It don't hurt. Not no more. It hurt going in real bad. But not no more. Not since you spit on it.'

'It's not hurting, Oysterman, because I know how to screw.'

Charley groaned, then asked, 'How do you know I'm an Oysterman?'

'Emmy talks about you, too.'

'She does? What she say?' Charley again groaned, admitting, 'You're getting deeper. It's good.'

'You're enjoying this, Oysterman. Maybe you'll be needing this on a regular basis.'

'I don't know. Men aren't supposed to be doing stuff like this.'

159

'All men are different, Charley. Just like your oysters. Some have a pearl in them, don't they? And some don't. Maybe you've got the pearl, Charley. You got the need, the need to get another man's dick up your asshole. Maybe you need it a lot, Charley. Just like my Emmy. Every night. Every day.'

'You give it to Emmy every night?'

'Just like this, Charley. Just like I'm giving it to you.'

'Up the ass?' Charley asked.

'Up the ass. Up that twat. In the mouth. Maybe you want to take it in the mouth, too, Charley.'

'I did already. Remember?'

'That wasn't taking it in your mouth, Charley. You were just looking at it. Shopping. Seeing it for the first time. Doing some tasting. Getting to be friends. You were still scared of it. You didn't know you loved cock.'

'I saw you playing in your pocket when I came in door. I saw your hand moving.'

'I recognize a man who needs dick. I can tell by his eyes.'

'Truly?'

'Truly, Charlie.'

'You could tell by my eyes?'

'I could tell you're no different from Emmy. That you were going to like this big dick as much as she does.'

'This does feel good. Maybe you're right. Maybe I do need it again.'

'Then you wouldn't need Emmy, Charley, would you? You'd just need me. Like Emmy does. You and Emmy would need the same thing. My dick. Maybe someday soon you're both going to be sluts for me.'

'The way you talk . . . I don't know . . . two guys . . .'

'Kneel, Charley.'

'What?'

'Kneel! Don't worry. I won't pull my dick out from your asshole. Just kneel on the bed like a dog.'

Charley moved - rose to his hands and knees - on the mattress. 'Like this?'

'That's right. Like a dog.'

'I can feel it . . . deeper.'

'Just like a dog, Charley. Just like my bitch dog.'

'Like this?'

'Just like a bitch dog.'

'This is good.'

'Bitch . . .'

Emmaline, tears brimming in her eyes, gently closed the door behind her as she stepped quietly out into the dark hall.

Emmaline paused on the boardwalk outside the building, thinking about Alain and Charley, completely forgetting about the man who had been following her in the buggy all evening.

The man sitting in the buggy alongside the kerb, asked, 'Is this where you live, Emmaline?'

Startled, Emmaline looked up and saw his face clearly for the first time; she felt her stomach churn - Cramer Crowley!

'Have you eaten your supper yet, Emmaline?'

Pulling the shawl protectively around her, she faltered, 'I was just . . . visiting a friend.'

'Can I give you a ride?' He was not smiling; he was not pretending to be surprised - or pleased - to see her.

'What are you doing here?' She did not smile at him.

'I've been in town for six weeks, Emmaline. Looking for you. After Jocasta's house burned down, I got seriously worried.'

'Jocasta?' Emmaline quickly told herself to pretend she did not know who or what he was talking about.

'The fire on Smoky Row,' he explained.

She shook her head. 'I don't know what you mean.'

Cramer Crowley had expected her to lie; he continued, 'Jocasta's still in jail, Emmaline.'

She blurted, 'Please, leave me alone. I don't feel good.'

'Emmaline, I want to help you.'

'Help me?' She laughed, shaking her head, 'I don't think so.'

'Emmaline, climb in the buggy. Let's go for a ride.'

'No. Please leave me alone!'

'If you're worried that I'm going to tell your mother and

father I saw you, don't be. I just want to talk to you. Help you try and see things other ways.'

Emmaline was getting both nervous and angry; she looked up and down the street; she said, 'Please go away! Things have . . . changed!'

'Nobody has to know about this part of your life,' he persisted. 'It can be over. Tonight. All over like a bad dream. You can leave. Now. Nobody need ever know about you and Smoky Row and this place and . . . Alain Summers.'

She glared at him. 'You've been following me? How long have you been following me?'

'Emmaline, please climb up into the buggy. Let me take you home.'

'No! I'm happy where I am. How I am. What I am.'

'I don't believe that, Emmaline.'

'I'm a whore!' she screamed at him, hysteria gripping her. 'I make love to men! For money.'

'Love?' he asked, staring at her. 'Do you know what "love" is, Emmaline?'

Panicked by his calmness, she became more wild, shrieking, 'And if Mama and Papa find out about me, I'll know exactly who told them! You! I'll know it was *you* who told them! You're the only person who knows about me! And if you tell them, I'll know you're not the good, perfect man you pretend to be, Cramer Crowley!'

'Emmaline, nobody's all good . . .'

'Go away!' she shrilled. 'Leave me alone! Can't you mind your own business for once in your life? Can't you stop playing . . . God?

He stared at her, surprised, wondering how long she had been harboring those feelings inside her – *God?*

Turning, Emmaline gathered her long skirt and ran down the block, turning at the corner, running until she found a dark alley, disappearing between the backs of red brick buildings.

Leaning against a cool red brick wall in the comforting darkness, Emmaline tried to catch her breath, to soothe her racing brain, but in the midst of her madness she visualized

162

Cramer and Sabrine Crowley, living in their big fine white house, wearing their silky white clothes, eating off their fine white china plates, drinking out of their white eggshell thin cups, sleeping on their monogrammed white sheets, sitting at the foot of their rolling lawn in their little white pergola. Emmaline realized how much she hated them, hated them for being so rich, so proper, so fine, so white, so white about everything, for having so much money, all the money in the world, all the whiteness, the power in the world. Oh, they were so glistening white, and, now, they had somehow found out she was so . . . dirty.

13 Southern Lightning

Emmaline awakened sick again in the morning, frightened
as she lay on the thin mattress thinking about Cramer
Crowley trailing her last night, worried that her whole
hidden world might be coming to an end; she lay half-
awake, trying to remember what her hopes had been when
she had left home, what she had expected to find in New
Orleans, and thinking numbly of how she had come to be
living in this room overlooking a cemetery.

Alain walked naked across the room, sipping coffee,
passing like a panther through shafts of bright, late-morning
sunshine streaming through the window; Emmaline
remained lying on the bed, her head resting on a pillow as
she watched Alain's body, the muscle flexing under his tight
golden brown skin as he moved, his long legs gracefully
joined to his slim hips and tightly rounded buttocks, his neck
rising like a thick column from his rippling back, his shoulders cupped with strong epaulets of muscle, the only part of
his anatomy which seemed to be out of proportion from the
rest of his finely chiselled body were his genitals – his penis
and scrotum, especially his penis, so long, so thick, swinging freely as he moved, the foreskin thinly covering the
shape of its crown.

The sight of Alain's body strangely revitalized Emmaline
as she lay on the bed, healed her sickness, gave her reason
to want to live another day, and she softly – adoringly –
called, 'You're so beautiful, Alain.'

The sound of the voice surprised him; he turned. 'You're
awake.'

Emmaline continued staring at him from the pillow.

Who was Cramer Crowley? Where was Longchamp Parish? Who cared about such things when she lived in the same room as Alain?

She said, 'I'm not even jealous.'

'Jealous?' He lifted the cup from the saucer, looking out of the window.

'About you and Charley.'

He sipped at the coffee.

She asked, 'Do you . . . like going to bed with other men?'

'Sometimes I have to.'

'Why did you have to go to bed with Charley?' There was no maliciousness in her question.

Alain, holding the saucer in one hand, the cup in the other, stood looking out of the window, staring down at the oddly shaped burial vaults inside the walls of the cemetery, death houses used on this soggy terrain instead of graves because graves would cave in before they had been dug; Alain studied the variously colored and sized houses, saying, 'You could always have run to Charley. He would have given you a home.'

Emmaline considered the idea. 'You're right.'

'Now Charley's the last person in the world you'd want to see.'

'Why?' She said the word as if it had two syllables.

'Charley's a pussy now. Like you.'

'That's why you left the door open,' she said. 'For me to see you.'

Alain finished his coffee in one gulp.

Her head still resting on the pillow, her eyes still admiring him, she said, 'You're right, Alain. The world *does* revolve around your cock. Anyway, for me it does.'

Walking to the oak table in the center of the room, Alain set down the cup and saucer, and fingered through the money which Emmaline had dumped into a blue and white china bowl last night when she had come home and he had already been asleep.

Estimating the amount of money in the bowl, he nodded, saying, 'You didn't do bad.'

The only way Emmaline had been able to forget about Cramer Crowley, about the fact he might tell her parents what she was doing in New Orleans, was to go back onto the streets, to resume hunting, looking, searching for men, to excel herself; she had thought that if people were going to say she was bad, dirty and no good, then she would be all those things, be lewd, abandoned and dirty. So Emmaline had stayed on the streets till dawn was lighting the sky; she had gone with eleven men, including three Black boys who had paid her with nickels and dimes; she had finally come home with nearly twenty-four dollars, dumping it all into the blue and white bowl, pulling off her clothes, collapsing onto the double bed alongside Alain's warm sleeping body.

Alain glanced at Emmaline still curled up on the bed; he jerked his chin at her. 'Come on. Get your fanny out of bed. It's almost noon and there's that big picnic in Congo Square. There's going to be a lot of horny hicks over there and you might even pick up something good and fast.'

Emmaline, remembering what Cramer Crowley had asked her about love, if she knew what love really meant, called, 'Alain, do you love me?'

'What makes you ask stuff like that?' He turned toward the curtain separating the kitchen. 'Because of that kid in your belly?'

Doctor Williams had told Emmaline she would give birth to her baby by December, definitely before Christmas, and that she would probably be showing a visible shape of pregnancy through her clothing in another month.

A month! The idea terrified Emmaline. And with her soft black ringlets piled high on her head, banked into a fluffy heap by small red combs, she swished her long skirt back and forth as she walked along Basin Street in the sunshine, headed toward Congo Square where Black slaves used to be allowed to dance on Sundays; Emmaline was no better than a slave being sent off, to perform with the permission of her own master.

Ignoring the large three and four storey bordellos lining Basin Street, Emmaline thought about Alain, wondering if he would get another girl to work for him in the next few months, or if he secretly had another girl working for him now in a crib or out of a room. She wondered if he would kick her out of their room when she started showing signs of being pregnant. If so, where would she go? Where would she get money to live on? She could still do mouth and hand jobs. But would she want to do that? Would it be good for the baby growing inside her if she swallowed semen? She hated, despised the idea that she was pregnant. But she did not want to hurt the baby, especially her own little baby growing at this very moment inside her womb. What would it be? A little girl? A boy?

Panicked by the idea of having no place to live with her baby, no money to buy food, she thought about Charley . . . And she then remembered Alain saying that he had buggered Charley to keep her from returning to him in case of an emergency. So that must mean that Alain did *not* plan to get rid of her . . . didn't it?

Emmaline tried to understand Alain but always failed. She knew better than to ask him questions. She hated people who pried into her life and she did not want to pry into somebody else's. But Alain was such a mystery. He never showed any warmth or love, so little tenderness and affection, and when he did, she seized it as if she were a sunflower turning to the sun, basking in it, feeding on it.

Hurrying along the boardwalk toward Congo Square, Emmaline glanced at the maids scrubbing the front steps of the fine bordellos on Basin Street, she looked out the side of her eye at the richly festooned curtains in the windows, the bevelled glass doors, the wagons, buggies, carriages drawn alongside the kerb.

On the street, one vehicle seemed to be keeping apace with Emmaline and, thinking about Cramer Crowley, she wondered what she would say to him if he again stopped her.

A woman's voice called, 'Emmaline!'

Emmaline looked to the street, seeing a carriage pulled by a team of white horses harnessed in shiny brass.

'Emmy!' the voice called as a gloved hand excitedly

167

beckoned from the carriage window. 'It's me! Lizzie!'

'Lizzie!' Emmaline threw both hands to her mouth and ran toward the carriage.

'Get in!' Lizzie ordered, opening the door. 'Let me give you a ride!'

Emmaline suddenly feeling shabby and cheap in her clothing, pulled the yellow Chinese shawl around her thin blouse, hesitating, 'No Lizzie. I can't. I'm just dashing out on an errand.'

'Balls! I know all about you and your errands! Now, Emmy, climb in this carriage this very minute!'

Reluctantly, Emmaline stepped into the carriage, immediately impressed by the padded velour upholstery, the thick dove-grey carpeting on the floor, the instant smell of wealth.

Lizzie, dressed in a beige suit trimmed with brown maribou feathers around the cuffs and high neckline, and wearing a feather-trimmed tricorn hat angled forward on her head, said, 'Two things first of all, Emmy. One. This is not my carriage. It belongs to Henrietta Gibson and she occasionally lets us girls use it. So don't be impressed. Secondly, I know all about you and your half-caste fancy man and the things he's making you do. So don't start inventing silly little stories about running . . . errands!'

'Alain is more than a "fancy man" .'

Lizzie frowned. 'Word travels fast, Emmy.'

'But I *love* him!'

'Don't apologize!' Lizzie held up both gloved hands, a velvet drawstring bag dangling from one wrist. 'I'm just stating facts! And the sooner you face facts, little lady, the better your life's going to be. There are lots of men – and women – living off us girls. And we love them all.

'Pimps. Madams. Drug-dealers. Doctors. Abortionists. Maids. Dress-makers. Boot-makers. Milliners. Jewellers. There's no end to our necessary evils. Or our evil necessities. But they're there. So don't whitewash them.

'But one thing you can do, Emmy, is stop fooling yourself. And you can begin by taking a good, long look at yourself in the mirror. Girl, you look a mess . . . considering how good you *could* look! Honey, you even looked better on Smoky Row. But no wonder. Consider what you're doing, how you're making a few dollars these days, being a street girl . . .'

Emmaline reached for the cord on the door saying, 'Lizzie, thanks for the ride. But I get out here.'

'Why does the truth hurt?'

Emmaline thought about Cramer Crowley last night and she flared, 'Lizzie, you're no better than other people!'

'Who's trying to be better? I'm just trying to tell you the truth. Oh, Emmy. I look around me at Henrietta Gibson's house – or at any of the other houses on this street – and I see hags, broken down old hags getting a hundred dollars for what you're probably doing for five.'

Emmaline sniffed. 'Most houses don't take colored girls, do they? There are city laws.'

'There's also city graft. Political graft. Police graft. You name it, and there's a pay-off for it, Emmy. There are ways to get around every stupid law made. Oh, it's not the laws that keep pretty Black girls like you out of the big houses. It's the White women working in them who make all the stink. They're scared you kids will take away their tricks. Emmy, you've got to start thinking with your head and not with your . . . twat!'

Tossing her head, Emmaline said, 'I'm happy.'

'Liar.'

'I *am*, too!'

Lizzie pointed a gloved finger out the carriage window. 'Basin Street's been in business for more than two, three hundred years. Since the first French settlers got here. The whores squatted here outside the old city and worked in a mud basin. That's why it's called Basin Street. And if it wasn't for what those enterprising, pioneering girls did with what they had between their legs, this street wouldn't be here today. And they did it in tents! But, honey, if it also wasn't for the brains a few of them gals had in their heads, whores would still be doing it in tents instead of fine big houses, those mansions you see there with stained glass windows and mahogany panelling and rich antique furniture.'

169

'You still forget, Lizzie, I'm Black. I'm *Black!*'

'And I'm a Jew! People hate Jews as much as Blacks in this town. Especially a Jew whose parents had the Star of David inscribed on her skin so she'd never forget what she was! I've had to learn to live with hatred, too, Emmy. And the women here hate as much, as hard, as mean as the men. So why don't you be a little braver and stand up to more people? Don't be afraid of getting hurt. Don't be afraid of people not calling you the cutest little girl on the block. Don't be afraid of somebody prettier, younger, more popular coming along. Don't be afraid that there'll be nobody around to protect you when somebody shouts "nigger"!'

Lizzie's words both stunned and surprised Emmaline. How did Lizzie know this was how she felt? That these were some of her fears?

Grasping Emmaline's small brown hand, Lizzie said in a soothing voice, 'Sweetheart, you're never going to pass yourself off as "Lady Elizabeth Louise". Who knows, maybe I'm not even doing it. Maybe people are saying behind my back, "Who does that horse's ass think she's fooling?" But, Emmy, I'm trying. I've been in the gutter and I hate it! I hate being poor and miserable and downtrodden. And I hate my friends to be, too. But what I hate worst of all is people not . . . trying!'

Quietly, Emmaline asked, 'What should I do?'

Lizzie, settling back on the buttoned seat, said, 'Don't get too excited, but Henrietta just happens to be having one of her big parties tonight. Actually, she's having *two* parties. One is very exclusive. And one is, well, not so exclusive.'

'You'll be at the "very exclusive" party.'

Fluffing the feathers around her neck, Lizzie said, 'It's formal white tie for gentlemen. Of course I'll be there.'

Emmaline said glumly, 'And you want me for the "not so exclusive" party.'

'Well, you've got to start someplace!'

'What do I do?'

'Henrietta needs special maids . . .'

'Oh, no!' Emmaline quickly protested, again reaching for the door cord. 'If I wanted to be a maid, Lizzie, I would never have gone to Smoky Row. I'd be peeling turnips on Carondolet Street, carrying chamber pots up and down the back stairs for the Shipton family.'

'Not *that* kind of maid, silly! These maids don't wear any clothes! Well, they do wear clothes. But not much. Just little French aprons and frilly hats. They stand around and look pretty and pass out free presents to the men. And, who knows? Probably you'll get the chance to slip out the side door with a big spender. These special "maids" aren't allowed to . . . entertain in the house. The regular girls would have a fit of hysterics. But no clever girl goes home empty handed.'

Emmaline considered the idea. 'When is this party?'

'Tonight. And, believe me, Emmy, it could lead to more work. I'm not promising anything. But it could lead to lots of bigger things.'

Emmaline remembered how only minutes ago she had been worrying about having no money of her own, no security for herself and her baby if Alain threw her out.

Lizzie added, 'Far be it from me to interfere in your life, but I do advise one thing.'

'What?'

'If I were you, Emmy, I wouldn't tell lover-boy.'

Taking a deep sigh, Emmaline asked, 'What time should I be there?'

'Early. Eight o'clock. We've got to fit you up in one of those French costumes.'

Emmaline frowned, nodding her head.

Many of the guests had already arrived by ten o'clock for the special evening at Henrietta Gibson's brothel on Basin Street, the larger group congregating in the two adjoining parlors on the ground floor, the second, more exclusive group ushered to a small room upstairs referred to as the Library.

Henrietta's staff of regular maids - Negresses dressed in long crackling black dresses and stiffly starched white aprons - circulated between the parlors with silver trays of champagne and bourbon. The men assembled in the brightly-lit parlors were in New Orleans for a dry-goods convention, raucous and loud-talking men looking for a good time; they grabbed for tumblers of bourbon rather than glasses of champagne, wanting the famous 'Southern Lightning'.

Henrietta Gibson, a small-framed woman with pretensions toward *ante-bellum* aristocracy, immediately saw that her parlor customers were going to be more unruly than the gentlemen in formal evening clothes being led upstairs to the Library.

She waved to the Black pianist to stop playing his lively music and she stepped onto a red velvet dais placed in the swagged archway separating the two parlors; she momentarily forgot her cultivated accent and summoned the voice she saved for dealing with back door pedlars: she bawled, 'Okay, guys! Let's have some order here!'

A momentary lull spread through the adjoining rooms.

Henrietta Gibson, smiling, positioned both tiny hands against the ruffled bodice of her Chantilly lace gown, proceeding in a polite drawl, 'Gentlemen, I do welcome you one and all into my . . . home.'

Applause greeted her words and she scanned the sea of upturned faces, noting with disapproval that most of the men wore checkered or tweed day suits, that many men were already flushed with too much alcohol, that they looked like any group of noisy conventioneers in New Orleans to raise hell – lambs to be fleeced.

Smiling, she continued, 'The theme for tonight's theatrical is "The French Revolution".'

'Screw the French!' shouted a man leaning against the upright piano.

Loud guffaws followed his remark.

'And *screw* is precisely what we're going to do!' retorted Henrietta Gibson. 'Plus a few little extras . . . Now, if you boys will cast back your minds to your school-days, you will remember that the French Revolution was a time of trouble and upheaval, a period of persecution and discord in that faraway land. So I have invited a special "executioner" in for the evening, a cruel disciplinarian known throughout

172

the best circles in this city for talents of chastisements as well as a masculine prowess –'

'Speak English, Lady!'

Henrietta, angered by the second interruption, blurted, 'He's hung like a horse and likes to beat lazy hookers!'

'Bring him on!'

The men cheered; more applause thundered through the adjoining rooms.

Henrietta, raising both hands for order, tried to continue through the uproar; she called, 'The courtesans . . . the ladies of the court . . . are dressed in genuine costumes of the period . . . but instead of the gallows, we will show you how the French bourgeoisie truly punished the fair sex . . .'

'Screw the French!' repeated the drunk by the piano.

Henrietta was becoming more exasperated; she glanced at Lizzie standing nearby, who, in turn, nodded toward the new girls hired for the party, gesturing for Henrietta to have the girls start circulating with their trays of gifts.

Henrietta, nodding at the suggestion, again held up both hands, calling, 'To reward you for being such an energetic group, I am now going to bestow a few gifts upon you, a few souvenirs for you all to take back home from your friends in . . . New Orleans!'

The men, at the mention of gifts, made way for the girls dressed in diminutive black satin corsets exposing their buttocks and lifting their breasts, with small white aprons, tiny caps, and heeled boots; the ten girls entered the parlor, smiling, carrying trays heaped with lewd postcards of women making love to other women, two men fornicating a mermaid on a beach, a mule prodding a milkmaid with his gigantic phallus, and an assortment of other gifts – bamboo canes wound with red silk handles, strings of Oriental vagina beads, thin brown leather condoms decorated with tufts of colorful feathers.

Henrietta, observing the men from alongside Lizzie, said, 'Look! They've completely forgotten about the French Revolution and my show!'

Shaking her head with disgust, Lizzie mused, 'You know what Maria Antoinette said.'

'Exactly!' Henrietta agreed, lifting the hem of her long skirt to ascend the stairs. 'Let them eat . . . shit!'

Lizzie followed Henrietta Gibson up the wide mahogany stairs, leaving the conventioneers milling downstairs, the rolling rhythm of the piano playing in the background, groups of men surrounding the girls handing out the gifts, and the brothel's prostitutes moving through the crowd, singling out their prey for the night, to begin the steady stream upstairs to the bedrooms and start getting the visitors' money.

A tall prostitute, with powdered white skin and wearing a maroon satin gown, sidled next to a ginger-haired man trying to pat Emmaline's buttocks; the prostitute said, 'Honey, there're plenty of coon gals back home. Why don't you try something special for once in your life?'

He answered, 'No coons at home cute as this one.'

Emmaline tried to ignore the ginger-haired man's hands, grateful for the white prostitute pushing a way between them, trying to edge out Emmaline.

But the man did not want the tall prostitute; he wanted Emmaline's attention and, lifting a tumbler of bourbon from a passing tray, he said, 'Hey, Blackie! Drink this in one swing and I'll give you five bucks!'

The prostitute grabbed for the tumbler. 'I'll drink it for ten!'

The man, ignoring the tall prostitute, reached for another full tumbler and said to Emmaline, 'I'll give you twenty bucks, Blackie, if you down this in one gulp.'

Emmaline never drank spirits; another guest saw her reluctance, saying, 'She ain't going to take you on, Jasper, for no money.'

The man named Jasper said, 'I bet she will for . . . what about fifty dollars, honey?'

Emmaline, smiling as she held her tray with only a few picture cards, slowly shook her head.

'A hundred?' he offered, pleased with his game.

Emmaline considered.

'Hey! See that?' shouted Jasper to his companion. 'She's hearing me all right!'

174

The second man laughed as Jasper quickly pulled a one-hundred-dollar bill from his wallet and extended the tumbler of *Southern Lightning* to Emmaline; she grasped it in one hand and shoved the tray toward the man for the money.

'One hundred cool dollars!' He dropped the money onto the tray.

Emmaline, holding the tray in one hand, lifted the tumbler to her mouth, closed her eyes, and tossed back her head – she emptied the tumbler in one long swallow.

Applause surrounded Emmaline from an assembling circle: another man called, 'Beginner's luck! Bet she can't do it again!'

Emmaline's throat burnt but she did not feel dizzy; she forced a weak smile, pleased now to see that the tall prostitute had disappeared.

The second man persisted, 'Honey, want another hundred smackers?'

Emmaline, feeling perspiration rise on her forehead, forced a wider smile and again held out the silver tray.

The second glass of bourbon was more difficult to swallow; but she kept her eyes pressed shut, gulping the bourbon till the tumbler was empty, set the tumbler on the tray, and picked up her second hundred-dollar-bill.

A third man shouted, 'Girl, you know why they called that stuff "lightning", don't you? That's how it hits you!'

More men pressed around Emmaline, waving money at her with one hand, holding tumblers of bourbon with the other. A new game had begun – Get the Pretty Colored Girl Drunk – and the group surrounding Emmaline became larger; she began to feel light-headed and her body was bathed with perspiration; but she looked at the hands waving money at her, and, waiting until she spotted another hundred-dollar-bill, she plucked it like a leaf from a tree, slapped it onto the tray, took a third tumbler of *Southern Lightning,* closed her eyes, and began to swallow . . .

Champagne was the only beverage served upstairs in the Library, and small ivory pipes of hashish.

Henrietta Gibson sat in a gilded armchair in one corner of

the dimly lit room, sipping champagne, savoring the pungent odor of the Eastern drug, and watched the greased body of Willy the Whip standing naked – except for a black leather hood, with two eye slits, covering his head – and dominating the trussed body of an Alabama prostitute, Junella, who had been shackled to a plank platform superimposed for the evening on the Library's Oriental carpet.

Earlier this week, Henrietta had sent a hand-delivered message to her neighbor on Basin Street, the Indian madam named Kuda, enquiring if Kuda's lover – the man who whipped prostitutes for money as well as pimped for many of the girls living in Kuda's bordello – would agree to appear at this special evening; Kuda and Willy the Whip accepted the proposal, and set a price of five hundred dollars for whipping the women in the Library, a modest fee considering the admission price of seventy-five dollars which Henrietta charged her select audience. Willy's fee for performing downstairs would be additional, but, now, considering that the plans for the dramatization of the French Revolution had been abandoned, Henrietta would try to pay him nothing, or perhaps only a small token fee, for the cancelled performance.

Willy the Whip had a firm body and his penis was famous on Basin Street not only for its size but for his ability to remain hard, to satisfy so many women in a single evening; but even more renowned was the White man's expertise with whips, lashes, canes.

A long oily black bullwhip cracked in the candle-lit room, snapping about Junella's fleshy pink buttocks, not striking her bare skin, merely making her tense with anticipation – and whetting the audience's appetite.

Henrietta did not personally enjoy receiving – or administering – physical punishment, but she knew many people did; she also believed that she understood the reason why corporal punishment was so popular in the South, not only in bordellos, but in the bedrooms of aristocratic Créole families, as well as on farms of poor White farmers, and in homes of many Black people freed from slavery.

Corporal punishment, a love to inflict or receive pain,

176

was an important part of the sex life in the South because of that land's heritage, because of its history of commercial slavery. Henrietta firmly believed that a tempo of cruelty had been set by Southern masters, by plantation overseers, by slave auctioneers and public whipmasters; the need for domination continued to this very day, a desire among people to master, to be enslaved, to concentrate passions, lust, sometimes even entire lives dominating – or submitting to – another person, someone stronger or weaker-willed, to seek the force of a whip, the search for the right partner in a pursuit of pain.

Prostitutes frequently were love slaves to their pimps. Henrietta even considered herself to be not unlike a master – a mistress – of a plantation in which the crop was not cotton, tobacco, rice, but sin, sins often including the sting of a whip, the slap of a leather paddle, the lash of a razor strop, a belt, a cat 'o nine tails, the rapid tattoo of a bamboo cane.

Junella's cries became more intense; Willy momentarily dropped the bullwhip to his side, his penis now bobbing with excitement from inflicting pain; the woman's cries had annoyed him; he reached for a small cloth on a table and, after using it to mop perspiration from his armpits, from his crotch, from the crack of his buttocks, he leant forward and stuffed the cloth into Junella's mouth, to gag her and stifle the cries; he then rose, pulled back the whip, and let it snake through the air, making a long neat line across her skin as if he were an artist executing one perfect slash of madder red.

Henrietta, pleased to hear the guests murmur their approval of Willy's action, rose from her chair and beckoned Lizzie to follow her from the Library: it was time to check the progress of the other guests downstairs in the parlor.

Henrietta and Lizzie paused on the mahogany staircase, staring at the confusion of men fighting one another, yanking at scarlet velvet portieres, throwing armchairs at the flocked wallpaper, smashing the etched glass cylinders covering the gas jets, crashing plant stands holding potted palm trees.

'Lizzie, send for the police,' ordered Henrietta. 'Then get the new girls out the back door.'

Henrietta had legal papers to prove that she provided living accommodation for fifteen women in a boarding-house, a ruse devised by a New Orleans alderman as a method to accept bribes from "landladies" to run houses of prostitution within the city limits of New Orleans. It was dangerous, though, for Henrietta to have more than the registered number of "boarders" on the premises during a police raid.

As further protection, Henrietta also hired young Irish immigrants to act as bouncers and, as the clang of police wagons filled the night, the Irish began tossing the conventioneers down the bordello's front steps for the policemen to pick up from the boardwalk; inside the bordello, the extra girls hired for the night were already being herded out of the back door.

Lizzie finally discovered Emmaline in a corner of the parlor, doubled over unconscious on her hands and knees, and a drunken man straddling her like a rider on a horse; he gripped a bottle of bourbon in one hand and slapped his other hand against her buttocks, trying to get Emmaline to buck, to throw him from an imaginary saddle.

Pulling off the man from Emmaline's body, Lizzie looked around the parlor for someone to help drag her outside.

The Library guests were quickly, discreetly, departing through a side entrance and Lizzie spotted Willy the Whip, buttoning his shirt, buckling the belt of his trousers, as he calmly strode down the wide mahogany staircase.

Willy helped Lizzie lift Emmaline from the floor, holding her limp body between them as they moved to his buggy in the rear stables; they left the sound of clanging police bells behind them, bumping along in the Basin Street night traffic, headed for the address Lizzie had given him.

Willy nodded at Emmaline leaning against Lizzie's shoulder; he asked, 'Didn't she used to work on Smoky Row?'

'Jocasta's.' Lizzie hoped Emmaline had stopped vomiting.

'I thought so. She's a cutie but always seemed a little bit lost. I had my eye on her and then she disappeared.'

'Forget about her, Willy,' Lizzie suggested. 'Somebody's already got her.'

'You only have a woman as long as you know how to keep her.'

Willy stopped his buggy behind the St Louis Cemetery, quickly stepping out to help Lizzie carry Emmaline into the building and up the dark wooden stairs.

Lizzie insisted in the darkness, 'Leave her here in the doorway. Her man might be home and I don't want to get involved in their business.'

Willy did not agree with abandoning Emmaline in front of her doorway, but Lizzie tucked Emmaline's clothes behind her for a pillow, and quickly led him back downstairs, and outside to his buggy.

Alain returned home shortly after midnight and did not recognize the woman dressed in the black corset slumped in the hallway; he smelled the reek of alcohol, the disgusting odor of vomit, and thought that some drunken woman had climbed the stairs and passed out in front of their door. Stooping to drag the woman down the hall, he saw the streetlamp's glow catch the sheen of a fringed yellow Chinese shawl and suddenly recognized that the woman was Emmaline; he quickly unlocked the door, picked her up in his arms, and carried her across the dark room to their bed.

Hurriedly, Alain dampened a cloth and dabbed at Emmaline's face as he worked to unlace the black corset, wondering where she had got such clothing.

He had only begun unlacing the top of the corset when money began to tumble from Emmaline's cleavage, falling to her lap, to the bed, down to the floor.

Alain stared at the money, and looked back to Emmaline's closed eyes, her open mouth, and he realized she had been at some kind of party.

As he unlaced the rest of the corset, more money tumbled from between her breasts, twenty, fifty, one-hundred-dollar bills, so much money that Alain guessed there was more than a thousand dollars stuffed inside the black corset.

Slapping at her cheeks, he asked, 'Emmy? *Emmy?* You okay?'

She lay limp on the bed, moaning.

Pulling off the corset, he saw more money fall to the bed, not only paper money, but coins rolling across the plank floor.

Smiling to himself, he knelt in front of the bed and began untying her tall boots, and still money appeared as he loosened the laces and pulled off a boot from her foot.

He was laughing; he had worked prostitutes in Natchez but never before had he seen anything like this. But, then, he thought as he pulled off the second boot and found yet more money, had he ever before met a girl like Emmaline?

Having undressed and washed her, Alain laid her on the sheets, looking down at her naked body in the yellow glow from the streetlamp, noticing for the first time the change in her shape which pregnancy was creating.

Falling to his knees alongside the bed, he studied the beginning of the protrusion of her womb, the rise in her body which he had never before noticed, and, which, in some strange way, was so beautiful, so natural on her body as she lay motionless on the bed.

Gently he leant forward and kissed Emmaline's stomach, and then carefully pulled the sheet over her nakedness. He gave her another kiss on the forehead, and fleetingly remembered being a child, kissing his mother goodnight after she had indulged in a drunken bout with a lover.

14   The Prodigal Son

Longchamp Parish swelled with the full blossom of summer; the pine forests were verdant, the earth beneath the boughs rich and dark, and scented with the evergreen's sharp aroma; the oaks were plump as lettuces; the cottonwoods, elms and poplars stood strong and tall alongside dirt roads cutting through the hilly wilderness, and bordered the creek beds shivering with cold water which rushed across black-and-white speckled stones, streams alive with wriggling trout, and fat green frogs jumping from rock to rock to log.

Sabrine Crowley sat forward on the seat of her buggy, holding tightly onto the reins of her lively mare, Trixy, as she hurried home to Belrose after spending the last few hours with Gemma Rickers. Sabrine had been returning books she had borrowed from Gemma, and making a long overdue call. During these busy days of summer, though, the people of Longchamp Parish forgave one another breaches of etiquette as crops were quickly ripening, many already into harvest.

Warren Rickers had been in the fields working with the migrant Black harvesters who moved south from Ketley in search of employment; Gemma allowed the harvesters' wives and mothers to prepare meals in the cabins which had once been the slave-quarters; as the migrant workers proceeded with their own schedule, Gemma entertained Sabrine in the kitchen, shelling peas while Sabrine sipped a cool glass of tea, comparing a strange little new book, *Uncle Remus,* to another recent novel which Gemma had also lent her a few months earlier, *The Adventures of Tom*

Sawyer. Most of Gemma's books came from friends in Philadelphia, and she confessed to Sabrine that her favorite new novel was the big epic, *Ben Hur,* but that she was also very fond of a colorful adventure story called *Treasure Island* and wondered if she should loan it to the Bluedaw family as she was certain the children would adore it. Both Gemma and Sabrine agreed that they were intrigued with the new Henry James novel, *Portrait of a Lady,* but Sabrine said, 'There's still something about his last story, *Daisy Miller,* which reminds me about Emmaline. Maybe because Daisy's such a riddle to understand sometimes . . . like Emmaline.'

Gemma, ignoring the remark, said, 'I took down another volume from the shelf for you this evening. As Emerson's just passed away, I thought you might want to reread his last volume of poetry.'

If Sabrine Crowley had learned anything about Gemma Rickers in the last twenty years it was that sometimes it was necessary to be persistent with her.

She said, 'Gemma, we were talking about Emmaline.'

Gemma reached into the colander for another handful of pea pods, continuing to shell them into her earthenware bowl, saying, 'Were we?'

'I was.'

'And I believe I had mentioned Ralph Waldo Emerson.'

'Gemma, I don't want to be rude but lately you've been avoiding all mention of Emmaline. Why?'

Gemma set the bowl next to the colander on the table; she rose from her chair briskly saying, 'Because there's nothing to talk about.'

Sabrine pressed, 'Do you hear from her?'

'No.'

'Do you write to her?'

'Sabrine, if we are going to talk about writing, may we please keep to the subject of poetry and novels?'

Sabrine knew she was being rebuffed; but she was not going to accept it, and she continued, 'Gemma, you and I have been friends for a long, long time. Since the first day you moved onto this land. It was the old Chatgrove place then, a home where I had been meant to live. But I never became the mistress of Candlewick Plantation. This land passed to you and Warren. And I was glad – thrilled – to have you as neighbors, friends, people I quickly came to love, respect, depend on.'

Gemma closed her eyes and sat down.

Sabrine recognized the pain in Gemma's face; she said in conclusion, 'Gemma, forgive me. I'm saying too much. At the wrong time. Just remember where I am if you need me.'

She rose, lifting the books from the table, and bent to kiss Gemma on the forehead.

Gemma, squeezing Sabrine's hand, whispered, 'Thank you, Sabrine. Just bear with me. Please.'

'I'll know you'll talk when you're ready.' Sabrine left the house.

'Oh, what's happening to everybody these days?' Sabrine wondered as she continued home to Belrose on the dusty parish road. Her husband also was behaving so strangely since he had returned from New Orleans, acting so mysteriously, replying vaguely to questions, avoiding many subjects completely.

Suddenly, Sabrine's horse shied in the road.

Gripping the leather reins to keep the animal from bolting, Sabrine steadied the mare as she saw a rider emerge from a side-road, a big, barrel-chested man, wearing a black felt hat, and a thick black moustache.

Dancing his chestnut stallion toward Sabrine, he called, 'Hello, little sister!'

'Junior!'

'Surprise you?'

'What are you doing back here?'

'What? No "glad to see you"? No "how long have you been back"?'

She repeated, 'Junior . . . Dehasset!'

Laughing, he said, 'Where's your family spirit, little sister?'

Sabrine, holding the mare under control, collected her wits and replied coldly, 'The same place yours was when I had to bury Mama and Papa!'

183

'Yes, I would've come home for Mama's services. The Lord rest her soul,' he said, reverently doffing his hat. 'But I didn't hear the news till two months after she was gone.'

'Nobody ever knows where you are, Junior Dehasset.'

'And probably don't much care!'

Sabrine glared at him. 'You still hate Papa, don't you? Well, I can understand why you only show sympathy for Mama. Mama always was quick to forgive you your wicked ways.'

'Let's hope you're as forgiving, little sister.'

'I stopped forgiving you a long time ago, Junior Dehasset. I stopped making excuses for you when you began dishonoring our family name. And if you've come home now like the prodigal son, expecting forgiveness and a warm welcome, don't look for it at Belrose. You will find no forgiveness there!'

Junior Dehasset smiled at Sabrine in the shade of his dusty, wide-brimmed hat. 'I wasn't thinking so much about you forgiving me, little sister. I was thinking about you forgiving your husband.'

'Cramer? What about Cramer?'

'I was mighty surprised to see Cramer Crowley strutting out – big as day – from a shabby little establishment in New Orleans.'

'You must be mistaken. Cramer is home.'

'Oh, I'm talking about a few weeks back, Sabrine. I'm talking about seeing your good, honorable husband coming out of a whorehouse a good month ago, some cathouse in the French Quarter specializing in . . . black tail!'

'Junior Dehasset, if that's all you have to say to me, will you please let me pass?'

Junior was no longer smiling. 'I have that to say, as well as that I plan on moving back to Longchamp Parish. That I've come home to claim Belrose Plantation as my rightful property.'

Sabrine flicked the buggy whip, charging past her brother's chestnut stallion with a loud clatter of wheels, leaving a cloud of yellow dust rising behind her in the parish road.

*   *   *

Sabrine jumped out of her buggy on the driveway which circled in front of the six Doric columns gracing the big house of Belrose Plantation; she stormed through the double doors, across the gleaming black and white marble foyer, barging into the study where she knew she would find Cramer. She angrily tossed Gemma's books onto a leather chair and, pulling off her suede driving gloves, muttered, 'Junior's back.'

Cramer looked up from his rolltop desk. 'Your brother?'

'I saw him on the parish road.'

'Just now?' Cramer leaned back with a creak on his swivel chair.

'Less than fifteen minutes ago. I was coming home from Gemma's and, suddenly, there he was in front of me like some dreadful . . . apparition!'

'What did he say?'

'That he plans to claim Belrose. And that he –'

Pausing, Sabrine studied her husband and asked, 'Cramer, is there something missing from our marriage?'

'Missing?'

She blurted, 'Junior told me he saw you in New Orleans. That he saw you coming out of a . . . brothel!'

Cramer studied his wife; she looked very attractive when she got an angry flush to her cheeks; he nodded toward the chair alongside his desk, saying, 'Sabrine, why don't you sit down. I've been wondering how I was going to tell you about something that's been troubling me. Who knew it would be your brother – of all people – to come to my rescue?'

Sabrine, sinking to the edge of the chair, stared at Cramer, her eyes dilated with anger and pain.

Cramer began his story with the account of the day he had taken Punkin Bluedaw to New Orleans to collect her possessions from the Shipton home; he told Sabrine how he had followed Punkin to Smoky Row and seen her emerge later with Emmaline, how he had gone back alone to the same house to meet the brothel-keeper, a coarse but worldly-wise woman named Jocasta, that he had learned nothing specific except that he had become more convinced than ever that Emmaline was a prostitute in Jocasta's brothel on Smoky Row.

He said, 'That's when Junior obviously saw me, when I was leaving Jocasta's.'

'Did you ever see Emmaline?'

'That's what makes the story so difficult. That night, following my meeting with Jocasta, there was a fire on Smoky Row. A very suspicious fire which the Army actually suspects was connected to the Ku Klux Klan – through those ladies wearing those veiled hats.'

Sabrine remembered Cramer telling her about the crusading women; she said, 'The bee-keepers.'

'Precisely. But after the fire I could not find any trace of Emmaline anywhere.'

'Oh, Cramer! You don't think –'

'No. There were no fire casualties. Of course I checked for that. Very closely. Then I started scouring the city. I looked every place for Emmaline. I tried other bordellos on Smoky Row. In those squalid little hutches called "the cribs". Big brothels on Basin Street. Innocuous whorehouses on Customhouse Street, Baronne Street, Conti Street. There is barely a block in the French Quarter these days that doesn't have some house of disrepute. Many people blame it on the carpetbagger politicians who came into power after the War. But people are too ready to forget that New Orleans is a port city, both a sea-port, and the mouth of this country's biggest river. New Orleans has always been a wild, wicked town, and there'll be no changing it.'

Sabrine asked, 'But what about Emmaline?'

Cramer shook his head. 'It seemed to me as if she'd suddenly and completely disappeared from the face of the earth. That's why I stayed so long in New Orleans. Also, I began to help investigate the Klan. Colonel Walsh asked me to study new files sent from Memphis. They are frightened of a political party growing out of these subversive activities. But, in truth, Sabrine, I was becoming increasingly more concerned about Emmaline.

'I was beginning to lose hope, thinking about coming

home when, finally, one night, I saw her walking through the French Quarter. It was quite obvious what she was doing. I followed and followed her and, eventually, I managed to talk to her.'

'The poor thing! She must have been embarrassed to death!'

'She was not so much embarrassed, Sabrine, as frightened. Terrified like a cornered little animal, and she started lashing out at me. Quite plainly she told me to stop bothering her. She warned me about telling her parents that I had seen her, saying that if they found out what she was doing that she'd know who had told them.'

'So she didn't try to hide the fact that she's a . . . prostitute?'

'On the contrary? She blurted out the word to me! Literally defied me with it! Flaunted it in my face!'

Sabrine stared at her husband, considering what he had told her, then said, 'Gemma knows, Cramer. I'm sure she knows what Emmaline's doing in New Orleans.'

'She knows?'

'I am absolutely certain of it. Gemma refuses to talk about Emmaline. She was on the verge of tears when I tried to discuss her.'

'But who could have said anything? Definitely not Emmaline. But do you think Punkin Bluedaw –'

Sabrine shrugged, asking despondently, 'Oh, Cramer, what can we do?'

He smiled. 'Another thing. Emmaline told me to stop playing God.'

'She . . .*what?*'

'She told me to stop playing God.'

'Well, Emmaline Rickers certainly sounds like a completely different person from the girl I remember.'

'Sabrine, we forget that children have minds of their own. That they form opinions we don't even suspect. And sometimes those opinions are not entirely wrong. Perhaps I should pay heed. Maybe I *do* try to play God and spend too much time trying to sort out other people's problems.'

Leaning back in his chair, Cramer drew in his breath,

saying, 'Well, we have our own problems facing us at the moment anyway. Junior is back, planning to claim Belrose.'

Sabrine, momentarily forgetting about her brother, rose from the chair, and said, 'Oh, darling, why didn't you tell me all this before about Emmaline?'

'I didn't want to worry you.' He patted her hand.

'But sweetheart! I love you.' She kissed him.

Glowing under her sudden attention, he confessed, 'You know, a little jealousy flatters a man!'

'But I am *violently* jealous over you!'

You are?'

Hugging him, she said, 'Of course! I love you!'

Sabrine and Cramer Crowley were finishing supper that evening when Hamilton, the Negro who had been acting as the Dehasset family's major domo for the past thirty-seven years, came into the plum damask-covered dining-room to announce that a distressed woman was asking to see them; Hamilton stated, 'She says her name is Mrs Hankley. Should I show her into the study?'

Sabrine and Cramer exchanged glances, realizing that their surprise caller was the wife of Gus Hankley, the man who had argued with Deke Bluedaw over the damming of Willow Creek; they had heard the parish rumor that Marjorie Hankley had moved out from her husband's cabin.

Sabrine said, 'Hamilton, show Mrs Hankley into the dining-room. She might want to join Mr Crowley and me for dessert. I believe Miss Flossie made a lovely blanc-mange.'

Hamilton bowed, returning a few moments later with Marjorie Hankley, dressed in a threadbare blue coat and grey worsted cap; she apologized profusely for her disturbance and refused a portion of dessert, but she did nod her head when Cramer suggested a small glass of peach brandy.

Taking a sip of the plantation-made liqueur, Marjorie Hankley again thanked the Crowleys for seeing her and then produced a brown parcel from her pocket.

Cramer, watching her nervously set the parcel in front of her on the table, said, 'Mrs Hankley, you obviously have something very urgent to show us.'

'Forgive me, Mr Crowley. Perhaps I should wait. I have upset your supper. It's not time to show you this.'

Cramer ignored her protests and held out his hand for the parcel; he unwrapped the wrinkled brown paper and, after staring at the contents, he passed it to Sabrine.

Sabrine immediately recognized the gold pocket watch.

Studying the inscription, her eyes misted as she said, 'My father gave this to Junior . . . the day Junior left with the Broderius boys for the War.'

She raised her head. 'Mrs Hankley, how did you get this watch?'

'Somebody found it, Mrs Crowley. Near Crowforks . . . on the body of a dead woman.'

'Oh dear.' Sabrine looked at Cramer.

Cramer asked, 'Who found it, Mrs Hankley? I assure you their names will go no farther than these four walls.'

'A boy. The grandson of a Black woman who used to be with us before the War. She took it away from the child, and, naturally, she was frightened of becoming involved. She buried the White woman and gave the watch to . . . me.'

Sabrine again glanced at Cramer. 'The woman acted very wisely.'

Marjorie Hankley sat forward on her chair. 'Oh, Mrs Crowley, I don't want to cause you distress. You're such a fine woman. You do so many good deeds in the Parish.'

'Mrs Hankley, my brother has caused enough distress in this parish for many people besides myself. I have to shoulder some of the responsibilities.'

Marjorie Hankley confessed, 'I understand about sharing responsibility – and shame, Mrs Crowley. It is no secret that Mr Bluedaw's recent accident was the result of a quarrel with my husband. I am deeply ashamed of what happened. But I have gathered my senses and I hope to persuade my husband – by fair means or foul – to give evidence to the law against the men who helped him harm Mr Bluedaw.'

The prospect of striking a blow against the Ku Klux Klan instantly excited Cramer and he asked, 'Do you think you can do such a thing, Mrs Hankley.'

'I don't know, Mr Crowley. But I am certainly going to try. It's the only way I see how we can redeem our names not only in the community but in the Lord's eye.'

She paused and, staring down at her lap, she said, 'There's also something else I feel I should tell you.'

Sabrine and Cramer waited.

'Mrs Crowley, I know the house where your brother is staying in Longchamp Parish.'

Cramer, rising from the table, said, 'I think we should go into the study. Hamilton can bring in coffee. I think we all have plans to discuss.'

Twenty miles from Belrose Plantation, Molly Bluedaw had finished bathing, applying fresh medication, and bandaging Deke's limbs for the night; she unknotted her hair from the top of her head, quickly brushed it, and crawled into bed alongside her husband.

In the darkness of their small cabin bedroom, Deke suddenly and unexpectedly asked. 'So what are we going to do about Punkin and Ben?'

Molly sighed, relieved that at last he was broaching the tender subject.

She answered, 'Thank you, Deke, for being so patient. I don't know if I could cope with big tempers. Not these days.'

'Tempers? No, Molly. I learned a lot of things in the past months. When something bad strikes a man, he starts seeing life different. He realizes that happiness is short, comes and goes so quick. Punkin is happy. I see it in her eyes. But she's scared. I also see that. Scared she's going to lose something precious. Oh, yes, Ben Hopper's a fine boy.'

'Ben is a good boy,' Molly agreed. 'A decent boy. You couldn't ask for better. But, Deke, there's still the color difference between them. We'll never be able to change that. Not for them. Not for the children they'll want.'

'I know, Molly. And I don't want them nor their little family getting hurt by not pleasing the wrong people. Not getting hurt like I was. Maybe worse. That's why I want to help them. I want to think of something good for those kids to do.'

'Deke, you're such a considerate man even to think this way –'

'Molly, I'm a father wanting happiness for my kids. But I can't get my brain working the right way. I can't come up with a solution. But there's got to be some solution. There's got to!'

'I've been thinking, too,' Molly admitted. 'And the best I can come up with is to ask Gemma Rickers for some advice. Gemma and Warren are good, sensible people. Being colored, too, like Ben, and being our friends, I thought they might have some suggestion for Punkin and Ben.'

'Funny, isn't it, how Punkin doesn't talk about Emmy?'

'Oh, she's probably too caught up with Ben. And then there's you, too, Deke. Don't forget, Punkin loves you deep and true. Like all your kids do.'

Listening to the crickets outside the cabin's window, Deke finally said, 'It's funny, Molly, when something bad hits, all the things you learn, all the things you lose.'

'We manage.'

'I'm thinking about you.'

'Me? Oh, Deke, I'm managing fine. I'm happy still to have you.'

'But what about loving?'

'Love? Who could ask for more love than I get?'

'That's not the kind of love I mean, Molly.'

'Deke, we solved other problems in the past, we'll solve that one, too. All in good time. All in good time.'

'The sawbones who cut me up made a joke, Molly. Doc Mackeson said I'd soon have all kinds of women chasing after me.'

'Deke, you know I'm not partial to jokes men tell. And to be quite honest, I'm surprised that a fine, respectable physician like Dr Mackeson told you some improper story, and inside a hospital! The shame of it!'

191

'Oh, I thought it was going to be a joke, too. But it wasn't, Molly. It wasn't. It was a downright true story. The doc told me there are women who actually go with men who got stumps for arms, that there are women who get satisfaction from a crippled man's stumps instead of a man's regular part -'

'Deke Bluedaw! I do not have to hear this story.'

'But I swear I tell you Gospel truth! The doc probably told me the story to brighten my spirit. Make me laugh. Or maybe to let me know I wasn't alone in the world. That there are other men like me. All kinds of men. Doc even told me there are special places - clubs I guess you'd call them - up in that New York City where men with stumps go and people with peculiar appetites pay good money to make love to them with their . . .'

'Deke, I'm going to forget what you've just told me. I'm going to roll over, say my prayers of thanksgiving for the night, and I suggest you do the same thing.'

'Molly, oh, Molly, my Molly. If a man don't know about the dark shadows in this life how's he going to appreciate all the sunshine? I was just telling you one side -'

'Deke! Enough's enough! Now say your prayers!'

Molly rolled over on the double bed, beginning to recite the Lord's Prayer to herself, *'Our Father, Who art in Heaven . . .'*

Deke's words crept back into her brain, though, his mention of knowing about dark things in order to appreciate the brighter things in life, and she added in her prayers a request for the Lord Almighty to help her see things more in Deke's open-hearted, broad-minded way.

15 Herc's Woman

Gemma preserved fruit and vegetables, scrubbed floors and washed walls, mended clothes and darned socks, helped the women in the old slave quarters prepare food for the harvest crew, doing any and everything to keep her sanity during these passing days of summer as she worried about Emmaline being a prostitute in New Orleans. The worst time was during the night's darkness, wondering what Emmaline was doing in New Orleans at that same hour, knowing that Warren was lying alongside her in bed, awake and thinking the same thoughts but refusing to discuss their daughter, unable to discuss her. Warren, also, was trying to lose himself in work, coming into the house late, tired and hungry, eating his meals in near silence, the same haunting silence prevailing throughout the rest of the night and at the morning breakfast table. Gemma tried to discourage all hope in herself of receiving a letter from Emmaline. But every sound on the driveway attracted her attention, and she glanced to see if there might be some word, a letter, a message brought by a stranger, even her daughter coming home. But all Gemma's hopes were futile, hoped and prayed for with no answer.

Gemma paid shiny pennies to the children from the harvest crew, hiring the earnest faced sons and daughters of the migrant workers to help her unearth carrots, radishes, early lettuces in her kitchen garden; she did not hear the carriage stop on the driveway and was surprised to see the blonde woman standing at the bottom of the pathway.

'Mrs Rickers?' The woman was not young, but her ivory complexion had been carefully protected from sun and wind, and she wore cosmetic paint which added to the youthfulness of her appearance without making her look garish; she was dressed in plainly cut, elegant clothing, a beige silk shawl graciously draped from her shoulders; the surrey behind her was driven by a handsome young Black man dressed in smartly cut gray livery, a servant who sat attentively on his seat, properly ignoring his employer's social call.

'Yes?' answered Gemma, wiping her soiled hands on her long calico apron as the children gathered behind her with large, inquisitive eyes, staring at the beautiful woman and fine surrey.

The blonde lady announced, 'I'm Marisse Summers. From High Hill, Mrs Rickers.'

Gemma, quickly sending the children back to the garden, tucked a stray strand of hair back up into the blue cotton bandana knotted around her head and stepped closer to her visitor.

Marisse Summers added, 'I'm Alain's mother.'

'I know who you are.'

'Mrs Rickers, I don't know what Alain's up to but I do know he drove your daughter to New Orleans and now the law's looking for him.'

'The law?' Gemma felt her knees weaken.

'A marshal from Natchez,' Marisse Summers explained. 'The marshal's been to High Hill saying that Alain stole a buggy.'

Gemma remembered Alain's yellow and red buggy as well as the story he had told Warren about buying the buggy with money from his first job as a book-keeper.

Marisse Summers proceeded, 'Alain apparently led a bad life in Natchez and, when he had to get out of town fast, it seems he took someboby's buggy to do it.'

'I'm sorry I can't help you, Mrs Summers, but I haven't heard from your son . . . or my daughter.'

'I didn't think you would've heard from my son, Mrs Rickers. But I thought that if you did hear from your daughter, you might write back and have her get word to Alain.'

'Word?'

'To warn him.'

Gemma was mystified.

'About the marshal,' explained Marisse Summers. 'That's the least I can do for Alain. I haven't been a very decent mother. Alain grew up knowing no father, just hearing that his mother had been "Herc's woman". When Alain was no older than seven or eight, he discovered that "Herc" was a field slave his mother had brought into the house, a Black man who had sired him, then was killed in a fight by some Cajun roué.'

Gemma remembered the fight at High Hill, the battle between the towering Black man, Herc, and the Cajun from New Orleans, a confrontation in which she herself had played an important – but secret – role. Marisse Summers did not even know that Gemma Rickers had been instrumental in the Cajun's arrival at High Hill. And Gemma wondered quickly if Emmaline's present conduct was part of the Lord's punishment against her for deeds committed long ago – even if those deeds had been committed to protect this land.

Marisse Summers explained, 'I feel I owe something to my son.'

Gemma, trying to collect her senses, faltered, 'Excuse me for not inviting you inside. But –'

'I am not here to socialize, Mrs Rickers. I just dropped by to say that if you can, please, help warn Alain that the law's after him. Nothing more.'

Gemma wanted to be equally honest and straighforward; she said, 'Mrs Summers, the simple fact of the matter is that we have not seen or heard from Emmaline since the morning she left here with your son.'

Marisse considered the fact. 'I remember Emmaline. The few times I saw her, I always thought she was a sweet, very pretty girl. Alain used to be sweet on her. Puppy love. I wonder if she's the one to give him the love and understanding he needs now.'

Gemma flared, 'Your son might not be in his present difficulties, Mrs Summers, if he had got more "love and understanding" from you!'

Marisse Summers studied Gemma; a wry smile spread across her face and she replied, 'If you haven't heard from your daughter, Mrs Rickers, perhaps too much love also takes its toll.'

Gemma opened her mouth to speak but words failed to come out; she wondered if this White woman spoke the truth, that she and Warren might have smothered Emmaline with affection and attention, that that was the reason she had left home.

Marisse Summers gathered her skirt and said, 'Mrs Rickers, I didn't come here for a debate about raising children. I came asking help. Also to offer some. We're both misfits compared to the rest of the parish, one way or another, so if ever you and your husband need me, don't forget I'm right up there behind those trees, still living, for better or worse, at High Hill.'

Marisse Summers turned toward her surrey and the handsome young Black man quickly jumped to offer his assistance.

An earthen jug of corn whisky stood on a wooden chair alongside a narrow bed; a tin can of lard rested next to the brown jug; the wood and leather phallus which Junior Dehasset called his 'whorebreaker' was attached to one of the four bedposts – pointing upwards – by leather thongs, and Junior Dehasset squatted over the phallus, his pants down around his ankles, his hand busily working his penis.

Masturbation was exciting to Junior Dehasset in this position. Working his thumb and middle finger on his penis – his sexual organ too diminutive to be satisfied with the grip of his fist – he held his eyes closed and thought of the 'whorebreaker', his mind momentarily picturing that the phallus was attached to a person, that a Black man was buggering him . . .

His mind spoke to his imagined seducer, '*Where'd you get that big pecker, boy? It takes a real man to take a pecker big as yours . . . a real man . . . a real man like me . . . so cornhole me, boy, cornhole that big bung you've got that pecker in . . . cornhole this man's bung . . .*'

196

The sudden sound of horse's hooves outside the cabin disturbed Junior's late night fantasies.

'*Damn it!*' he thought, wondering who knew he was staying in this cabin which had once belonged to his old friend, the late Sheriff Laird, who had also been a member of the Knights of the Camellia.

Quickly standing up on the bed, Junior pulled up his twill trousers; he untied the 'whorebreaker' from the post of the bed and hid it under the bed.

At the second loud knock on the cabin's plank door, Junior Dehasset stood holding a Winchester forty-five rifle in his hands, calling 'Who's there?'

A man's voice answered from the other side of the door. 'Dehasset?'

'I'm armed!' shouted Junior. 'Don't try no smart business!'

A woman's voice called, 'It's Sabrine! Open the door, Junior!'

Sabrine? Now how did that meddling bitch find out where he was staying?

He called, 'What the hell do *you* want?'

The man spoke again; Junior recognized him as Cramer Crowley; Cramer said, 'We want to talk to you.'

Junior realizing he had little choice, turned to make sure that the 'whorebreaker' was safely out of sight, then pulled back the bolt on the door and stood looking at his sister and his brother-in-law, backed by six armed men on horseback.

Cramer said, 'We've come to make certain you don't cause any trouble.'

'Trouble? What the hell you two talking about?'

Cramer nodded toward the men behind him. 'This is Sheriff Bleeker from Palmetto Landing. The sheriff remembers your old friend who used to live on this place. The sheriff doesn't have much respect for him - nor for any of the other hooligans who used to ride through the night with you and Laird.'

Junior grunted. 'You come all the way out here just to tell me this crock of shit?'

Sabrine said, 'Sheriff Bleeker has something that Papa

gave you, Junior. A pocket watch being used in an investigation into the murder of a woman named Ivy Bravo.'

'A pocket watch?' Junior felt a trap closing around him; he quickly lied, 'That damned thing was stolen . . . years ago!'

Sheriff Bleeker, a lean man with a drooping moustache and wearing a tall crowned hat, turned to a rider alongside him; he asked, 'Frank, is this the guy you saw leaving Ivy Bravo's?'

The rider nodded. 'Same man. And saw him on more than one night.'

The Sheriff asked, 'You'll swear to it?'

'On a stack of Bibles, Sheriff.'

The sheriff and his men raised their rifles; the sheriff said, 'Mr Dehasset, you'll have to come with us.'

Junior Dehasset looked from the Sheriff, back to Cramer and Sabrine; he muttered, 'Don't think you've won. Oh, no! Belrose is still going to be mine.'

The overseer from Belrose Plantation, Melvin Hanks, sat in the darkness of the same night with twelve armed riders, down the parish road from the Laird place; the men waited in the moonlight, keeping to the shadows near the sharecropper settlement of Crowforks. Cramer Crowley had sent Melvin Hanks and a group of workers from Belrose - an assortment of trustworthy Black and White men - as protection against a vigilante gang who might try to seek vengeance for Junior Dehasset's arrest. But when no riders appeared by midnight, no peaked hoods or crosses of fire, Melvin Hanks guessed there would be no immediate leak in the sheriff's office in Palmetto Landing to the local Klavern of the Ku Klux Klan, that no blood would be spilled tonight at Crowforks because a woman's mutilated body had been found nearby by the fat child called Washtub.

Part Three

The Best Street In Town

16 Good People

Ben Hopper was more talkative than Gemma had expected him to be as he drove to New Orleans; the two of them had left Longchamp Parish in early morning darkness, planning to stop no longer on the road south to the delta country than the time it would take to allow the horses to rest, and Ben virtually talked the entire time.

Cotton. Slavery. The French Créoles. His grandmother on his father's side. His grandfather on his mother's side. How good the Bluedaws were to him. Prospects of war again with the North. What his mother said about White ladies. What his father said about President Garfield. What his younger brother said about his father. What his older sister said about his younger brother. How he worried about his sisters and that they shouldn't worry about him.

Gemma, listening to six hours of the scarcely unbroken monologue as Ben continued driving Warren's buggy from Junctionville toward Centipede, began to realize that what made the young man so talkative was that he had not been alone with another Black person since he had arrived in Longchamp Parish and had kept so many things locked inside himself.

'Ben, you're starving for conversation.' Gemma wore a cotton print dress for traveling, something she felt would be both cool and not show much dust from the road; she wore a scarf knotted at the nape of her neck.

The words surprised Ben and he asked, 'What do you mean, Mrs Rickers?'

'Why you've been talking as if you haven't spoken for weeks.'

'Well, I haven't. The Bluedaws have their own concerns. Besides they're . . . White.'

'Ben, you must learn to talk to White people as equals,' she scolded. 'Has it ever occurred to you, Ben, that the Bluedaws see you not as a Black person, but as just another human being?'

Ben was momentarily stunned.

Gemma had long ago recognized a natural intelligence in the young man, and she now felt free to advise. 'Don't make the mistake so many Black people do, Ben. A mistake I'm afraid I made myself. We too often defer to White people. We still treat them as masters, as if they have privileges and powers denied to us.'

'Respecting your opinion, mam, but . . . don't they?'

'Yes! Of course! But how are Black people ever to achieve equality with White people if *we* don't treat them as equals? If we don't behave as their equals?'

Her words both impressed and amused Ben; he grinned widely, his white teeth flashing.

'Oh, you laugh, young man. You laugh. But I have a neighbor, that very nice lady, Sabrine Crowley.' Gemma bounced with the sway and jolt of the buggy. 'Sabrine Crowley and I have been friends for so long I often think of us as sisters – at least cousins. I told her one day that I never felt the slightest racial difference between us. And she said that only once in her life had she ever considered me "colored", and that was the day when she had first heard that a Black family had moved into the parish. From then on, she had thought of me as nothing but her friend.'

Ben's broad, handsome face showed no bitterness, no resentment when he said, 'I wish that was the case with the Bluedaws. Everything would be so much simpler.'

'Don't you go selling the Bluedaws short. They're not trying to break up you and Punkin. Quite the contrary. Molly Bluedaw has even asked me to help.'

'To help? To help do . . . what?'

'Don't be blind, Ben. They know what's happening between you and Punkin. So did Warren and I when we first met you that night at their home. It's plain as the nose on your face that you're no migrant worker there to help with crops. Good Heavens, boy, even eleven-year-old Marianna Bluedaw spotted it!'

Ben pressed, 'So how did Mrs Bluedaw ask you to help?'

'Molly and Deke Bluedaw want Punkin to be happy. It's quite obvious that Punkin is head-over-heels in love with you. Her parents worry, though, about you two remaining in Longchamp Parish. So Molly came to me and I promised to give it some thought. And I have.'

Ben held his eyes on the road. 'May I ask what your thoughts are, Mrs Rickers?'

'I have a brother living out in San Francisco. His name's Jay. I wrote him a letter.'

'California?'

Gemma nodded. 'It's a long ways away from Louisiana. But I understand California is a big, different new country, what people truly mean when they say a "melting pot".'

Excitedly Ben said, 'But Punkin and I have even *talked* about running away to California! Punkin doesn't want to leave home yet. Not with her Dad being like he is. But California is one of the places we considered living.'

'Ben, please don't mention any of this to Punkin. Not until I hear from Jay. You seem like a conscientious, level-headed young man, and I thought you should know.'

'Oh, Mrs Rickers. Punkin said you were a fine lady, the finest lady she'd ever met. And you are. You are!'

'I'm flattered, Ben,' Gemma said. 'Judging from you, Punkin Bluedaw is a fine judge of character.'

Ben, excited – slightly flustered – by the possibility of moving with Punkin to California, said, 'I can't believe that Mrs Bluedaw approached you! I thought you asked me to drive you to New Orleans because the Bluedaws wanted you to help get rid of me.'

'No, Ben. The Bluedaws are very pleased with you. I even had second thoughts about taking you away at this time. But Molly insisted when I told her I needed somebody to drive me.'

Briefly hesitating, Gemma explained, 'You see, Ben, I have a very personal matter to attend to in New Orleans. It's

203

taken a long time – maybe too long – to decide I have to make this trip. My husband doesn't agree with me. He thinks I'm wasting my time. But for the moment, please understand I don't want to talk about it.'

'Yes, mam,' Ben said, suspecting that the trip to New Orleans involved her daughter and the secret which Punkin had told him she had unwittingly divulged to Mrs Rickers.

Gemma said more brightly, 'Your family does know you're coming home, don't they? You did write them a letter?'

'Oh, yes, mam.'

'Your mother and father must be very excited to see you.'

Considering her words, he said, 'Mother's letters have been a bit guarded. I know she and Father were definitely not pleased about me going to help Mr Bluedaw. You'll understand more when you meet them.'

'I look forward to the honor.'

'They'll want you to stay at the house.'

'We'll see,' Gemma said, being uncertain about the days ahead of her. 'I'm going to New Orleans with one purpose in mind, Ben, and I pray for the strength to see it through. Only the Good Lord knows at this moment whose hospitality I will be accepting – and whose wrath I'll raise.'

They rode silently in the buggy, Ben lost in his dreams about moving to California, Gemma not allowing herself to have any doubts about her decision to go to New Orleans to find Emmaline.

The idea had sprung instantly into her mind when she had first learned from Punkin what Emmaline was actually doing in New Orleans; she and Warren had discussed the prospect of one or both of them making the trip, then they had decided it would be the wrong thing to do; the thought had remained like a seed, though, at the back of Gemma's mind, and the passing weeks, then months, had nurtured the idea, and with the same force by which Gemma had originally discarded the idea, she was now pursuing it.

Samuel Hopper was a tall, husky man, with a wreath of white hair encircling his coffee brown head; Miriam Hopper was short, slender, stern-faced; their eyes betrayed displeasure that their son, Ben, had left home to work for a White man who had been injured by the Ku Klux Klan, and that Ben had intentions of marrying that White man's daughter.

Gemma sat in the large parlor of the Hoppers' home located in the north west section of New Orleans, beyond Claiborne Avenue, a neighborhood once called 'back-of-town' that had been an area where emancipated Negro slaves lived; but now it was quickly becoming incorporated into the growing metropolis, a quiet neighborhood for both Black and White families.

The Hopper home was a large wooden house, with deep porches both front and back, a house simply but comfortably furnished. Gemma accepted Miriam Hopper's offer of coffee and pound cake in the front parlor, a formal welcome to New Orleans for Gemma – and a stiff welcome home for their son – attended by the five other Hopper children sitting politely on straight-back chairs, listening quietly to the adults' talk of weather, the long evenings, the appearance of yellow jacket bees being a sure sign that it was going to be a difficult winter.

Gemma, feeling an ample amount of time had been passed in making polite conversation, said, 'Mr and Mrs Hopper, I wonder if you'd mind if I spoke to you alone?'

Miriam Hopper turned to a willowy girl with her hair neatly braided over both ears. 'Beth Ann, why don't you take Ben and show him the new rabbit hutches. Hiram, you and the other boys see that Mrs Rickers' horse-and-buggy is attended to'.

Gemma, waiting until she was left alone in the parlor with Miriam and Samuel Hopper, began, 'I will speak plainly and save us all time. My daughter originally came to New Orleans to work with Punkin Bluedaw as a maid in the Shiptons' home – a house I believe you know, Mr Hopper – but my daughter turned bad, and I've come to find her.'

Mrs Hopper did not offer an opinion on Gemma's blunt announcement; she asked, 'Do you know the city, Mrs Rickers?'

'Not very well. And certainly not the section where such activities are prevalent. For one thing, I would like to be pointed in that direction – if that is possible.'

Miriam Hopper began, 'Mrs Rickers, you strike me as a decent church-going woman, and no decent, church-going woman can set foot –'

'Mrs Hopper, excuse me for interrupting you but I have lost a daughter. The only daughter – the only child – I have. I mean to find her. And if the Good Lord intends me to find her, I will be safe. If I am to come to harm, that is also His will. I have both prayed and thought on this matter. I do not embark on the task lightly. It is my decision.'

Miriam Hopper looked at her husband sitting quietly on the stool in front of the upright piano, his back to the keyboard and the lace square hanging in a triangle from its top.

Samuel Hopper, speaking for the first time since the children had left the parlor, said, 'Oh, I know the districts you want to see, Mrs Rickers. Those women there buy fruit and vegetables from me same as other women. Sometimes more. Never haggle about prices neither.'

Gemma said, 'I would appreciate any help you could give me, Mr Hopper. The sections of town I should see. The names of streets I should know.'

She stopped and, looking back to Miriam Hopper, she added, 'I do not arrive in your home to sow contention. I understand your hesitation, your warning. I would feel and say the same. Nor do I intend to be a burden on you. The only other request I have to make is for the name of a rooming-house, a decent, respectable place where my husband would feel I would be safe.'

'You will stay here.' Miriam Hopper sat primly, hands folded on the lap of her darkly printed dress.

'No, Mrs Hopper.' Gemma shook her head. 'You have a big family. Also, your son has just come home after a long absence. You need your privacy.'

'Mrs Rickers, you brought Ben home.'

'Yes, Mrs Hopper,' Gemma said. 'But I might also be instrumental in helping Ben leave again. As you know, he's more than infatuated with the Bluedaw girl. They intend to get married. I have been asked to help find them a place to live. I have a brother in California to whom I have written.'

Mrs Hopper made a quick, almost inaudible intake of breath; she lowered her eyes, picked some imaginary lint from her dress, murmuring, 'At least you're an honest woman, Mrs Rickers.'

'Honest, but perhaps not too wise. I have one child. I lost her. That's why I want to help Ben and Punkin. There would be too much against them living in the South. I am not saying that life for them will be easier out West. But a war has not been fought there. That faraway land is not drenched with the blood of Black people, and of White people who fought for us.'

Miriam Hopper, turning to her husband, said, 'Sam, make out a list of streets Mrs Rickers should know. I've got a city map someplace around the house. A street guide left over from the church raffle.'

She turned back to Gemma saying, 'One of the boys will take your bag upstairs, Mrs Rickers. I'm sorry it's only a small room. But if you leave the windows open, there'll be a cross breeze and you'll be comfortable. Stay as long as you need to accomplish the work which takes you away from your home.'

Tears of gratitude welled in Gemma's eyes; she began to speak, then lowered her head, saying, 'I understand why Ben is such a fine young man. He comes from good people. Very good people. Thank you, Mrs Hopper . . . Mr Hopper . . . thank you very much.'

17 A Stern Mistress

For Emmaline one joy of being pregnant was that she did not have to milk a man's penis, to twist it for a dribble, checking for gonorrhoea; she was now into her eighth month of pregnancy, too big to make love by having intercourse, and refusing to swallow a man's seed.

More customers came to the room on Liberty Street than had ever been there before; neither Emmaline nor Alain knew who sent the men; they were strangers whom neither had previously known, men who made no sexual demands on Emmaline which she could not easily cope with, customers who mostly wanted 'hand jobs', to be sucked, to shoot their semen onto her face, in her hair, over her hands, having orgasms which in no way would affect the child she carried in her womb.

During these days of heavy pregnancy, Lizzie also visited Emmaline in the room on Liberty Street, but she pleaded ignorance about who – or what – might be prompting these strangers to arrive; and whenever a man was questioned, how he had heard about Emmaline, he answered that a friend had told him, or that he liked to have sex with a pregnant woman.

Emmaline not only looked more beautiful – more youthful – during these days, but it was no secret that many men considered pregnant women to be extremely erotic.

Nevertheless, a few of Emmaline's visitors on Liberty Street were men from Smoky Row, old customers she had seen in the French Quarter and who had asked where she now lived and worked; that was how the small, bespectacled White man had resumed cleaning for Emmaline.

It was a pleasant, only slightly humid, New Orleans afternoon; Alain had gone to the Fair Grounds for the horse races; Emmaline wore a white cotton shift and lay on the double bed, one leg crossed over the knee of her other leg, swinging her small foot back and forth as she watched Henry Peele down on his hands and knees scrubbing the floor. Emmaline hoped she would remember how Alain had taught her to use the whip he had brought her.

The sound of the whip had awakened Emmaline from a late morning sleep a week earlier; she had sat bolt upright in bed when she had heard the loud crack and saw Alain standing naked in the middle of the room, flicking a long black leather bullwhip across the plank floor.

Sleepily rubbing her eyes, she asked, 'What in God's name are you doing?'

The whip again cracked, and Alain had a smile on his face.

'Alain? What are you doing? Where did you get that whip?'

'From the party money.'

Their sudden cache of savings was referred to as 'the party money', the money which Emmaline had brought home from Henrietta Gibson's party in her corset and which now was kept in a tin biscuit box under a floor board. The only reason Alain tolerated Emmy's friend, Lizzie, suffering her feather boas, heady perfumes, and arrogant manners, was that he suspected Lizzie might be helpful in the future to find Emmaline work at parties on Basin Street after she had her baby. But, when Emmaline worked her next party, Alain planned to tell her how to make some arrangement with the bartender, to drink only diluted alcohol.

Alain, flicking the whip, reminded Emmaline, 'Jocasta thought you should whip Henry Peele. Well, the little shit's back down on his hands and knees, and I'm going to teach you how to whip his ass.'

'And how do *you* know how to use a whip?'

Alain flailed it again, making the plaited leather roll, move like a snake, flicking with a loud snap; he said, 'Don't forget my father was once overseer on High Hill. He laid

209

leather onto the backs of his field slaves. And he probably took a bit of skin now and then off the back of dear -' Alain snapped the whip - 'mother!'

Alain then spent the rest of the morning teaching Emmaline how to stand, how to pull back her arm, how to flick the whip over her shoulder, as well as how to toss the whip underhand, as if she were throwing a ball across lawn, to use the whip in a variety of ways without allowing it to snap against her own skin.

'Is that all, madam?'

Emmaline looked and saw Henry Peele in the middle of the room, the knees of his baggy trousers wet from scrubbing the floor, his brown bristle brush and his wooden bucket by his feet.

Knowing the moment had come to force herself to act like a plantation's stern mistress, Emmaline glanced around the room, her eyes finally studying the four chairs grouped around the oaken table; she said, 'Did you dust the chair rungs?'

'No, madam . . . I spent today doing the floor.'

'There's more here than a floor!'

'Yes, madam, but -'

'Do I have to tell you to do everything?'

'Madam, I'm sorry.'

'Sorry? What good is "sorry"?' Emmaline rose from the bed, ordering, 'Bring me my whip!'

Henry Peele jerked his head at the fact that Emmaline might possess a whip.

Pointing across the room at the curtain separating the small kitchen alcove, she said, 'There's a whip hanging on the far side. Fetch it for me! Now! And take off your shirt!'

Emmaline, watching Henry Peele move toward the curtain, sat on the edge of the bed and extended her hand for the whip.

Henry Peele, keeping his eyes lowered as he obediently brought the whip toward Emmaline, stumbled on the bucket, spilling water across the floor.

Emmaline angrily snatched the whip from his hand, scolding, 'Now look what you've done, you stupid little fool!'

Peele fell to his knees, begging, 'I'm sorry, madam! Please forgive me, madam! I didn't mean to make such a mess, madam!'

Emmaline, feeling true anger at him for spilling the water, began to beat him before she even unfurled the whip, bringing down her hand, repeating, 'You stupid little fool! You stupid little fool!'

Crouched on the floor in front of her, Peele buried his head between his hands.

Emmaline lifted one bare foot, kicking his buttocks, sending him sprawling flat on the floor and, remembering what Alain had taught her about inflicting punishment, she began to flail the whip in longer, more evenly-timed strokes, continuing to flog Peele even as he anxiously pulled down his soggy trousers, eager to bear the full brunt of his mistress's fury.

It was too perfect, Alain thought. None of the men arriving in Liberty Street made demands on Emmaline which she could - or would - not fulfil. The men had started arriving shortly after Emmaline had worked the Basin Street party with Lizzie, and although Emmaline had told Alain everything she could remember about the party, he was still suspicious that there was some fact she had not told him, some detail she perhaps had not even been aware of herself, and he was determined to learn the true reason why she suddenly had so many visitors.

Surprising even to Alain, Emmaline excelled in telling stories which excited men, whispering lewd accounts to them as they knelt at her feet, kissing her toes, licking her legs, caressing her thighs, masturbating as they listened to her voice. Emmaline later reported to Alain what each man enjoyed, and early one Autumn afternoon Alain waited downstairs to see an office clerk who visited Emmaline during his lunch time, a young man particularly interested in hearing Emmaline tell him stories about her lover's penis, and how he made love to her. Charley the Oysterman had disappeared after Alain had seduced him; this new young man, though, was as eager, as curious, as perversely excited to hear tales about Emmaline enjoying Alain's largeness.

Since unlacing Emmaline from the French black satin corset on the night she had come home from the Basin Street party, since putting her to bed and first noticing the change which pregnancy was making in her body, Alain's attitude toward Emmaline had altered. Lately, he was finding it more difficult to be cruel in his domination toward Emmaline. He still enjoyed exerting masculine authority over her but he had a new feeling, a protective feeling for her.

Despite this growing tenderness, Alain still felt a professional claim over Emmaline, a right to her body which he fiercely guarded.

Having learned in Natchez how pimps and brothel-keepers poached on one another's territory, Alain suspected that someone might be trying to lure Emmaline away from him, and he had been waiting for the right moment to find him – or her.

The right moment had finally come when Alain heard about the store clerk spending his lunch time listening to stories about his penis.

Alain, waiting for the clerk to leave the building, called him alongside the doorway, 'You like my woman?'

The clerk, sandy-haired and neatly dressed, stared at Alain.

'The girl upstairs,' Alain explained. 'She's good to you?'

The young man's gaze dropped to the crotch of Alain's tightly fitting trousers.

'Anything else maybe interest you?' Alain stood taller.

'It's . . . it's . . . you she talks about?'

Alain gently worked one hand over his crotch and nodded.

'Are the stories she tells me true?'

Beckoning the young man down the alleyway, Alain pointed toward a far doorway and began unbuttoning his trousers.

The young clerk fell to his knees, opening his mouth, ready to enclose his lips around the head of Alain's penis, when Alain flicked open the knife and pressed its long, thin blade toward the man's throat.

He demanded, 'Who sent you?'

The man pulled back his head with surprise.

'Who sent you?' Alain demanded. 'Tell me who sent you or I'll slit your throat ear to ear, you little cock-sucker jennie-boy.'

The kneeling man looked from Alain, to the knife, to the penis hanging in front of him; he nervously asked, 'Can I play . . . with myself?'

'No, cock-sucker! You can't do anything! Not until you tell me who sent you!' He pressed the tip of the knife closer to his neck.

The man gulped. 'His name's . . . Willy.'

'Where does he live?'

'Basin Street . . . He's a pimp at a bordello.' The young man stared hungrily at Alain's penis, excited by the knife, repeating 'Can I play with myself now . . . *please*?'

'What bordello?'

'A big house on Basin Street . . . That place owned by the octoroon woman who claims she's an Indian . . . Her name's Kuda.'

'Kuda?'

The young man nodded. 'Willy's a pimp there . . . He's called Willy the Whip.'

'Why "whip"?'

'Because he whips hookers.'

'He sent you here?'

Nodding, the young man said, 'He knows what I like . . . that I like to hear good stories . . . stories about pussies and big pricks and . . .'

Raising his eyes to Alain, he again begged, 'Can I suck you now . . . *please*?'

'No.'

'I promise I won't tell anyone. Not even Willy. Especially not Willy.'

Alain smiled and, lifting his penis, he began slapping it across the man's face, saying, 'They call me "the whip", too.'

The young man offered his fair face to be slapped by Alain's darkly-skinned penis, holding out his tongue, his eyes pressed shut, his hand now quickly working on his own penis, remaining kneeling in the alleyway even after Alain had hurriedly tucked his penis back into his trousers and was running toward Liberty Street for his buggy.

A Black maid answered the door of Kuda's brothel, a large yellow and white house on Basin Street surrounded by a porch and fronted by an iron fence and painted to resemble ripe cornstalks. Alain barged past the maid, but she grabbed for his shoulder, saying, 'Hold it, sonny. Colored boys ain't allowed in here.'

Alain, shoving off the woman's hand, stopped at the foot of a spiral staircase and looked up past three storeys to a stained-glass dome; he shouted, 'Kuda! I want to see the woman called Kuda!'

'She's out shopping for the afternoon,' said the maid. 'So don't you cause no trouble, boy, or –'

'Shopping?' Alain turned, holding his seven-shot knuckler in his hand. 'Then I'll wait for her to come home.'

The maid, seeing the small pistol, began shaking her head, saying, 'Boy, don't you cause no trouble for me. I just work here. Don't you cause no trouble for me.'

A voice called from overhead. 'Jessie! Who's down there?'

Alain raised his eyes and saw a tall sunken-cheeked woman, with long straight black hair, looking over the bannister.

He called, 'You Kuda?'

'That's me,' she said, flicking her long black hair with one hand. 'What you doing barging into my house this time of day?'

'You've got a son-of-a-bitch here named Willy. You tell him to stop sending tricks around to my place. You tell him we don't need charity.'

Kuda asked, 'You got a name, boy?'

'You tell Willy the message came from Liberty Street. You tell him, too, he's not king pimp in this town. Not with my girl, anyway.'

'I'll pass on the message, boy.'

Kuda turned away from the bannister and walked into a room.

Kuda's voice was hushed, muted as the faint twilight filtering through the raspberry gauze curtains on her bedroom windows, soft as the aroma filtering from the Turkish opium pot.

She asked, 'What's the gal like, Willy?'

Willy sat in a deep armchair across from Kuda's velour divan, his fingers steepled in front of his pensive face, his grey-green eyes studying Kuda lying on the divan.

He answered, 'Young. Tender. New to the game.'

'What's your game with her?'

'I told you. But you aren't remembering too good these days. You got to stop taking all this dope, Kuda. It's making you rummy.'

Kuda, ignoring Willy's advice, lay on the divan, asking, 'So what's your game with her?'

'She's that kid who worked for Jocasta on Smoky Row. The girl who turned up at Henrietta's party. The one who got sick and I took home with the Jew girl.'

Kuda dreamily ran her fingers through the pampas grass standing in a vase next to the divan. 'Can I use her?'

'Not yet.'

'No, but after she drops her baby? Is she good stuff?'

'Oh, she's good stuff all right. Real good stuff.'

'Dark?'

'No darker than you. But her hair ain't straight like yours. She can't pass for no Indian.'

'Maybe I can still use her. Maybe I can say she's part Cuban. Or from someplace down in South America. Oh, these White bitches, why do they make life so hard for me, Willy? Why? Why are they so tough on Black girls? They scared? Are White pussies scared of Black stuff?'

'You'll get by.'

'You be careful of that mulatto buck, Willy. I don't need him shooting you. Don't you send no more tricks around to – what's that stuff's name?'

'Emmy.'

215

'Emmy.' Kuda raised herself on one elbow from the velour divan, holding out the squat water-filled jar to Willy.

Taking the jar, Willy set it down on the kerosene brazier next to his chair and relit the flame; he waited for the water to boil inside the heavy jar, creating heat for the opium inside the jar's silver lid; he took a tapestry square to lift the jar from the brazier and handed it back to Kuda, cautioning, 'Careful, it's hot.'

'This stuff, Willy, this stuff is Heaven.'

'I take good care of you, Kuda.'

'You know where this stuff puts me, Willy?' Kuda had already inhaled fumes.

'Where, baby?' Willy asked. 'Where does this stuff put you?'

'The best street in town.'

He watched her inhaling the fumes, seeing her eyes become pale and dreamy as the opium began affecting her brain.

He said, 'Sugar, you put yourself on the best street in town. Basin Street's the best street in town. No dope put you here. You did it yourself.'

'Who's talking about Basin Street? Shit, I ain't talking about no Basin Street. I'm talking about the street where you go and nobody finds you. The street where you go where you can hide from the world. That's the best street in town. Your street. My street. Secret Street. That's the best street in town. Secret Street.'

Kuda closed her eyes, inhaling the fumes deeper, and Willy the Whip continued studying her from his chair, his own mind becoming a jumble of thoughts, thinking how Kuda had grown so addicted to her drugs that he had to keep her supplied without killing her, and how today he had been given a new name – King Pimp.

King Pimp! He liked it. King Pimp living on the best street in town! He liked it a lot. So maybe Kuda wasn't so crazy after all, he thought, watching her swoon on the velour divan as she drifted farther into 'Secret Street.'

18   Needle in a Haystack

Gemma expected to find ignominy but not squalor; she stopped as she turned from Bienville Street into Burgundy Street, staring at the shabby, tumbledown cottages lining the garbage strewn street, looking at the gaps between the houses heaped with rubble, the boardwalks running at odd angles, the gutters deep with waste.

Only moments earlier, she had left the busy hum of late morning traffic behind her on Canal Street, the hustle and bustle of clanging streetcars, merchants arranging their wares in store windows, the boardwalks thronged with shoppers, business men, waiters delivering trays of coffee and baignettes.

But, here, only a few blocks away from one of New Orleans' busiest thoroughfares, was a stretch of houses which looked as if their inhabitants might have suffered from a plague, as if the houses were vacant, as if some blight had hit this part of town – Smoky Row.

Lifting the hem of her dress to avoid stepping in a pool of slop, Gemma raised one hand to shade her eyes against the morning's sun and looked at the street-marking on the side of a house, checking to see if she indeed had come to the correct spot, the place which Samuel Hopper had told her about, the spot which Miriam Hopper had pointed out on the city map, the street where Punkin Bluedaw had told her she had last visited Emmaline in New Orleans.

According to Punkin's directions, though, the spot where Jocasta Liddle's bordello should be standing was no more than a vacant, rubble-strewn lot.

Gemma noticed charred boards and rain-soaked ashes in

the heap as she went to the small shack next door; she moved cautiously up the boardwalk and knocked on the front door.

Receiving no answer, she wondered if the derelict house was even inhabited; she knocked again, calling, 'Anybody here?'

A lowered shutter opened next to the door; a Black woman leaned out her head, demanding, 'What the shit you want, bitch?'

Surprised, Gemma collected herself and said, 'I'm looking for a woman named Jocasta – Jocasta Liddle.'

'Next door.' The woman reached to pull close the shutter.

'Wait, please!' Gemma quickly said. 'There's no *house* next door!'

'The fire cleared her out.'

'So where can I find her? Or anybody else from that house?'

'If you're a bill collector, lady, you're too late.'

'Was anybody killed?'

'Killed? No such luck. Jocasta's thrown in jail and the rest flew the coop.'

Gemma said, 'I'm looking for a girl named –' she forced herself to say the name – 'Emmaline Rickers.'

'You and half the world, lady.'

'Excuse me?'

'You and half the world are looking for somebody. Do it someplace else.' The louvered shutter slammed shut.

Gemma, determined not to be discouraged by this first encounter in Smoky Row, walked briskly down the wobbly boardwalk, opened the gate, and went to the next house on the block; she rapped firmly on the front door, waited, then knocked a second, and a third time, knocking again until another Black woman – young, prettier than the last woman, wearing a lavender dressing-gown, and holding a small yellow kitten to her breast – opened the door.

Gemma said, 'Excuse me, miss, for disturbing you but I asked next door about the house that burned down on the corner –'

'Jocasta's?'

Gemma nodded. 'Yes.'

'Too bad about that. It happened a month, six weeks ago. Maybe longer. I don't rightly remember. My mind ain't been too good lately. Booze makes my brain play tricks on me. But I did hear Jocasta got tossed in the calaboose.'

'Excuse me?'

'Calaboose. Jail. Jocasta's got pitched in the jail house. Oh, I tell you, those White ladies are bound and determined to save their husbands from us Black gals!'

The young woman, stroking the kitten, studied Gemma more closely, saying, 'But you ain't looking for Jocasta. Who you looking for, lady? Your kid or something?'

'Why . . . yes.'

'Let me give you a little advice.'

'Thank you, miss. But I don't need advice. I need help. Names.'

'Your girl work for Jocasta, you won't find her on this street. No parlor house gals here no more. No crib gals here from across there . . .'

Stopping, the young woman said, 'Parlor house, honey, that means whorehouse. Cribs is them hutches across the street. But you look like a nice church lady. Why don't you go home and say your prayers? You'll do more good that way than traipsing around New Orleans beating down doors and asking a lot of questions.'

'I intend to find my daughter, miss.' Gemma knew she sounded prim, perhaps even foolish, but desperation left her with little pride.

The young woman tilted her head, asking, 'You ever hear about trying to find a needle in a haystack? Well, if your little girl's on the game, you'll have as much luck finding her in New Orleans as finding that needle in a haystack.'

'Thank you.' Gemma turned on the porch.

The young woman called, 'Hey, lady? You don't need a kitten, do you? Got three left! Cute little things. Ain't charging nothing. Just looking for good homes.'

'No thank you.' German moved toward the gate.

'Sure wish my Mama would've come looking for me,' called the girl.

Gemma could not glance back; she realized the young woman was probably little older than Emmaline.

Remembering the first woman on Smoky Row saying that Jocasta Liddle had been thrown in jail, Gemma decided to ask a policeman on the street for the directions of the nearest jailhouses in the vicinity, and not feeling hungry for lunch, she walked until she reached the St Charles Street Police House.

The desk officer, a fair-skinned Irishman wearing a white shirt and no hat, was not helpful with information about Smoky Row; he smirked at Gemma's hesitation in asking about prostitutes, finally suggesting that she hired a detective.

Looking the policeman straight in his blue eyes, Gemma lied, 'I hate to pay some detective good money that might go back to the Catholic Church, sir. Our priest gave money to find Jocasta Liddle, and I thought you might have a record of the good soul who paid her bail.'

At the mention of the Catholic Church, the policeman reconsidered Gemma's request and sent her down the hallway to a glass door marked, 'Records', telling her to say that Sergeant Reilly said to help her.

Reilly's name was effective in the small office, and Gemma was soon handed a piece of paper bearing the name and an address of the person who had paid the bail for Jocasta Liddle – 'Luba Belle, 1011½ Crown Street, New Orleans.'

Proud of her ingenuity, Gemma again consulted her map and saw she could take the St Charles Street Car to Harmony Street, which led into Crown Street; hurriedly, she walked to St Charles Street car stop, not even angered when she had to sit in a car designated by a star as the car for colored people.

Gemma tried to imagine what this woman, Luba, was like, hoping she could direct her to Emmaline; Gemma alighted at Harmony Street, her heart beating fast as she hurried down Harmony Street, turning right onto Crown Street.

1011½ Crown Street was an abandoned warehouse.

Miriam Hopper proved to be both a friend and a source of strength for Gemma; Mrs Hopper never questioned Gemma about her day, and always had small but demanding chores

220

which needed to be done when Gemma returned depressed to the house in the late afternoon, small chores usually given to children, such as sifting grit from lentils for soup, mending a broken sugar bowl, plucking pin feathers from a boiler hen. Gemma gladly helped, and even cancelled her forays into the city on laundry day, insisting that she do the washing and ironing, saying that it was the least she could do for her board and room.

The atmosphere at the Hopper home was a welcome relief for Gemma as she saw more of the city life in New Orleans; she had always suspected the city to be a wicked place, an out-post in the New World, founded by French and Spanish adventurers, the age-old haunt of pirates, flat boat river men and paddle wheel gamblers, and the center for slave-traders; New Orleans had been further ravaged by Union soldiers during its occupation in the Civil War.

Gemma made it a rule not to go out after dark; she saw enough prostitutes in daylight hours when they were supposedly resting, and she felt she was not obliged to endure seeing them plying their trade. She would rather not find Emmaline than discover her in the throes of degradation.

Also, Gemma had quickly learned that the New Orleans police were going to be of no assistance to her; she did visit three private detectives, though, all of whom impressed her as being no more than charlatans, opportunists eager to prey on people in distress, men who made little effort to hide their racial prejudices.

Convinced she would do her best work alone, Gemma stopped keeping track of time after three weeks in New Orleans, working her way through the streets on the city map, asking questions, following any suggestions, achieving nothing, but driven to continue her search.

Going through an iron gate to a brick house on Conti Street, Gemma rapped a brass Egyptian-styled knocker and was not surprised when a Black woman wearing a bright orange wig answered the door; Gemma had grown accustomed to seeing outrageous outfits, dyed hair, gaudy jewellery – all the plumage of prostitution in New Orleans.

'Hi, honey,' said the woman.

Gemma still possessed only two prostitutes' names to link with Emmaline; the mention of Alain Summers' name had only drawn blank stares in the past weeks, but Gemma had discovered that Jocasta was rather infamous on certain streets, and that a few people even nodded at the mention of Luba's name.

Gemma announced, 'I'm looking for someone from a house on Burgundy Street, a woman called Jocasta Liddle.'

'Smoky Row?' The woman frowned.

'Yes.' Gemma also had learned that the stretch of tumble-down houses on Burgundy Street was considered to be a ghetto, even in the eyes of other prostitutes.

'You won't find a girl like that . . . here!' The woman tossed up her nose.

She said, 'Forgive me, I'm sorry.'

'Oh, no need to be too sorry. I heard of that bitch, Big Jocasta.'

'You have? Perhaps you can tell me –'

'Only thing good I can tell you about Jocasta is that the bitch would give her right arm to have one of these!'

The woman in the orange wig lifted her robe and exposed a penis dangling between her legs, showing that 'she' was not a woman but a man in female clothing.

Gemma, staring at the penis, realized with shock that there must be brothels in New Orleans staffed with transvestites; then she thought how, until now, she had never seen another penis except Warren's.

A letter arrived from Gemma's brother in San Francisco, a reply to Gemma's second letter, answering that Jay had not only found work for Ben Hopper in the community of Santa Clara near San Francisco but also a part-time job for Punkin in that picturesque area originally settled by missionaries.

Gemma sat in her room at the top of the Hopper house, holding Jay's letter, waiting until Miriam Hopper finished putting her smallest children to bed before going downstairs to report Jay's good news, as well as the other information she had to tell them tonight.

222

'Excuse me,' she said, finally peeking her head into the parlor. 'May I come in?'

'Mrs Rickers! Certainly!' Mrs Hopper was seated in her favorite chair with a knitting basket by her felt slippers; Mr Hopper sat across from her reading the *Daily Picayune* in the glow of a kerosene lamp.

Gemma took a chair, announcing, 'I got a letter.'

Miriam Hopper kept on knitting. 'Mrs Crowley must be such a good friend of yours. She writes so often. Did they finally settle that trial about her brother? Poor dear woman!'

Gemma had chosen to write Sabrine about the reason she had come to New Orleans, finding it easier to express in written words that Emmaline's life had taken an abruptly ugly turn, to write that she had come to New Orleans to try and find her. Sabrine had written back to Gemma, relating her own bad news: the reappearance of Junior, his threat to seize Belrose Plantation, and then the incident about the murder of Ivy Bravo and the trial to be held in Ketley.

Gemma, gripping Jay's letter, answered, 'Mrs Crowley's brother has been found guilty. He's in Federal Prison.'

Samuel Hopper said, 'Yes, I'd seen something about that murder here in my paper a week or two back.'

Gemma continued, 'But that's not the reason I wanted to talk to you. My brother wrote saying that he's found Ben a job in California.'

Miriam Hopper's knitting needles paused; Samuel Hopper looked up from the newspaper, staring at Gemma through the wire spectacles on the tip of his nose.

Gemma continued, 'Of course, I haven't told Ben anything about it –'

Miriam and Samuel Hopper exchanged glances.

'I thought you should be the ones to tell him first. You can show him the letter after I leave.'

'Leave?' Miriam Hopper put aside her work.

Gemma nodded. 'I'm taking the stage coach home in the morning. I made inquiries today about departures from the Canal Street Post House.'

'Mrs Rickers, you're welcome to stay,' Miriam Hopper said. 'To stay as long as you need.'

223

'Thank you. But it's time I went home.'

Samuel Hopper said, 'I wouldn't want Miriam here traveling all alone on no public stage, Mrs Rickers. I'm sure your husband thinks the same way.'

'No, I've been here - what? Six, seven weeks? That's long enough. Long enough for many things. I learned in that time I could spend six *years* in this city and not find my daughter. But I tried to find her. I tried. Now I know my place is at home with my husband.'

'It's a long trip to make alone,' said Mrs Hopper.

'There's only one overnight stop. In the little town of Junctionville. There's a lady there, Miss Spooner, who takes in overnight guests. The stage coach continues the next morning to Bossburg. I can walk home from there. The Lord knows, I've done it before.'

Gemma rose, shaking hands with Samuel Hopper, bending forward to kiss Miriam Hopper on the forehead, saying, 'Of course I'll see you in the morning. But I wanted to thank you both personally - privately - tonight. And to give you this letter to pass on to Ben after I go. It has all the instructions, the addresses, the information he should know.'

Gemma left the letter on top of the upright piano, again saying goodnight, then gently closing the door behind her, she went upstairs to the small room at the top of the house and wept.

19   King Pimp

Alain stood inside the door of the room on Liberty Street, his hat still centered on his head as he stared across the shafts of bright December sunshine at the empty bed; he smelled the redolence of perfume in the room and instantly knew where Emmaline had gone, who had taken her away.

He loaded his seven-shot knuckler, buckled the leather knife scabbard to his leg, knotted the whip to his belt under his long jacket, and finally glanced at the Winchester repeater rifle leaning in the corner, but decided against taking it, knowing he could not get into Kuda's bordello carrying a rifle.

The Negress maid, Jessie, answered the door and, remembering Alain from a few months earlier, pleaded, 'Go away, boy. Don't you come back here no more making trouble –'

Alain barged past her, taking three steps at a time up the staircase.

'Boy!' called Jessie from alongside a coat rack made from bull horns that was in the hallway.

Alain banged on the door behind which he had seen Kuda disappear the last time he had been here; he banged again with both fists, shouting, 'I told you to leave my woman alone! I warned you! *I warned you!*'

A voice spoke behind Alain. 'Get out of here, coon.'

Spinning around, Alain saw a White man with curly yellow hair and instantly he knew who he was.

'Where's Emmy?'

'Get out of here,' repeated Willy.

'Emmy's in this house!'

'It's no business of yours where that girl is.'

A door opened across the landing; a woman's face momentarily appeared, long enough for Alain to recognize Lizzie, and the door quickly shut.

Moving toward the door, Alain said, 'She's in there, God damn you all to hell! She's in there! You brought her here to have . . . *my* child!'

Willy blocked his path.

Alain shoved him with one hand, reaching into the pocket of his long jacket with the other hand.

Willy grabbed for him, tightening the grip and pulled back his fist.

Alain ducked the blow, and gripping the small pistol called the knuckler inside his fist, he caught Willy on the chin with a strong jab, sending him falling back against the bannister.

Catching his breath, breaking his fall with both hands on the bannister, Willy lunged forward, muttering, 'You Black son of a bitch . . .'

Alain turned the pistol to fire at Willy, but Willy tackled him and the weapon clattered to the floor, while Alain tumbled backwards.

Pulling up his knee, Alain aimed for Willy's groin and grabbed for his neck. But Willy began driving his fists angrily against Alain's face, landing one, two, three, four heavy blows.

Locked into a knot, the two men rolled across the floor, along the bannister, passing Kuda now standing bleary-eyed in the doorway to her room; she stood staring dumbly at them slugging, kicking, pummeling one another, only screaming when she saw them reach the top of the stairs, and begin to tumble downwards.

The clatter of their rolling bodies brought sleepy-eyed prostitutes from their rooms, edging along the bannister to watch the fight as Jessie the maid stood at the bottom of the stairs with a broom.

Alain, his face cut and running with blood, jumped to his feet at the bottom of the stairs, jerked the whip from inside his jacket, and pulled his knife from its scabbard.

Willy snatched the broom from Jessie's hand, took a wide swipe at Alain, then grabbed a carpet bag from the foot of the coat rack and pulled out a long cowhide whip.

The two men faced one another, both crouching forward, circling the hallway, and, inside the parlor, a piano started playing, a loud, thumping song to cover the sounds of lashing whips.

The piano music rose from the parlor, a steely roll of the treble, a loud pounding thump of bass.

Lizzie stood alongside a rosewood bed, mopping perspiration from Emmaline's forehead as the midwife worked to ease the child from between Emmaline's legs.

Emmaline had adamantly refused all morning to take any tonics or drugs to ease her pain, fearing that medication would harm the birth of her baby; she had clung onto Lizzie, crying that she was frightened she was going to die.

Lizzie urged, 'Relax, honey. Just let it come.'

'Lizzie, I'm not going to make it.'

'Sure you'll make it.'

'I'm going to die, Lizzie.'

'Honey, where's your fight?'

'Lizzie, I want you to write my Mama and Daddy. I want you to tell them to come get my baby. I don't want my baby to be an orphan, Lizzie. Please don't let my baby be an orphan with no mama.'

'Don't talk this way, Emmy. You're going to be fine. Kuda's going to give you a job. You're going to be fine.'

'Lizzie, you know where to write,' Emmaline insisted. 'Mr and Mrs Warren Rickers . . . Bossburg . . . Longchamp Parish.'

Emmaline's fears and persistent demands had stopped two hours ago; she now passed between unconsciousness to fits of hysteria; she was unaware that the head of the baby had finally appeared, that the midwife was already working to keep the cord from wrapping around the infant's neck, pulling hard to bring the child into the world.

Lizzie was holding Emmy's body in her arms, knowing

she had died during the moments the midwife had been slapping life into the child.

The piano music tinkled, trilled, crescendoed, a feeble attempt to cover the sharp snaps of the whips; Alain, his clothes now torn and smeared with blood, cracked his bull-whip at Willy: Willy, having pulled a knife from his boot scabbard, jabbed it menacingly at Alain; both men bent forward as they circled one another – the blond White man, the slim half-caste man – and moved from the entry hall to the parlor, through an archway to the second parlor, each man holding a whip in one hand, a knife in the other.

Willy concentrated solely on his younger opponent, his confidence shaken only moments earlier by a successful strike against his back – the first time in his life that Willy the Whip had ever felt the biting sting of leather against his own flesh.

Alain, his jealous eyes cooled into determination to win, kept jabbing the point of his steel blade at Willy, hoping to weaken him, to tire him, to wear him down before moving in for cold-blooded murder.

Willy carefully stalked his opponent, slashing suddenly at Alain's knife hand as he simultaneously swung his whip with a crack.

Alain pulled away, cursing.

Willy, extending his left foot, tripped him.

Alain fell backwards and his knife clattered across the shiny mahogany floor.

Plunging toward Alain with his own knife, Willy shrieked as he charged, emphasizing the movement he hoped would be fatal for Alain.

But Alain rolled quickly on one hip, only allowing Willy's knife to scratch his shoulder through the torn fabric of his shirt.

Springing to his feet, Alain reached for a fringed cloth covering a round table, shoving a lamp and a collection of bric-a-brac toward Willy, creating a diversion to give him a moment to catch his own bearings.

Willy leaped to his feet, though, armed only with his

whip, and cracked it down hard against the wooden floor, making the whip snap loudly and, in a flash, recoil only inches away from Alain's blood-covered cheek.

Momentarily stunned by the flash of Willy's whip, Alain did not move. And Willy again snapped the whip, this time striking across Alain's back, drawing blood which instantly blotted his shirt in a large stripe of red.

Alain, receiving the painful hit without screaming, grabbed his own whip with both hands, gripped it like a garrotte, and rushed toward Willy's neck as he brought up his knee at the same time to protect himself from another kick of Willy's leg, to pound his own leg hard against Willy's crotch.

'Pimp . . .' Alain muttered, tightening his whip in a choke around Willy's neck. 'Dirty no-good White . . . pimp.'

Willy's whip dropped to the floor; his hands struggled, groped, grasped to push away Alain's constricting grip on his neck, the tightening whip pressing against his wind-pipe.

Alain's hold became stronger, his eyes burning with hatred; he smiled thinly, firming his jaw as he watched Willy's face grow red, the White man's eyes bulge as the whip strangled him, strands of saliva beginning to drool from the corners of his mouth.

Neither Alain nor Willy had noticed Kuda descending the staircase; they did not see her raise the gleaming pistol in her hand.

Kuda fired the Smith and Wesson .44 once, twice, a third time at the center of Alain's back, continuing to work the pistol even after Alain collapsed to the floor, blood gushing from his chest onto the burgundy and maroon pattern of the Oriental carpet.

Willy, gulping for breath, teetered above Alain's bleeding corpse and stared at Kuda as she silently turned to ascend the bordello's staircase, still clutching the pistol, and flicking her long black hair from her face.

'I'm going to marry Emmaline Rickers when I get big, Mama, when I'm old enough to have a house of my own.'

'No, Alain. You're going to marry your Mama. Because your Mama will have nobody and you don't want Mama to be

229

alone, do you? Poor Mama will have nobody if you marry Emmaline, Alain. Mama's your sweetheart. Never forget that. Mama's your girl-friend.'

Marisse Summers thought of this long-ago exchange between herself and Alain as she sat wrapped against the December chill in the outer office of her lawyer in Ketley, Louisiana. She had received news that Alain had been accidentally shot in New Orleans, that Emmaline Rickers had died giving birth to a child, interrelated stories which had come so quickly, in such horrid succession, that she had been too shocked to cry, only thinking that, yes, Alain's wish had come true in some strange macabre way. He had finally married Emmaline. Their union was unholy, gruesome, but at least they were together, although not on this earth. But wishes did come true for some people, Marisse Summers realized, and wanting to help the dreams of the child whom she firmly believed to be Alain's progeny, she had come to her lawyer to bequeath High Hill to Alain's and Emmaline's child, a fact only to be made public at her own death. She felt it was the least she could do in recompense for tutoring Alain from childhood to love her, a woman who lived like a whore, perhaps even making her son turn the one person he had truly loved into becoming the whore he had been taught to love.

20 The Lord's Strange and Mysterious Ways

The fact that the stranger, Lizzie, wrote to meet Gemma in the same hotel in New Orleans as the one into which Sabrine and Cramer had booked themselves before sailing for Europe, convinced Gemma that the Lord truly worked in strange and mysterious ways.

The St Louis Hotel, located on Royal Street in the French Quarter, had been the centre for rich planters before the Civil War, and the scene of many slave auctions.

The main lobby was a vast hall of black and white marble, fine Grecian columns supporting a glass rotunda. A winding marble staircase rose from the lobby to the grand balcony, the walls decorated with elaborate frescoes of cherubs and nymphs.

Sabrina Crowley, standing behind the tall windows of the parlor in the suite of rooms on the grand balcony which Cramer had taken for their visit, looked across Royal Street to the house purchased by Créole loyalists for Napoleon to live in after his planned escape from prison on the island of St Helena.

Raindrops slid down the window panes as Sabrine asked, 'Do you think Junior will try to escape from prison?'

The fact that her brother had been jailed for murder still haunted Sabrine. But she did not know if she was more troubled by the fact that Junior had been convicted of murder, or by the fact that he had not been executed for the crime, that he could still escape – or be paroled – by members of the Ku Klux Klan placed in High Federal positions, and that he could still carry out his threat about seizing Belrose Plantation.

Cramer Crowley moved alongside his wife. 'I made you a promise that I would not talk about politics for the next months. And you promised me not to talk about your brother. Remember? We've decided to concentrate on completely new worlds - Pompei . . . Rome . . . Florence . . . Venice . . . Vienna . . . Paris . . .'

It had been Cramer's idea to take the European trip, to sail from New Orleans for Naples, following a southern route across the Atlantic in hope of avoiding inclement weather, to disembark in southern Italy and then travel north through Europe as the seasons warmed.

Gemma Rickers sat in the Crowley suite of rooms in the St Louis Hotel, watching Sabrine and Cramer standing side by side at the window; the thought of her good friends seeing Etruscan treasures, Vatican pomp, the baroque splendors of Austria kept her mind off the meeting she had in a few hours' time with the White woman who had written her a letter, this stranger named 'Lizzie.'

Then, too, Gemma also had the prospect of Christmas to occupy her mind. She had brought gifts to New Orleans for the Hopper family, small presents she had made on the farm especially for them; she had already sent parcels west to Punkin and Ben, as well as to her brother.

Cramer, turning from the window, said, 'Gemma, I spoke to the desk clerk, to the hotel manager, and the assistant-manager. They know you are staying here tonight, and that our carriage will collect you at the front door tomorrow morning and take you back home to Longchamp Parish.'

Gemma smiled; she still harbored mixed feelings about saying farewell to Sabrine and Cramer, wondering how she would fare without them at this critical point in her life.

She said, 'I wish you'd at least let me come to the pier and wave goodbye.'

Sabrine, dressed in her long travelling coat and hat, moved from the window. 'Oh, why aren't you coming with us, dear Gemma?'

Clasping Sabrine's hand, Gemma said, 'It's Warren who needs to travel and see new places.'

They all were concerned about Warren; he had spoken little in the last few months, having just been emerging from the shock of hearing about Emmaline's life in New Orleans when, now, suddenly, he was faced with her death.

The orchestra in the hotel lobby was playing *The Blue Danube Waltz* as Sabrine, Cramer and Gemma descended the staircase; Sabrine clutched Gemma's arm, whispering, 'I feel as if I'm in Europe already!'

Gemma, dabbing tears from the corner of her eyes, kissed Sabrine goodbye one last time as Cramer had a final word with the desk clerk; Sabrine and Cramer put Gemma in a horse-drawn cab to take her to the Hoppers' home, and then they left for the Bienville pier to board the *S.S. Guardi* for Naples.

Two hours later, Gemma returned to the St Louis Hotel and announced herself at the desk; a uniformed page collected the red-tasselled key for her suite of rooms, and Gemma had gathered the skirt of her long black coat and was about to ascend the wide staircase when the desk clerk called, 'Mrs Rickers.'

Gemma turned.

'Your guest –' The clerk held out his hand, announcing, '– Lady Elizabeth is here.'

Gemma saw a tall, exquisitely dressed young White woman approaching her, carrying a bundle clutched to her breast.

'Mrs Rickers?'

Gemma stared at the bundle.

'I'm Lizzie,' said the young lady. 'And here is your . . . grandchild.'

Smiling, Lizzie held out the small bundle to Gemma.

Taking the infant in her arms, Gemma looked at the little brown, sleeping face.

Lizzie said, 'Have you ever seen such a doll?'

Gemma shook her head, her eyes misting with tears, as she asked, 'And you knew . . . Emmaline?'

'Yes.'

'Please come upstairs. I don't want to let go of this little

233

baby. But please do come upstairs. You've been so good. So wonderful to write us. At least let me send for some coffee, some tea, something so we –'

Lizzie shook her head. 'No, Mrs Rickers. Thank you very much. But I don't think so.'

Gemma asked, 'Are you certain?'

Lizzie fondly gripped Gemma's wrist. 'Most certain.'

'Thank you, Lizzie, for all you've done.'

'If only I could have done more, Mrs Rickers.' Lizzie turned and moved quickly toward the doors.

Clutching the child, Gemma followed the porter up the marble staircase to the suite of rooms on the hotel's grand gallery.

The winter days in Longchamp Parish were chilly, with darkness falling early over the hills, and ground fog spreading from the swamps, covering the fields and pastures. Warren was sitting close to the kitchen stove, a birch fire crackling, when he heard Gemma step onto the back porch.

Shutting the kitchen door with her foot, Gemma kept her eyes on the bundle she had brought from New Orleans, now watching the baby yawn, imitating the child's mouth with her own, then nodding her head, saying, 'Yes . . . yes, we're . . . awake now . . . we're awake . . .'

Curiosity was too much for Warren; he rose from his chair by the stove.

Looking down at the child, he finally poked a finger toward the small yawning face, saying, 'Hi there, Smoky.'

Gemma stiffened at the mention of the name. Smoky Row?

Warren glanced at her; he demanded, 'What's the matter with you? Don't you like "Smoky"?'

Gemma quickly realized that Warren knew nothing about Smoky Row, nor about Jocasta Liddle, the house where Emmaline had lived in New Orleans.

Looking back to the tiny child, she asked, 'How did you know he's a boy?'

'Anybody could tell that's a boy!'

Warren reached for the infant, adding, 'And what's the matter with the name "Smoky"? I had a good friend named Smoky when I was a kid.'

Looking down at the small wrinkled face, Warren said in a lighter voice, 'Hi there, little Smoky. You and Grandad going to be friends? What do you say there, little guy?'

Gemma soon had supper sizzling on the stove, hot water boiling for tea, milk warming for the baby; Warren sat behind her at the kitchen table, playing with his grandson, and Gemma wished fleetingly that Emmaline were here with them.

Yet, remembering that this was not the life Emmaline had wanted, Gemma returned to the steak she was frying in onions, to the water boiling for tea now that Warren was complaining about coffee keeping him awake at night, to the milk warming in a pan for Smoky.

Yes, Gemma thought as she worked busily at the cookstove, the 'house at three o'clock' was once again feeling like a home, and – as a prayer – she privately thanked Emmaline for the miracle.

THE END

A SELECTED LIST OF NOVELS
AVAILABLE FROM CORGI BOOKS

While every effort is made to keep prices low, it is sometimes necessary to increase prices at short notice. Corgi Books reserve the right to show new retail prices on covers which may differ from those previously advertised in the text or elsewhere.

The prices shown below were correct at the time of going to press.

ORDER FORM

All these books are available at your book shop or newsagent, or can be ordered direct from the publisher. Just tick the titles you want and fill in the form below.

CORGI BOOKS, Cash Sales Department, P.O. Box 11, Falmouth, Cornwall.

Please send cheque or postal order, no currency.

Please allow cost of book(s) plus the following for postage and packing:

U.K. Customers—Allow 45p for the first book, 20p for the second book and 14p for each additional book ordered, to a maximum charge of £1.63.

B.F.P.O. and Eire—Allow 45p for the first book, 20p for the second book plus 14p per copy for the next seven books, thereafter 8p per book.

Overseas Customers—Allow 75p for the first book and 21p per copy for each additional book.

NAME (Block Letters) . . . .

ADDRESS . . . .

. . . .